some
kind
of
black

Diran Adebayo

ABACUS

An *Abacus* Book

First published in Great Britain by Virago Press in 1996
Reprinted 1996 (twice)
Published by Abacus 1997
Reprinted 2001

A CIP catalogue record for this book
is available from the British Library.

ISBN 0 349 10872 2

Typeset in Garamond by M Rules
Printed and bound in Great Britain by
Clays Ltd, St Ives plc

Abacus
A Division of
Little, Brown and Company (UK)
Brettenham House
Lancaster Place
London WC2E 7EN

For my mother

contents

acknowledgements

Props, for their tales, support and all that good stuff: The Big Bonsu, Clare H, Kodwo E, Ian and the Cook clan, Alex L, Greg Tate, Max C, Winston S, Nana Yaa M, Essie O, Ellen and all my family (especially Fola).

And a big thank you to the professionals: Bill Scott-Kerr, Marsha Hunt and my editor, Lennie Goodings.

'Now black is . . .' the preacher shouted.
'Bloody . . .'
'I said black is . . .'
'Preach it, . . . brother.
'. . . an' black ain't . . .'
'Red, Lawd, red. He said it's red!'
'Amen, brother . . .'
'Black will git you . . .'
'Yes, it will . . .'
'. . . an' black won't . . .'

Ralph Ellison, *Invisible Man*

'Across the diaspora, young people are trading complex identities for tribal affiliations'

Danyel Smith, *Vibe* magazine

nothing
can
contain
me

DELE LOOKED down at the pile of discarded cards on the table, then across to his friend. Concrete had a big, unwieldy hand but could barely hide a smirk on his face. There must be something tasty there. Dele would have to speak now or not at all.

'Come, padre. It's your turn,' said Concrete.

Dele held out a card and hesitated.

'Problem?'

'Might be,' said Dele.

Whenever the two played blackjack there was drama over the rules. Dele went by what he liked to call the traditional Queensberry rules. But some years back, Concrete had introduced some wild excursion on the version that seemed to take the game into rummy territory. Basically, you could hoard little sequences, then play them all in one go. This way, even if your opponent had pure cards in his hand, and you were down to, say, just one, you still couldn't rest easy.

Eventually, they had reached a compromise: Queensberry in north London and Concrete madness in south London. And true, they were in Camberwell right now, so Dele couldn't really grumble. Only he reckoned that, somewhere in the course of the five consecutive games he had lost in the past half-hour, his man had slipped in some new piece of slyness. Probably best to let it ride until he had pinpointed the devilry.

Dele laid down a weak four of spades, which Concrete set upon. First a five, six, seven of spades, then a brace of eights and a couple of royal sets. One flashy flurry and he was out.

'Oh Gosh! Me *hot* this year!' Concrete leapt up, flicking his fingers in triumph. 'Check it though, Del. You may be the BooksMan, but when it comes to dis ting here – ' His voice trailed off as he disappeared into the kitchen of his friend, whose flat this was. The guy himself seemed to have breezed out a while back but he had left them his car keys and that was the main thing.

Concrete, so-called from his time as primary school headbutting champion, had been talking about a quality new set of wheels for a while, but there was still no proof of it, so he was forever trooping down to Camberwell of a weekend. Now the two were set up with the mobility desired for a night's raving.

Raving was what they tended to do these days, when they were in one another's company. They had been pretty tight at one stage, but then Concrete's family had moved south, and Dele had been despatched to the grammar school in Enfield, thirty minutes away from their Tottenham home, door to door, then he'd gone away to college. So now Dele mainly belled Concrete when he was blitzing London on weekends. His spar definitely had access to the most parties.

'It's for you,' said Concrete, returning to the sitting-room and handing Dele his bleeper.

'For me? Who can that be?'

Dele was puzzled. He'd only been in town for a couple of hours and nobody knew he was coming up here. But his face broke into a little smile as he read the message on the display:

Mista D,
    Your presence is required. I am in D-wing again for my

sins. Don't say you're not there 'cos I know you are.

Soon come?

May you be guided by the pigeon-fancier.

'It's just Dapo. She's in hospital again. She wants me to go round – '

'Why she waste her dollars with all that foolishness?' asked Concrete, peering over his shoulder.

Dele shook his head sorrowfully at his friend. 'Concrete, man. It's the foolish bits that I like.'

'So what you gonna do? Pass by?'

'I think so, yeah,' Dele clicked his teeth as his mind returned to an ugly memory. 'It's a bit tricky though.'

There was just an off-chance that his father might also drop in to see Dapo. And if the old man caught him in town when he should be in Oxford studying, without having been forewarned, Dele would catch a load of grief.

Once, a couple of summers ago, Dele had been just perched in the small park by Russell Square, chatting over a cigarette and a drink with an old friend, when suddenly his old man strode past, booted and suited in those wide seventies' lapels. He was with a couple of what Dele assumed were work colleagues. Dele's mouth dropped; he just froze. He somehow had the presence of mind to drop the cigarette, but he didn't know if he had let go of it quickly enough. Not that it would have made any difference. His Dad just picked him up by the scruff of the neck, didn't look at his mate or the colleagues, and frog-marched him to the tube station. They didn't exchange a word on the way home. Dele just stood behind his old man on the escalator, his dome dizzy and light from fear. On the bus from Seven Sisters to home he pissed in his pants, and the wetness trickled warm and sticky down his right thigh. On the doorstep Dele collapsed and his father dragged him in, banging his head on the entrance.

His mother had rushed from the kitchen shouting, wondering what the commotion was, but the old man pushed her away. In the front hall he tore Dele's clothes off, grabbed the thick wooden stick and flogged him and flogged him, on his butt, across his back and, when Dele put his arms up in a pathetic plea, on his arms and hands. Now Dele sported a fat bump on the ring finger of his left hand. The doctors wanted to break the finger and reset it, but Dele didn't want the pain. He still couldn't make a fist.

After a time his Dad had stopped and walked away. He still hadn't said a word. Dele had lain on the floor, sobbing and wondering how the human body could absorb so much pain. He was hoping to lose consciousness, but it never happened. He had tried to use the block-out technique that Dapo had passed to him: 'Repeat lines from tunes that move you. Lines to help you slip away . . .'

She had so many lines, often culled from devotional Rasta classics. Scraps of the Old Testament filtered through reggae's dulcet singers, the Abyssinians and the Dennis Browns:

Here I come
With love and not hatred
Surely goodness and mercy
Shall follow I
All the days of my life? . . .

Dele mouthed his mantras and did not resist when his mother picked him up and led him to the bathroom. She had boiled a kettle and a pan and poured them into a bucket. Then she soaked pieces of cloth in the water and wrapped them around his bruises to reduce the swelling. Dele fell asleep, his head in her arms, as she sung to him in a language he did not understand.

When he woke up he was in bed, and his Dad, head heavy with homilies, was standing over him. No rest for the wicked.

'I've no more time for you, boy. Tch! You are an ill-trained, degenerate little boy. Complexed, you are complexed and bring shame on the family. You are no son of mine.

There is a saying in my country: the well-born child does not walk in the dark. Do you understand what that means? I will not be here to pick up the pieces when you fall to earth. I have done my best for you, but now I wash my hands! You can lead a horse to water, but you cannot make him drink. Enh-henh! But for your mother, I would throw you and your complexes out of the house, until you understand that you're an African, not some Follow-Follow boy! It were better that you spent some time in Africa and then you would know. If I ever see you, or hear of you being in London when you should be at college studying, you will not be let off lightly. Are you with me?'

Dele had mumbled back.

'Is that clear, boy?'

'Yes, sir,' he said.

And the old man had left the room.

Concrete located the phone and Dele called his Mum at her workplace.

'Ah-ah! De-le! Where are you calling from?'

'College, Mommy. Where do you think!' he said. 'I heard that Dapo is in hospital. Is that right?'

She confirmed that his sister had been admitted two nights ago after a sickle-cell crisis, and no, she didn't think that the old man would be visiting her this evening. Dapo had only got out two weeks ago and they didn't understand why she had got sick again so quickly. Maybe it had something to do with the sudden passing of Parmesta, Dapo's good friend and another sickler, who had haemorrhaged shortly after giving birth to her first child. The whole disaster had begun with a gangrenous infection in her foot.

'Oh, but Dapo became so down-hearted. I have never seen her spirit so low.'

'Listen, Mommy. You must tell me when she goes in, you know. Everytime, straightaway. It's just not fair otherwise. Dapo wants me to know anyway – '

'Dele, we do not want to disturb you from your studies. Please, you will do this for me.' She was talking about his final exams, which were only a few months away. 'You know I will do anything in my power for you, Dele. Do this one thing for me and we will all shine in your glory.'

'Alright, alright, Mommy. Don't fret, seriously. I'll be fine.'

He replaced the receiver and puffed out his cheeks. Best he headed now, when the coast was clear and it was just getting dark. He said he would bell Concrete and maybe he could pick Dele up later someplace?

Dele was annoyed with himself for snapping at his mother. But he just knew the only reason she didn't keep him up to speed was because of some silly stipulation of his father's. Dele had been getting especially touchy on this issue ever since his bid for semi-detachment from the domestic dramas had borne fruit with the place at college.

These dramas mainly revolved around Dapo. Sometimes she'd be struck down in the evening, or on her bicycle reaching for the shops. Her joints or chest would seize up and then she'd be on the floor, writhing and crying with so much agony on her face you didn't believe she could live. Twice the pain of childbirth, the consultant said. And Dele would just sit there and tell himself not to freeze, and offer up various unlikely sacrifices to God or Satan (he was never too sure about how the theology of it worked), and try to force water down her body, and wait for an ambulance or a cab or their neighbour Femi, the van driver, to take her down to the hospital. Sometimes the diamorphine pills she'd have belted down when the crisis started would suddenly kick and lay her out on the floor, her hand intertwined in his or their mother's.

The attacks weren't predictable. They came like a thief in the night, although since her mid-teens' resurgence of a kind of faith, Dapo said she was prescient now, like she had an idea God would let her know when her time was up. But Dele didn't like her talking about that. They made a vow not to discuss anything they could do nothing about. So they didn't chat much about her runnings any more, mainly his. He was the one with the options.

Clutching two fistfuls of fruit, Dele was greeted in the lifts at Middlesex Hospital by Marie, an English girl and a regular from his previous visits. Marie was most always pregnant on the theory that no doctor was going to deny her the methadone she craved for fear of harming the child. So here she returned to jack-up the green sap and hang out with other detox casualties from the Merchant Navy and the West End. She had a real lived-in, sat-upon look.

'Alright Marie, what you saying?' smiled Dele, looking at the needle marks on her arms. 'Been into the sharps box again?'

'Yeah man, yeah!' she screamed. 'Tryin'a shift some goodies. Y'interested?' She took from her pocket a rag-tag collection of tablets: tranquillisers, diazepam and heminverins – the last prescribed to stop her deliriums.

Dele shook his head. 'I'm looking for my sister. Is she in her room, do you know?'

'Nah, she's in the TV room.'

Dapo was lying back in an armchair, decked in the regulation prison-blue pyjamas, staring at the ceiling. Her short, natural hair was uncombed, with picky-picky bits peering out at the top, and her eyes looked whacked out on diamorphine. Her right forearm, worn, rubbery and blotchy from countless needles, hung over the side. Her ankles and lower legs had swelled up badly, very dark and thick. On days like these, with the tubes and drips all around, it seemed that triffids were squeezing her softly. Dele didn't like it one bit. He planted a big kiss on her cheek.

'Whassup, whassup, whassup natty dread?'

'Mista D! Alright, Trouble.' They hugged, and settled into their usual gentle bickering.

'I'm not talking to you anyway, as it happens,' she said. 'You're in the dog-house. You haven't dropped me a line for how long? You've sacked the whole household!'

'Who, me?'

'Actually, some other guy. You're always doing that "Who, me?" when it's perfectly clear who I'm talking to. It's 'cos you're so used to stalling for time.'

'Don't hot me, Miss D. I come in peace – '

The door swung open. Trevor, a thallie, was waddling towards him and they touched knuckles. Only twenty-three, Trevor couldn't have much time left. Iron had seeped through his organs, into his kidneys, and now his stomach had blown up to a grotesque balloon. Dele had seen Trevor from time to time on other visits but they had warded off discussing how it was now the end of the road for him.

In a small room at the back, Dele could glimpse an old woman wheezing grimly, with a bank of flowers by her side, and what he assumed were her husband and relatives all gathered round.

'I see they put you up with all the bright young things. Still, maybe it beats living with Papa Doc. Although word is he's announced a set of liberalisation measures after the life-long state of emergency – '

'Has he fuck!' She kissed her teeth. 'Let's leave that, it's too much. So how's grand old Oxford then?'

He shrugged. 'I'm just frying time there now. Anxious to get out, move on to the next gripping instalment. Next year I return to purity.'

'You and your resolutions. They have a half-life of about three days.'

'How did you know I was around, by the way?'

'An educated guess. It's Friday, isn't it?'

He handed her a present he had been meaning to give her – a book about life in Kerala. Dapo had seen a holiday show about that part of southern India and decided she wanted to know more. Her bag, book-wise, was travel, history, middle-brow fiction, and manuals on spiritual redemption by holy men and quacks. As she leafed through the pictures Dele quizzed her on her love-life. She tutted with irritation.

'Still interviewing. At this rate, best ask me in five years' time. If I'm here in five years' time – '

It was strange for her to say that. She rarely said anything morbid, or even talked about her illness.

'It's all off, Dele. I can't stand it, you know.'

'Hey! Enough with that.' He got up decisively and kneaded her shoulder. 'Come on, let's get out of here – '

Cutting-out incognito to a local bar or café was a little cherished ritual of Dele's hospital visits. They headed to the ward where Dapo changed, her left leg moving with a heaviness.

Dele helped her disengage from the drips and machines, and button up her duffel-coat. She was a bit worried about the desferol in the pump as she was supposed to absorb it for a further half hour, but they persuaded themselves it didn't matter.

'So, you're going back to your roots this time?' Dapo said, returning to the previous theme.

'Did you hear anyone mention roots? I just said "back to purity", that's all. I swear, if I had a puff for every time black folk drone on about "roots this" and "roots that". I'm more worried about my branches, you know. It's the branches that bear fruit and tilt for the sky.'

'Oh, very poetical. As usual, more pretty than sense. "Nothing can contain me!" she mocked, throwing a line he had once used in a high-spirited moment back in his face, as she twirled, puffed-up legs and all, in a crazy pirouette.

'Now, that's a slap. You know what I mean. It's just that, you know, remember what we always said? Once we get out of the house, we can go anywhere!'

'So why are you unhappy then, if you're so busy branching out? 'Cos don't tell me you're happy, otherwise why are you down here on the regular?' She shook her head. 'You haven't looked on top form this past while. I wish you'd be careful.'

'It's one thing always telling me to be careful. It's another to tell me *how* to be careful. Don't worry – '

'If I had a puff for every time you say "no worries" . . .'

They padded round to The Greystoke, an old-style saloon bar around the corner. They said their brief hallos in the back room, where Marie and other hospital hustlers were clustered around some busted-looking guys shooting pool, then passed through the linking doors to the quieter part.

Dele got his sister an orange juice and himself a double brandy and coke.

'So what's eating you? Mummy told me about Parmesta. I'm so sorry. I know you moved together and that.'

Dapo nodded. 'I told her. You don't know how many times I said, "Parmesta, don't even *entertain* the idea of getting pregnant!" Slight, sick thing that she was. And that gash! It was septicaemia, you know, it wasn't even the crisis. She was in and out of clinics but they didn't pick up on it. They seem to think if you're a sickler you can't get anything else!'

'And she'd only just turned twenty-one, wasn't it? 'Cos I remember you did that do – '

'That's right.' Dapo sucked her teeth. 'It was because of Shorty, I think. You met her guy, didn't you? He's one nice man but you know how he just wasn't getting any work and he's thirty-odd now and I think their whole situation was getting so uphill she thought a kid would help. She knew the risks.' She shook her head. 'Now she's gone. I'm sorry, it's just set me thinking. I mean, Lord, what's gonna happen to me? I need for so many miracles to happen just to get started, put a foot on the rung. This has to ease up so I can leave home and get to college. Then *this* has to ease up so I can hold down a job and get money, then find someone to take care of me, and who's gonna want to do that if this shit doesn't ease up? I mean, I'm not exactly looking like Miss Nigeria UK, am I?' She stared straight ahead, her eyes rimmed with tears.

Dele placed a hand on her shoulder, then cast his eyes around the bar to see if anyone was noticing the distress in the corner.

'All this moaning isn't your style. What's happened? Tell me.'

'I'm sorry, Mista D. I just feel such a way at the moment. How did I get into this state where they can't use my veins any more? Riddle me that. I don't get any light pains now, just heaviness rushing me from all directions. So spiteful. They're writing about me in the *Lancet*, talking about a new kind of sickling – '

'Is it?'

She nodded. 'They gave me good blood two weeks ago, for God's sake, and then my count just dropped straight off and bang! – I'm back in. Before, it would be months before they saw me again. I've got this bronchial cough that's burning my chest up in the middle of flippin' summer, my knees have packed in, my lungs are thick and mucusy. It's just the spite of it!'

Dele didn't know how to boost her. He cursed off her doctors, but she said you mustn't shoot the messengers, they were only doing their best. He asked her about SuperSoulSis, the local socialising group she had got off the ground, but this only upset her again. SuperSoulSis was Parmesta's baby too, she explained. The two had got it up and running in the face of dire indifference from their friends, who were only prepared to come on board if somebody else contributed the enthusiasm. Dapo didn't even know what was going to happen to SSS now.

'You can be everything you want to be. I can't be nothing I want!' She looked down and tapped her empty glass. 'If all this could just stop now, you know.'

A prickly loner, forever answering back to the guys, Dapo had passed through that teenage phase where you hug your difference greedily. That way of being had conspired with her hospital terrors to exhaust her, render her socially immobile. It had emerged as a kind of moody sloth. People would ask Dele, 'What's up with your sister? She needs to loosen up,' they would say, 'take care of herself . . . Oh, but your sister is too harsh-oh! Enh! Young women should not be like that. She will end up an Old Maid . . .' It was these last comments that really wound Dapo up. She thought it was their mother's docility that was her greatest mistake, and Dapo was damned if she was going to suffer to the world in the same way.

The boggling frenzy of the year before had been Dapo's first foray out from the corner of the room. She, like other 'decent' girls, had started checking the reggae dances and SuperSoulSis was her bid to build on those adventures.

Dele bought another round and changed the subject, because all these sad pills were too much to swallow.

They walked back a long way round. Up Tottenham Court Road towards Goodge Street, taking a left into the School of Oriental and African Studies, where they sat themselves on the lawn and Dele built a smoke for the stunning sliver of moon in the sky. Any excuse would do really, but nights were always a bit special to the two of them. From the days of their youth spent messing around or smoking on the stoop in the small hours when the old man slumbered. He passed her the puff.

'I shouldn't be doing this, you know. And you shouldn't be letting me.'

'I know, I know,' he said, and they shared a rueful smile. But he didn't know for sure that everything was alright again until Dapo started creasing up on account of something and threw out their currently favourite mantra, taken from the West Coast Funkateers: 'It's good. It's all good!'

He took her back, then bucked up with Concrete. Dele slipped into his party rags as they drove south to Sydenham for the night's main event.

It took the pair a full five minutes to push their way through the throng that rammed the stairs leading up to the three main rooms. Stories he had heard of the New Cross house fire a few years back flashed through Dele's head and he prayed there was nothing too combustible in host Samantha's house. But by the time they had found a spot to call their own, Dele was as happy as he could be. True, you could hardly move or breathe, but wherever you looked you got an eyeful of sweetness shaking a leg. Young, sassy neighbourhood saplings clad in leather mini-skirts, printer shorts and batty riders, or calf-length black boots, clingy lycra tops and bomber jackets. There was a slightly older crowd, fitted in more sober fashion, in the room set aside for mellower R & B sounds. Some of them still had black wraps dangling over their trouser suits, as if they hadn't yet decided if they were staying or going. But even they were very nicely turned out – a welcome relief from the unwashed grunginess that was carrying the swing back at college.

Dele wasn't really a part of this scene, so he didn't feel any pressure on his head. If it was a Nigerian do now, he might have to pop outside for a smoke; the sounds would be down and the chat would be thick and fast: who was doing business in Germany or in America on a Master's course, and whose family had been spotted in the papers bringing shame on the homeland. He would be introduced to eligible Nigerian-Nigerian girls, now at Buckingham University or Holborn Law Tutors, in a meaningful way. And Dele would turn to Dapo or any other renegade UK Africans in the house and bemoan the fact that there weren't enough of them around to have a party all their own.

'This is the boomiest dance. You always deliver,' said Dele, turning to his friend. They were standing with a whole heap of other guys at the back of the main space. Behind them, little rivulets of condensation ran down the black bin-liners that covered the windows. It must have been about two but punters were still flooding in.

Concrete smiled, his eyes like red slits after hours under the sensi. He was chomping away on a plate of rice and dried fish, so it took him a moment to reply. 'You know dat! No need for speech-speech tonight. The way these girls stay, anyting can happen.' He cackled, and burped quietly, with the contentment of the full stomach.

Dele clocked his spar furtively, wondering if there was anything in Concrete's style that he had missed. For although anything could happen, they rarely seemed to happen to Dele. These tough, brawly girls, with 'Yard' stamped on their foreheads, attracted yet intimidated him. Underneath the great edifices of hair that was relaxed and coiffed and coiled and set and wedged at angles you hadn't known about, that was so totally *worked*, stood faces set in granite. Mind you, if he was living in Peckham, as half of them did, he'd probably be the same. Some of these women would be crying out for a relatively decent, employable guy such as he to enter their lives, but you still had to come correct. And Dele didn't feel that he had much of a purchase on the strict rules of engagement at these raves. No good coming to them with small talk about his history course and what did they think of the new world order? Even if they were on that level, you couldn't really discuss anything of import with all these decibels pumping in your ear. No good representing like some rude-bwoy, as there were enough genuine badness around to rumble that cover at any moment. And no good just being yourself, because being yourself didn't get you checks – unless you were the cutest guy out there or your clothes carried the promise of a hefty disposable income.

But Concrete! He was already getting rubs with some browning no more than a yard away. Dele was gutted. He'd been talking to the man only a minute ago. He seemed to have these cool and deadly skills.

Hold on, though. Maybe he had a couple of possibilities too. One – a mampie stalking the room in a shocking satin two-piece that had her resemble some flipped-over fairy god-mother – could easily be discounted. But the second, who stood with her hand on her hip, was fine. She had given him a once-over and she didn't look sick with him either. The trouble was she was with three other girls, and packs like that were pretty difficult for a guy to operate in. Dele went to the kitchen to get a brandy and consider the situation.

He was just hunting in his pockets for some change to pass over to the women behind the hatch when this shambolic dread hustled himself to the front of the queue, with 'Easy, blood, easy!' blandishments, and 'Gimme some of dat Martell now, sista.' Dele wasn't going to stand for that, so he pushed himself back ahead and the two eyed one another evenly, wondering how far the other was prepared to go in the battle for pole position. Dele's challenger was a good inch taller and no Ryvita. But soon enough, the dread held up his hands.

'Alright, alright!' he said. There was a strange something in his manner – you could see he didn't have the full whack. 'Sometime the man in front get shot, and the man behind don't get shot, y'hear?' he added gnomically, shaking his finger at Dele. 'And sometime the man who gives way gets a-way!'

What the hell was *that* about, Dele wondered as he made his escape. Pure Rasta Metaphysics, as he and Dapo had christened this quasi-mystical style in which a lot of Caribs, especially the older locksmen-type, discussed matters. Give them half an inch and they'll be telling you that time is longer than rope.

Back inside, Dele strode straight to the girl from before and begged her a dance.

'Wha'?' she barked. Her arms were folded now and she seemed altogether less interested than ten minutes ago.

'I said, do you fancy a little dance?' His voice fell to a whisper as his conviction weakened.

She glanced at him, glanced at her crew, busy fanning their faces in the heat, and then stared into the middle-distance. 'Too late already!'

He shuffled away, muttering defensively about mutton dressed as lamb, fired a cigarette and contemplated the increasingly ugly scenario. He had early morning moves to make – back to college to do some work and then the Rites of Summer party in the evening – and had been banking on Concrete dropping him off for the bus back. Now he faced a future trudging off on his jack jones, kicking cans . . .

Ragga-time had started again, with the DJ dropping original takes followed by their female answer versions. First, Beres Hammond's quick-step 'One Dance Can Do', running into Audrey Hall's honeysweet response, and then the Stress/Vex combination of more recent vintage. And Dele was just thinking what a neat idea this was when a pretty, dark girl appeared out of the shadows, flashed him the briefest smile, and just started grinding her backside up against him. The shock of it made him lose the rhythm of the dance for some seconds, until the DJ came to his aid by freestyling his own chat in and out of the answer tune to create a third monster mongrel that had some folk flicking their lighters in approval. They knew that this pleasure was privileged and private. Well, after that Dele was just fine. He led on the rough-voiced bits, his arms above her head, and she countered vigorously when the women rode the rhythm, butterflying so closely to him he could feel the tensile strength of her buns.

He glanced up triumphantly at Concrete as the tune faded out. His girl still had her back to him, and he was just running a quality check on the lines he had in store by way of formal introduction when a rangy red-skinned guy, who had been observing them all this while, sidled up, tugged and whispered in her ear. Dele didn't catch the chirps, but in a few moments the interloper was leading her by the arm out of the room.

Dele stood the next number out, forlornly hoping the red guy and the girl were just long-lost cousins, until Concrete appeared through the gloaming. 'You looked like you were sorted,' said Dele.

'Nah-nah. She my bredren's girl. You know Marcus? If I trouble dat, then blood must run, you get me? And you, you was flexing with some fitness back there!'

Dele sucked his teeth. 'This smoothie just came along and whipped her away. I can't believe it. I thought I was on for a little spurt and desert.'

They spotted his brief encounter an hour later, on the estate forecourt. She was nodding like the living dollyhead at the guy, who sat back in proprietorial fashion behind the wheel of a red BMW. So Concrete teased Dele mercilessly about how he was just a shambling bus-pass boyfriend who couldn't even keep a local slapper under manners, until he dropped him off at Marble Arch for the Citylink coach.

mr
mention

THE GAMES that white folk play on blacks are straightforward enough and well documented; the games that black
folk play on whites are equally obvious. But the games that
black folk play on one another! Well, that's something else
again.

Dele had some knowledge of the first and scant purchase on the third. But, come the second now, and our man
was a connoisseur. Nearly three years in Oxford town had
honed those skills. So it was with something of the world-
weariness of the dab old hand that Dele strolled to the stereo
situated at the back of Tabitha's cavernous sitting-room. The
Motown selection had just played out and the punters parted
and smiled expectantly at the brother as he moved through
the crowd to exercise his inalienable prerogative. He shook
his head in avuncular but firm fashion when a guy, with due
deference, held out some doomy Nick Cave and The Bad
Seeds vinyl for his inspection. 'Nah, man. That can't work.
This is a dance, not a wake!' Dele sighed. He dug deep into
his baggy pockets and unearthed a clutch of tapes. Rule number one, he thought, if you're going to a student's rave, always
bring your own sounds.

'Hey!' squealed an approaching voice.

'Easy, Tabitha.'

Tabitha, with her freshly-scrubbed, Enid Blyton Five-Go-On-Frolics face, pecked Dele on both cheeks. 'Thanks for taking over, sweetie. What are you putting on? How about The Godfather Funkmaster? That'll get them dancing.'

'Please! Enough already with James Brown. If I hear 'Sex Machine' one more time it'll be too many. We want something with an up-to-date '93 lick. Trust me,' Dele soothed, pointing to a tape marked *Breaking-Up at the Basement*, 'this is pure west London sounds.'

The Basement was a club that played to a Love Has No Colour crowd in London's Ladbroke Grove. The Basement was Tabitha's spiritual home although, hailing from Tewkesbury, she had never been there. 'That sounds wild, Delboy.' Her face was patchily ruddy; a combination of the liquor and the fall-out from the first sunny day of the year. 'We're over there.' She pointed to a little stage erected in the back garden, where a small group was showboating to the tunes. 'Your presence is required!'

'Okay. Very soon.' Dele smiled. The bogus Basement label worked every time. In fact, the tape sticker was a cover for tunes altogether more hardcore and X-rated but this way you could slip them on and no one would complain. His task completed, Dele found a vacant piece of wall, settled himself down with a shot of peppered vodka, savoured its flavoured hit, pulled out some Rizla papers to build the customary five-sheeter, and took a predatory look around.

Tabitha's jamboree for the talented and beautiful was now in full swing; posh people, clubbers, budding journalists and actors, all were milling around her north Oxford place. Tabitha was neither talented nor beautiful, so she was forever having to host raves for the bright young things to keep her hand in. Dele wasn't necessarily talented or beautiful either, but up here there just wasn't a big enough supply of brothers to go round. Well, there were the bloods who laboured at the British Leyland plant and lived on the big estates down

Cowley way, on the east side, but they didn't count in the student scheme of things. Up here, Dele was what you'd call a Mr Mention. A player. X amount of invites to events and launches littered his college pigeon-hole.

After three years of sharing his sensi and flexing across the city, Dele was now the undisputed number one negro. For sure, there had been some competition along the way, like that guy Tetteh, whom he could glimpse now in a side room, tinkling a Scott Joplin rag on Tabitha's piano to a little crowd. Tetteh was stocky, strong, cobalt-dark, with unnerving obsidian discs for eyes. With Ghana's Minister for Transport as his old man, his long-time mixing in English 'Society', and his weekend trips to Paris and Geneva for exclusive parties, Tetteh was the living Supernegro. Entering college straight from Harrow public school, Tetteh had arrived with a reputation and a crew of school chums already in place – a big advantage. Then there was Deidre, the busty coffee-coloured thing profiling her chest, on the stage with Tabitha and the others. Deidre was a permanent fixture on the scene. No one quite knew how long she'd been around, how old she was, or where she was from – sometimes she said Ivory Coast, sometimes Gambia – or indeed what she was doing in town at all. Rumour was that she'd studied at the poly or a secretarial college back in the day. Certainly, she wasn't leaving town until she'd persuaded one of her rich part-time lovers to slip a ring on her finger. Or Colin, of Bajan natural parentage but adopted by a liberal English couple. Hitherto lumbered with a nondescript mid-Afro, Colin had gone AWOL and returned only today sporting long, braided extensions. He was shaking his funky locks around and twirling a canapé by the food table. But still, with his Home Counties burr, his cords and his brogues, Colin was coming like an English gentleman of the old school.

This was the problem with his rivals, Dele reflected as he pulled on his smoke. They were all too speaky-spoky, as Oxford as yards of ale. But most students didn't want to hear that. No, sir! Be they Chelsea girls or strident left-wingers, they wanted danger, they wanted to play away just once in their lives. It was best to homey the hell out of them, indulge their romance of the real nigga!

Dele hadn't always been like this. He had arrived here to begin his history degree nearly three years ago open-minded, totally up for these new runnings. He had embraced new musics, styles and fashions. But various things had led him to review the situation. The first problem, he'd have to confess, was there were precious few checks in it. And even those few were with these grungey types. And second, there was the celebrated occasion when Dele had been rucking violently to a twangy-guitared Smiths song at a college bop and cannoned into Jonathan, a languages student from another college, standing in a corner. Now Jonathan was about the only person around who had had anything like a similar background to Dele's own – West African descent, inner city (albeit Liverpool), elevated post-GCSEs to a state grammar school – and Dele was keen for them to get better acquainted. So it had bothered him slightly when he had smashed into Jonathan at the dance and soul-man Jonathan had stared at him with a kind of pitying astonishment.

Shortly afterwards, when they bumped into each other on Holywell Street, Jonathan had let on by immediately launching into a reworking of the chorus of 'This Charming Man', an old Smiths hit:

> I would go out tonight
> but I haven't got a stitch to wear
> My name is Dele
> and I may be black
> but I don't care – aa-are!

Jonathan had sung mockingly, his bare arms clenched above his head, rucking and rotating around like some Nubian New-Age Traveller.

A joke thing then, if still with a sting. But they had become friends and Dele had been at his right hand when Jonathan had set up an informal Black Students Discussion Group in their second year. The problem was that people came – those who came at all – with different agendas. Deidre said why did we need to have our own discussion group anyway, and it was inverse racism. Tetteh said look, let's be realistic, there really aren't any problems for us, are there? And he was right, in a way. For Tetteh, with free flights to Accra when he wanted and prosperous dual futures ahead, there was no problem. And Ruby, the ferociously militant mixed-race girl, she was for severe, separatist action. Only nobody took her seriously, as she was known to fling down the cream of European manhood behind closed doors.

It was funny, though. There was a certain wanky air of self-satisfaction bubbling under the surface at these Black Chats. Folk felt that whatever the problems had been out there, *they* had overcome them, they must be the *crème de la crème*. As an evening wore on and tongues got loose, some would invoke hoary myths of the integrity of strong African cultures and contrast that with the Caribs' lack of a coherent identity to explain their minuscule representation there. But when he checked it, Dele could barely find a person in the room, himself included, who was truly sorted. Most of them were unreconciled either to their families or to their role here, if any. Their heads were mash-up, frankly. It was quite possible that the only thing they were really sorted about, were good for, was taking exams. But you couldn't linger over thoughts like that. The implications were too troublesome.

It was after that group foundered that Dele lost the thread a little. In some barely acknowledged way, he lost commitment to the place, took it less seriously, and began donning different hats to see how they fitted. Oh, there he would be at a dinner party with liberal friends, and wait until the second course had been served and chat was free and comfortable, then hush the room in an instant with some choice Race facts. And the smiles would be replaced with flurries of worry and concern, and they would say, 'Gosh, Del! Is that really how it is? I can't believe black cabs think they can get away with that! You should write to the papers . . .'

But, truth say, he didn't really feel that a history of slavery and low-level grief around town made him a bona fide candidate for Black Rage.

He had grown tired of this game, tired of sitting with his peers, worthy and curious, and explaining to them bits of experience that he knew about already. So he had started moving with a less right-on crowd, and here Dele had developed a range of broader comic roles. He'd been a fool, he'd made few close friends, he could see that. He was unhappy although he was having a nice time. But he felt that he was on the case and was fond of telling Dapo of his imminent return to purity. The trouble was that he endlessly deferred.

The night's event has been hyped as the last great blowout for the student hip set before they settled down to prepare for their final exams. Like a dictator of the thirties, Tabitha engaged in a tireless quest for *lebensraum*. She and her empire of kissy-kissy friends were set to graduate and keen to seal contacts for life. The five-year plan was to recreate the same scene in west London's Notting Hill. Her place had the usual nods in the direction of downward mobility that no cool posh girl these days could do without: a Student Loans Company policy plastered prominently on the kitchen wall, a 'Can't Pay/Won't Pay' sticker defiantly underneath, and guests in their polished Doc Martens and lumber jackets. All this jarred slightly with the glassy clink of cherry, lemon, and peppered Polish vodkas and champagne being iced in the bath, the boiled quails eggs, and tomatoes stuffed with roe all ripe on the table, but who gave a shit? Not Dele. That wasn't what he was invited for.

Scoping the vibe, he was assailed by a growing sense of detachment from proceedings. He didn't know why. These sights and sounds that he had waded into knee deep were now beginning to defamiliarise themselves. These same old shapes – greys clad in Levis that their flat-jack backsides could not properly fill out – reasserted their difference. No rumps and no lips, never mind a stiff upper one. How did they build an empire?

Dele's reflections were interrupted when the bars of a popular tune started up and the company on the podium by the open French windows shouted for him to 'Stop hiding yourself down there!' He grimaced at this loud, long-distance acknowledgement of his role as court entertainer and sauntered over to do his stint.

As he found a few free square yards for his self on the stage, Dele was dimly aware of Tabitha and this guy he recognised with a dark-brown mop of hair, looking at him and giggling loudly, 'How much do you think he's worth then? Five, fifteen . . . I reckon he's worth thirty if he's worth a penny.' But Dele's attention had been distracted by the first sight of a potential chirpsee.

She was fairly tall, five feet six or seven, auburn hair tied in a French bun, black polo neck under the check jacket, black flimsy elephant pantaloons rounded off with a pair of black leather boots. She leant gracefully against a table. Twice she had looked up at him and smiled. The first, a too-ready open beam, Dele had read as a 'I don't have any problems with black wood!' smile. The second, just as borderless and full but more focussed, was a 'So who are you? I might be interested.' But just as he was mulling over some lyrics, four or five pairs of hands grabbed and blindfolded him, knocked him off his feet and carried him off the stage to the back of the garden. There were cheers and he could hear Tabitha singing 'Surprise, surprise!'

Dele steeled himself for a practical joke. Why were these people distressing a perfectly nice do with these silly japes? But the full ugliness was only revealed when a hand slipped the blindfold off and Dele found his shirt-crumpled self in front of a sniggering throng and standing opposite the nerdy Grant Knowles, Tabitha's college union president.

Grant was wearing a judge's robe and pince-nez with the executioner's black cloth perched on his head. To his left, behind a long table, stood his lieutenant, the union treasurer, suited and booted, with a gavel. A blackboard was mounted on the grass, and Dele's name was up there, above a number of others, with starting-price pound signs by their names. A length of rope cordoned off a section of the garden where four members of the university rugby team sat shackled together. Among them, grinning inanely, was John Omiteru, star rugby winger and Supernegro. And Deidre, now clad in a low-cut leopard-skin number, scuttled seductively around them, cracking her whip to keep them in line.

Damn, Dele was thinking, it must be the rag week's slave auction. A yearly ritual of obscure origins, it involved auctioning off participants as 'slaves for the day' to the high-est bidder. Sometimes the bidder was a group, sometimes the slaves were a group. If you were a lucky guy, you might get four fit young ladies to hire you for a day and strap you to their four-poster bed. But no one had ever been lucky. 'Look, Tabitha. I'm not doing this. No way,' he muttered quietly to her.

'Oh Delboy! Relax. It's all for charity, you know – '

'Fuck charity, Tabitha! It's not my bag. You shoulda told me you were planning this. It's so out of order – '

'You shouldn't take yourself so seriously. We're not dunking you in the water tank or anything.'

The girl he liked had wandered down to the scene. She looked amused. Not you too, thought Dele.

'Really, Del!' huffed a friend of Tabitha's. 'It's not as if Deidre and John aren't joining in.'

'So what do they have to do with it? They're not my business.'

'Oh why are we wai-ting?' sang Grant, with mock im-patience. Then he turned to the crowd and said, 'Time to start early bids for this lot. What do you say, Ladies and Gentlemen, to this real live black person?'

'And why did you even let that ignorant fool in here in the first place!' said Dele sharply.

Until then, all the exchanges had taken place within the accepted cut and thrust of slave-auction foreplay, but this last remark chilled the temperature. Dele sucked loudly on his teeth and stomped back inside. He felt to walk out altogether, but then people would notice and think he was making a big deal out of the incident. So he propped himself up by a speaker and tried to look relaxed while his mind ticked away. Boy! John and Deidre, the shame of it! Is that really how he's been coming these past three years for Tabitha to think she could run that slave fuckrey past him? Is that what everyone thinks? Funny how he thought it was he who was taking the piss . . .

Dele glanced around, suddenly nervous of the import behind the old, knowing, indulgent looks; his eyes finally settled on the girl he'd liked from before and he ambled over.

Her mouth was wide and her lips full for one of the Caucasian Persuasion. This was the only hint of wantonness about her person, for everything else came across starchy. Her tones were Home Counties clipped, like she thinks her shit don't stink. He took in the strict lines of her face, and the dainty manner she dangled her cigarette, as she rapped with her friend. She was a bit of a luvvie, peppering her chat with hyperbole and dramatic stresses – 'Oh, well, I *do* think that Joseph's behaviour really *is* utterly peculiar sometimes . . . Oh, you *must* come! It'll be such tremendous fun . . .' – but Dele liked that. She made him think of jodhpurs, formally cut sports jackets, country hunts and empire; the living vision of the shires. She pressed all those buttons.

She looked up at him one moment as her conversation waned and he used the opening to move in between them and lean towards her, casually throwing an arm against the wall above her head, in street condescension. 'Psst! What's happening? Talk to me, what's your name?'

She looked at his arm and then at him, startled. 'What?' she said.

He'd kicked off too fast, Dele could see that, but he'd started so he'd finish. 'I said, "So talk to me". Hey, relax. This is as bad as I get,' said Dele.

Her eyes were grey and cold. 'Do you mind?' she said. 'I'm trying to talk to my friend.' But her friend had already given up the struggle and wandered away. Dele was about to give up too, when she unexpectedly threw him a lifeline. 'You're Dele aren't you? I've heard a lot about you.'

Dele grinned and nodded. Things could be safe from here. She said her name was Helena, and she'd come to a couple of his promotions, and wasn't he studying history? He confirmed that he was but, no, he didn't know what he was gonna do by way of a career, but what about her? She was set on some big gig at the United Nations, but first she would have to brush up her French at a private language school in Grenoble. She came from Southampton where her old man was a surgeon and her Mum, social evenings at the Women's Institute aside, did very little, really. All very pleasant, but his mood was making him mischievous. He felt like dropping a little ghetto jive on her, just for the crack.

'My Dad? Well, my old man's inside the house of many slams. The Scrubs. Doing life. We were all just sitting there one evening in the living-room. I remember *The Price is Right* was on the box. My man was just polishing his A-K, nothing strange, when he ups and says "I feel to do you something right now!" Then Booyacka – Booyacka! And my Mum is just lying there on the floor. It was terrible, terrible.' Dele's voice broke a little, and Helena placed a sympathetic arm on his.

'Oh gosh, I'm so sorry! I don't know what to say – '

'Don't say anything, Helena – '

'How could you possibly recover from something like that?'

'Save it, H. I was only messing with you.'

She stood there, looking mighty vexed. Her eyes bored dum-dums through his temples. 'Oh, why don't you just grow up!' she said and stormed off.

Dele stood there for a moment, licking his wounds. Nobody seemed to have noticed the contretemps but someone had hijacked the boombox and the tired strains of 'Play That Funky Music, White Boy', filtering through for the hundredth consecutive Oxford party, only added to his discomfort. The track was being greeted with the whoops and shameless whirring of limbs that signalled anthem status. He slipped out into the small front drive, saying he needed to catch some fresh air.

He shuffled through Jericho's little village streets, reaching for the city centre. In the late April twilight, with some church bells banging away in the distance, and the streets free of Saturday night nastiness, this postcard town was doing a fine imitation of itself. Oxford, just like he pictured it.

Dele hummed on a rhythm and sought calm in the whisper of the breeze tugging at his clothes. The red and green patched Click suit, over Caterpillar lug boots and topped with a matching woolly hat, was his pride and joy. It was one of only three pieces of his wardrobe in which he actually liked the look of himself. And it was the first ever rudebwoy gear he had brought home, slipped on, and gone downstairs in, looking at his father as if to say, 'So wha'cha gonna do?'

Students in little groups moved all around him. Some, their gowns flailing in their wakes, were heading to get changed after their formal dinners; others were consulting times for the pictures, or clustering around bars; there was an older VIP-style crowd outside the Sheldonian Theatre, waiting patiently for the doors to open on an organ recital.

On the corner of Broad Street he whipped on his shades hurriedly when he glimpsed a couple of guys sandwiched around a gesticulating girl up ahead, all rolling their bikes along beside them. But too late, they were coming his way. He didn't know the guys but, judging from their bleachy, acid-washed denim jeans and polished white PVC shoes, they must be African graduate students. The blonde, Josie, was familiar.

A friend of Tabitha's, Josie had come bounding up to Dele at some do when he had first arrived in town and invited him down to the Afro-Caribbean Society. It turned out her old man was one of those Europeans headhunted by multinationals, and dispatched to Africa post-independence to lord it over thousands of equally qualified natives. So Josie had passed much time as a youth in Lagos, Port Harcourt and Harare when it was still called Salisbury. Her proposition had seemed a good idea so the two of them had reached. Only Dele had been taken unawares by the scene that greeted them. He had expected a darkened room rammed with fly boys and girls, and the odd Old World paternalist, happily mingling; an evening of relaxed networking, lightly garnished with cultural reasoning. With this in mind, he had nipped back to London to purchase a new cap and some prime draw especially for the occasion.

Instead, he had entered the strip-lit junior common-room to find the place holding a score of intense Africans. Some had matted hair, like they had just jumped off the stowaway container. The men, all older than himself, carried all the sombreness of folk whose sponsors were paying untold pounds sterling in overseas fees for graduate places, and who were still too near to their homeland's tragedies to lighten up even in an ivory tower half the world away. They saw themselves as leaders in waiting, preparing to lead their countries out of their horrors. Part of it was just the same self-importance that infected so many of the student crews in this town, but the context gave it a poignant edge. Dele worried that his own haircut, a short fade with razor cuts at the back, had introduced an unwelcome note of levity to the proceedings.

There were three African women in the house, two with short, natural hair, one in braids, but most of the females present were erstwhile expatriates like Josie. Caribs were conspicuous by their total absence.

The chair had opened that evening's discussion on the motion that Kwame Nkrumah, twenty-one years after his passing, was still the most relevant figure for today's Africa. Interesting enough, really, but the discussion was spoilt by anal adherence to the formal rules of debate; pompous rulings from the chair, a battery of interruptions on points of order and of information by the opposing speakers, barely a chance given to the audience to get a shout out. It was as if the Afro-Caribbean Society believed it was playing the same high-falutin' game as the University Debating Society up the road. Dele was reminded of the way his father's accent would hop up the class rung whenever he spoke to a white person on the phone. As the evening wore on, he had become intrigued by the stubborn spittle that rested on the chairman's lower lip. He'd been all but prompted to exclaim, 'Either dry your lip or close it up, man!'

The debate had ended with a vote in Papa Nkrumah's favour, followed by a few drinks and a dance to Zimbabwean jazz. With an air of benign amazement, Dele witnessed all these African-Africans cleaning up to right and left of him, even the ones in the white PVC shoes, while he, dropping his inner-city blues, got no purchase on the situation at all. People just weren't interested. Luckily, he had managed to enveigle Josie back to her rooms, where they had enjoyed vigorous doggie-style dealings. Her ass had been as hard as rock, he remembered, on account of her constant cycling around town, posting up flyers for WOMAD and 'Small is Beautiful' aid projects in the developing world.

In the morning he had burnt off and dabbled no further in that scene. But he would still see Josie around occasionally. Every time she was in tow with a brother ever further along a gradient ending in Mama Africa's bosom. She had started with him, a Londoner yet to set foot in his home country. She had then moved on to John, who at least went back to Nigeria during the vacations. Then she had sacked Anglophone Africa and shacked up with a Senegalese folk painter, a guy in Oxford as an artist in residence at Josie's college. And now, to judge from the men she was introducing him to – whom she chatted with in a Swahili-English mélange – she was close to sacking any brother with a manor-born track on Europe at all. Like she was desperately seeking some dark continent concentrate.

'Are you coming to the meeting tonight?' Josie enquired. 'You know we've got Nad from the ANC's London office coming down? He's going to take us through the blueprint for change. You must come. There's only a year to go.'

Dele shook his head. 'I'd love to, Josie, but what it is, you know, I've really got to push on with my work. Pick up the pace and that. I just haven't got the time tonight,' he replied, unconvincingly, as his breath threw out thick shafts of reefer and liquor.

The three others condemned him with a 'Playing the fiddle while Rome burns' look and moved on. Dele cut down a side street and traced the walk back to Jericho.

Josie and her crowd were just one of the many options not pursued in his time there. He didn't feel so fretful about it. It wasn't as if the other paths were so appetising, but he still regretted the lack of a comfort zone. It was crazy, that, with all these worries, there was no place out there which could ease them and relax him. How could he have been so reckless? He thought back to the time when he had brought Concrete up here, only for his spar to sulk monosyllabically all the time. Not get into it at all. It had triggered their first serious beef. He had accused Concrete of having a ghetto mentality only for Concrete to curse him for being a blood chameleon. And Dele had smiled at the time and thought 'That's right. Nothing can contain me!' Now he didn't feel so clever.

Turning into the road of Tabitha's house, Dele all but tumbled into Jonathan, loitering on the corner with someone. Quick as a flash, Jonathan began doing his trademark skit: 'I would go out tonight . . .'

'Easy, Arnie. Ze good pumping is better than ze coming!' replied Dele in a bad Austrian accent. Dele called Jonathan 'Arnie' because Jonathan was a body-building buff, and he was prone to quoting nuggets of Schwarzenegger approvingly. Even now Jonathan sported a sleeveless Nike T-shirt, tucked into jeans, for that solid six-pack effect.

They punched knuckles and Jonathan smiled. In the battle of cuss-words, he reckoned the charge that Dele was a disciple of dodgy indie music was a dis far weightier than Dele's feeble 'Arnie' comeback. After all, Black Man was supposed to have top abs.

'This is my bro, Gabriel, come to visit for the weekend. Got to show him the sights, you know.' His brother looked a few years older and leaned casually against the wall, drumming his fingers. He wore a flat Kangol cap with the brim at the back, a sheepskin jacket and little round glasses. He could have been some boho beneficiary of the United Negro College Fund. 'So what's the coup, Del? What badness have you got lined up this weekend?'

'Ah, boy, nothing much. Quiet night tonight.'

'You going up there?' asked Jonathan, pointing to Tabitha's place.

'I been there.'

'What's it like?'

'S'alright. It isn't all that. The usual thing, you know – '

'I wouldn't know. I don't get invited to those parties.'

'Well, come up if you want. It's no problem,' said Dele.

The ice-cream sounds of happy house greeted them. Dele grimaced as he led them on a tour of the house. He shook a dozing friend awake and introduced him to Gabriel. He looked for Jonathan but Jonathan was already working the room, eyeing up the pretty girls, the plucked eyebrows and bare midriff culture. When he returned, clutching a round of shorts and mixes, he was beaming like it was Christmas. Gabriel wasn't impressed. 'Hold it down, man. You're acting like your dick's been on the dole since the Stone Age.'

Dele and Gabriel made a connection straight off. Within minutes, in their little space on the sofa, they were thick in reasoning. As usual, music was the motor. So often Dele privileged music, used it to carry the burden of conversations. With new acquaintances, it was a way of quietly probing them, and setting out your own stall. Music was a means of sharing intimacies without overstepping the mark. What Dele liked about Gabriel was that he didn't give you any of that cultural-nationalist nonsense about how black folk should listen to this, but not to that. It was like people who checked for Dionne Warwick and Aretha Franklin, but couldn't be dealing with The Carpenters, even though Burt Bacharach scored tunes for all of them, said Gabriel. Or his friend who frowned if he played Cat Stevens or Barbra Streisand, but when a reggae artist's lovers rock version of the same tune came out, this same friend would be bigging it up.

Dele built another blunt, passed it to Gabriel, and revealed his fantasy project for the nineties: a pamphlet on drugs and black music aesthetics. From Duke Ellington, through the urban blues and Chicago when it sizzled, taking in the dubmasters, and ending with hip-hop's current sensified embrace. Gabriel puffed away and nodded, said that dub was his favourite thing and did he know that producer Lee 'Scratch' Perry, his dome fuzzy with herb and Rasta Metaphysics, would bury freshly pressed records in the soil and bake tapes in the sun to increase their potency?

It was all good, only they were periodically interrupted by people coming up to Dele and enquiring solicitously if everything was alright with him now. He would have worn their concern better if these hadn't been the same folks laughing at him so vigorously before in the garden. One woman, lurching drunkenly around, her hand dangling limply, was moaning to no one in particular. 'Erica said she'll bring someone to dance with; I need a dancer. Are you a good dancer?' she asked, spotting Dele and tugging at his shirt. He motioned to Gabriel and replied to this insistent stranger, 'Another time.' At the last, this curvy brunette, wearing white spandex leggings, suddenly plumped herself down beside them, and began declaiming, in a cod-Jamaican accent, 'I and I! Dem and dem! Man and man, Lion and Lion! Ting and Ting!'

'What?' said Dele.

'You must know Linton, yeah? He's my baby – '

Dele did indeed know Linton. A guy from the year below, Linton was the number one Negro-elect. Dele had followed his progress with interest. For Linton's sake, he would give this seemingly barking girl a few moments' grace.

'And Bluey, from Global? You *must* know Bluey and all the London crowd. He's my baby too!'

Global Nation was an acid-jazz band, popular with multi-culti clubbers. Dele shook his head, but this turned out to be the wrong move as she proceeded to rattle off a long list of her other babies, before concluding that Linton was her most precious one.

By now Gabriel was looking agitated so Dele swiftly moved them on. 'Who does she think she is? Is that the kind of shit you put up with here? You can't have people thinking you're a pushover.'

Dele shrugged, then nodded. He didn't want Gabriel to think badly of him.

They shifted to Tabitha's master bedroom, where a little gathering was already in place. Everyone was conversating on the future, their plans after the final exams. They were utterly assured the world owed them a supremacy. Most actually subscribed to the adage that it was never enough for themselves to succeed, but that their dearest friends should fail, only they kept this a secret. Some guy behind Dele was banging on about the offer he had received to do research at Tory Central Office as if the ship of state would sink without him. Tetteh was headed to a big city firm of solicitors. Another, Tamsin, was coolly explaining, amidst an envious hubble of hacks, how she had landed a traineeship with the *Chronicle* newspaper.

'Have you actually written anything, Tamsin?'

'Well, I've done bits and pieces,' she equivocated. 'Anyway, it's potential. They said I had fantastic potential and I'd travelled widely. They said my experience of other cultures was invaluable. They said they've got me in the frame to be Hong Kong correspondent in the run-up to '97.'

Tamsin's old man was a big bod in Hong Kong, she, just another fair-to-middling Chelsea girl.

A friend pulled out two wraps from his pocket and passed one to Dele, who unfurled the paper and cut the white grains of speed into long lines with his cheque card. He unfurled a £10 note, crouched over a desk and snorted absent-mindedly, more out of habit than logic.

'Damn! Who's that?' Gabriel was looking at Deidre, who had just swanned in, wearing a clingy, short black dress. Her second change of costume.

'Oh, Deidre. I'm sorry, my man. No joy there.' Dele coughed a little and sniffled as he tasted the initial sourness of the speed and saliva journeying down his nose and throat.

'She's a strict Europhile. Plus you gotta have serious change for her to even give you the time of day.'

Gabriel nodded and smiled. 'Introduce me to her, though.'

They were just returning to their little spot when Tabitha, bubbling still, grabbed Dele's arm, whispered, 'I know somebody who's well up for you,' and led him back to Helena before he could protest.

He expected her to be embarrassed, but she was unfazed, which he liked. He brought her a drink and passed her a smoke.

'Oh, so you're gonna be nice to me this time,' she said, those wanton lips framing a half-smile.

'So what are you actually doing next year?'

'Oh God,' she rolled her eyes with the look of someone who's always being pestered by an insatiable public about her future plans. 'India.'

'India?'

'That's right. I'm travelling out there. Not as a tourist, but for my personal growth. I think it's awfully important. I mean, I'm not into that whole tourist attitude to India. I'm going to be a schoolteacher for a while. My uncle Horace runs a school in Calcutta. And you?'

Dele begged her a dance.

At the stereo he made a detour, brooked no argument and slipped in a Sergio Mendes tape for some Latin flavour. He took on the fiery look of a stern dance-master, grabbed Helena and glided with her, tango two-step, across the floor. She laughed, as they enjoyed a little rock and lock. With the next tune, Dele tried on some matador struts while Helena eased away and moved on her own. She wasn't winding to kill or anything. In fact she was barely dancing at all, just more pouting and styling saying 'Look at my body'. But Dele was down with that, seeing as her body was a shapely thing.

'Oh God. I bet you everybody is watching us!' she said.

They took a break. Gabriel had returned, looking perturbed by the wall. Dele sidled over to see what was up.

'I tell you, this place is the craziest place I been in! I was talking to that girl you know, Deidre – just chatting about interests and that. Then she kind of starts with me and goes, "I'm not interested in nasty black guys who like dub. I only go for Eurotrash." Okay, I know you told me, but it's still a shock when you hear it. And then she asked me what I did and I said I was a photographer and I did a bit of stuff for an agency but, you know, there wasn't much work around and I was still signing on. And she looks at me and goes, "Unemployment! That's all that the black guys here know about." And then she said what people did when times were hard where she came from was to leave the city, go to their farms, and work on the land for a while. So I said "Not every-one has forty acres and a mule", she goes "What?" and I go "Never mind. Where do you come from?" She goes "Gambia", and I say, "Funny thing, that's where my people come from. What part?" And she says "I didn't say Gambia, I said Ghana", and walks off.'

Dele cracked up, throwing a glance around. It was only about three in the morning, but folk were already slipping, heaving noisily in the garden. He offered to continue the session back at his place, but Helena said she was tired and wanted to go home, but why not meet for tea tomorrow? Gabriel said they would buck up another time in a saner place, i.e. London. Dele should drop round and reason further. They parted company. Stoned was the way of the walks.

Back in his college rooms, Dele fired his nightcap spliff as his brain coursed through the events of the evening. He felt like someone was unravelling a carpet, ironing out the creases in his dome and then through his body. It was a funny smoke – some skunky medicine weed – but it sparked him nicely.

He slipped on Warren G's 'Regulate', his sketchy condi-tion giving him unprecedented purchase on the track. With smoke, you could play ball or tennis with ideas. The riffs and takes become so light they levitate.

'Regulators. You can't be any geek off the street. You got to be handy with the steel, if you know what I mean . . .' It began by sampling a snatch of dialogue from Young Guns, a forgettable Hollywood film, gleefully claiming the codes of the Wild West and the male bonding of the outlaw for the ugly urban dramas of Los Angeles. This was the tale of two spars overcoming would-be muggers, but Warren G was also working in a local nod to the internal world of hip-hop and reggae massives, the world of soundboy-killings and lick-shots of applause; where the ability to be a lyrical murderer, handy with the steel of your poetical techniques is the ultimate accolade.

And the music! . . .

Warren G had hijacked Michael McDonald's eighties pop standard 'I Keep Forgetting', coating the tune in doo-wop harmonies, breezy synthesiser lines, and a lazy, sparse bass; the style was kingly slack, the bounce of a low-rider convertible on a cloudless day. It was so instantly definitive you couldn't imagine summer in the city had ever had any other soundtrack than this 'G-Funk'. You just nod your head, nod ya head . . . Dele laid down on his quilt, lost himself in hip-hop's lush pastures and drifted to sleep.

Things ran swiftly between Helena and Dele after that first night. They were seen frequently together on the last days of the circuit. But the real coup was altogether less pleasant. Helena thought she was on a level with Dele, but Dele didn't think so. It happened that she subscribed to the line that you should only enter into a relationship if you could learn something from it. She was highly curious about other cultures, only had had little field experience of any. Her previous boyfriends had been bland, sturdy public-school types, and she had had enough. So she seized the main chance, peppering him with questions on his upbringing and background. Unfortunately, he'd simply lost the will to meet her half-way. Not in this space.

That evening at Tabitha's had set the seal on Dele's disaffection with his Oxford career. He would have liked to be easy-going with Helena, but he didn't want her to think he was the type of brother who believed there weren't any problems in affairs like theirs. To have treated her right would have required a free and frank discussion about *everything*, only he was too frustrated with himself to be emotionally forthcoming to this woman who seemed to him emblematic of his experience there.

He worried that if he told the whole truth, about his home life and the rest, it would lead to such a shift in the balance of power. It would have been an invitation to Helena to respond to him on the level of pity or sympathy, the way contrary black critics said that white people got off on Toni Morrison books. He was too proud to let it come to that. Fuck it. Even Dapo, who had the cause, resented it if people came to her like that! No, it was best that he and Helena dealt with each other with a quickness and done.

But this was the problem. Dele wasn't getting his. The furthest he reached was the occasional lickey-love. Forever linking, almost cloying in public, Helena would clam up once they retired inside.

'It's not that I don't like you, Dele darling,' she would say, rubbing her finger along the outline of his lips. She was forever touching his lips, or running her hand down regions of his soft, smooth body, as if trying to come to terms with the sheer negritude of it all. 'It's just that, well, that kind of sex is a very special thing. It's the greatest intrusion into my personal space, and, well, I don't think we're ready for it.'

Dele, lying next to her, would take his hand from her shoulder.

'What is this? So putting my dick inside you is oppressive, but giving you head isn't, is that it?'

'Dele, don't shout at me – '

'I'm not shouting!'

'Just hear me out, will you? One, of course there's a difference between this and everything else – '

'I can't believe this. So you're on some bogus new woman tip now? Before, you had no problem with beer-crazy rugbyheads.'

'Don't you dare patronise me! You get so agitated sometimes. All I'm saying, Del, is that before you get inside me I need to get inside you. You never tell me anything about your family – '

'There's nothing to tell. Okay, I've got a younger sister and then two parents. They think I'm gonna become a lawyer but they're very much mistaken. And that's about it.'

'Tell me about your parents. And your sister.'

'No stories, H. My sister leads a storyless life. I'm sorry,' he added sarcastically.

'Alright. Be like that! It was a perfectly harmless request,' said Helena decisively, turning over, away from him.

She was within her rights, he could see that. He hadn't paid his dues to her, he hadn't shared inside information – what could he expect?

He liked looking at her back, though. Front-on, he had to contend with the blue veins that ran through her hands like fault-lines, the individual qualities of her face and speech. But her back was a smooth slab of alabaster and he could hug up to it, inhale its perfumes and make play with images of an incoherent revenge. He had her teasing the snatch of his claws only he couldn't make the kill, the steal. He wanted to fuck Helena, he wanted to fuck English history, like some horn of Africa.

It took a good little while to placate her.

'Boy, what else again? What do I need to do? We are not amused. We are certainly not amused,' teased Dele.

'Del, you know how much I like you,' said Helena finally, 'but there's just something about us at the moment, and I need to feel really relaxed if . . . you know. We'll know when the time is right.'

Dele cursed silently. When he first met her, he had assumed that this wariness was part of some temporary coy routine. With this in mind, he had devised his most elaborate three or four scenarios yet. Scripts would have to be written, theatrical costumiers ransacked . . . Now all this would have to be put on hold. He clambered out of bed and shuffled moodily to the bathroom. She didn't call him back.

Maybe he should change tack with her. Maybe he wasn't bad enough. Perhaps he should drop the dress of his Queen's grammar and go for pure ragga blather? Or maybe go for the vulnerable, Woody Allen, mildly tortured tip?

He knew what Concrete would advise. But advice from an if-it-bleeds-tek-it merchant was not what he needed here. He puffed his cheeks, washed his face and chided himself. Helena was all right and he shouldn't have gone down this dumb-assed road with her. He felt to knock the thing on the head, but he didn't want her to think he was sacking it just because she wouldn't give it up. What on earth had prompted this latest piece of vainglory he couldn't figure.

Probably he didn't like her enough. But the way he was acting these days he was unlikely to meet, much less notice, someone that he really took to. It was like, which came first, the chicken or the egg? This was the dead-end street, and here the hole he had dug for himself.

He decided to pop up to London. Dust up his head and get a wider perspective on the situation. Consult Dapo. She would sort him out.

home
and
away

THIS TIME Dele thought it best to head home straight. Creeping through London undercover for yet another weekend would be tempting fate. And it would be nice to touch base with his folks. His Mum would feed him up. Eba and turbo beef stew . . .

Dele got down on one knee, lowered his head slightly and said 'Good evening, sir.'

'Good evening, son,' replied the old man and Dele got up. 'How are your studies?'

'They're fine. I'm just up here because tomorrow a group of us are being shown round some of the barristers' chambers in the Middle Temple. You know I'm thinking of applying there for a grant for law school,' he lied.

The old man nodded and continued, 'You are now on the last and most important lap, Dele. Concentrate your mind on the riches to come. You must not let me down. I have spent thirty years in this country, forgoing the lifestyle to which I was accustomed. Blood money, blood money! I trust you will not spit my blood in my face.'

The old man was settling into his groove now, hurtling words at his son and – he not being the kind to slip in a few interrogatives amongst the rhetoric – Dele could afford to let his mind cruise. Judging by the wafts blowing from the kitchen, his mother was on the case. He was just wondering why Dapo hadn't come down to greet him when his Dad dropped the bad news.

'Your sister is in hospital. She had a crisis two nights ago. We did not want to tell you, of course. We do not want to distract you from your studies.'

'How bad is she?'

'It seemed a little worse than usual at first. We had to call an ambulance to take her away. But your mother has been seeing her every day and she says she is much better. After dinner, we shall have our service to pray for her. Now you should go upstairs and ease yourself.'

Dele poked his head quietly into the kitchen. His throat tickled at the dense pall of chilli peppers, enough to fell a casual visitor. But never his mother who was unconcernedly chopping up vegetables. Whenever Dele returned home, it seemed that time had stood still. He would find his mother in five or six stock positions, most of these on her feet. She was swiftly topping and tailing stalks of okra, the spindly, etiolated type you got in the Indian greengrocers. They must have been out of the bulbous Kenyan ones. She preferred those; they gave off a stronger flavour.

Seeing her sent a familiar twinge of melancholy down him. She had kept her petite figure, but the yellowing sadness of her lined eyes told of the toll of the struggle. In her moments of pique, she chided her husband for never having given her a day of relief in this country. She said that she would die of hard work and they'd all be sorry, don't say they hadn't been warned. But these minor outbursts were rare and really just registerings of the facts. They were not made with the slightest expectation that her regime would be relaxed. The children always doubted they were doing enough to relieve the pressure but they understood the big powers were not in their hands. One day, they promised, there would be a glorious payback.

When she noticed Dele she rushed over, cradled his head in her hands, danced over him and sung her little greeting-song. The words were lost on him, but its every cadence and inflection was reassuringly familiar.

Her breath exhaled a little liquor sweetness. She had granted herself her irregular reward that evening – a miniature bottle of brandy bought and guzzled at some mysterious point on her journey home. Not that there was an outright ban on alcohol to his knowledge, but none of them seemed to drink it in the open. Dele mock-fainted under the fumes and she placed her finger to her mouth, smiled and pointed next door to the dining-room.

The prayer for Dapo was squeezed in between Psalms 23 and 129. A song of ascents:

> They have greatly oppresed me from my youth –
> let Israel say –
> they have greatly oppresed me
> from my youth
> but they have not gained the
> victory over me.

The old man followed up with his ten-minute thought for the Sabbath Tonight, a particularly bilious attack on the Church of England, and the overtures its leaders were making to the Pope. (The closer it got to the second coming, the angrier his sermons had become, for some reason.) But his Dad said this had all been predicted in Revelations 13 and Isaiah, and signified the Countdown to Armageddon had begun. The shit would swamp the fan, if not by the year 2000, then certainly in his children's lifetime. But God had made a covenant, a promise passed down from generation to generation, and the good would be protected.

After dinner, his father eased himself into a straight chair and beckoned to his son for his regular chore. Dele dried his fingers, stood behind him and set about disentangling and picking the grey and white hairs from the expanse of black curls. His Dad sat with his arms crossed, staring straight ahead. Every now and again he might direct Dele to a particular cluster that he felt required special attention.

If Dele felt his father had been troubling or hurting him unduly, he might pick his hair with as vicious a snap as he dared from his blunt fingernails. When Dele's friends had 'bad hair days' they would shove it all under a tammmy or a wrap and make lightning raids to the shops until they could get to the salon and sort it out. So Dele would entertain himself with a wicked little fantasy where his Dad was forced to don Dele's Kangol and rush to work. But when he was in a good mood, or feeling positively towards his old man, he would linger over the hair, really do it thoroughly. And his father would respond to such a peace offering with inchoate intimacies of his own.

For sure, there would be the usual exhortations about Dele's future, but also lovingly detailed remembrances of Nigeria. Stories of street-boxing (his father had been a keen bare-fist fighter in his youth, and dripped anecdotes about every glovesman from Mandela to Muhammad Ali), bed-hopping, academic triumphs, and the histories of his own parents. Of Dele's grandfather, who had had a vision in Oyo State that their family would settle across the globe and prosper.

The old man came as close as he ever did, at these hair sessions, to passing on to his son the reason why things had not gone quite to plan. It was not that Dele thought his family a special case, but he wanted, and felt he deserved, his father's own gloss on it. Every now and again, his father might interrupt a lengthy silence by hinting at some indignity he had endured in perfidious Albion – problems with landlords or interview panels for jobs – but Dele never got the whole fullness.

Maybe this was because his father was no fan of conspiracy theories. He was a One Nation Heathite Tory Man, and proud of it. He liked nothing better, on a good hair day, than to chat affairs of state with his son, the history student. After all, Baba Dele fancied himself as yet another President-of-Nigeria-in-waiting and – after a loud session conversating and drawing correspondences across continents and time – he would jump up, slap his hands on the table, or shake them vigorously, saying 'Yes! Clever boy!', and beam at his son, adding '*That* is why we have children!'

Tonight was a so-so hair night. Dele was preoccupied. His father contented himself with an amusing story about how, when he first arrived in England, he was staggered to find all these Jamaicans here called Winston, named after Britain's wartime premier, when over in Nigeria Winston Churchill had been castigated as a reactionary, who could not bear to dismantle the Empire.

Hearing him with his erudite flourishes, Dele was confused and wondered if it were possible, still possible, to grab the closeness that he craved with this man who bestrode their worlds like The Colossus. But probably too much had happened already. And again, he was afraid.

He fetched his father a mirror so he could study Dele's handiwork. His father looked at his dome, front and back, and declared himself satisfied.

Time to repair to the sitting-room, the nearest thing to his father's perfect world. In some of his friends' places the sitting-room – kept so pristine, with the prayer scrolls, and cloth maps of the Caribbean – carried so much family pride you could only go in there on Sundays. Theirs you could enter any time but, from the moment you stepped in and were bulldozed by this battery of educational achievement laid out on the walls – the school sports medals, the framed college photographs – you realised this room was a concept you didn't fuck with.

They sat down in silence in front of the telly, Dele fidgety, wondering how soon he could legitimately leave. He stared at the framed letter of acceptance that Dapo had received from Sussex University granting her a place, which her ill health had forced her to defer for a year, and thought 'How bathetic!' She hadn't been sure which college to go for and he had advised Sussex or Essex because there were supposed to be quite a few black students there.

His Mum had already nodded off. Shirts and trousers, destined for the ironing-board, waited in a huddle around her feet. Her mouth lay half-open, head lolling to one side, utterly shattered from the day. Her children were her big joy but, other than her brandy, she seemed to have lost all interest in creating space for little local happinesses.

He didn't even know exactly what she did. His folk saw no need to tell him about stuff like that. All he knew was that it was some lowly personnel gig for a firm in the City. The key thing was that it was clerical, and not manual. If you asked Mum, or her home country friends who dropped round the house what they did, they would reply, 'Oh clerical, clerical!'

Whatever it was, it was some degrees beneath the level that her erstwhile sparkle and quickness had merited. Before she became so cowed that she dozed off in front of the box by nine. He tried to remember when this had begun to happen but it was too long ago now. Dele couldn't stand it any more. He mumbled his excuses and left the room.

That night Dele found it difficult to get to sleep. He wanted to play some tunes, but they weren't supposed to use electricity on the Sabbath, barring necessities. He was gutted about Dapo. Her shit was beginning to look very serious. He stretched out on the bed that the two children had used for years before, until Dele had got so big Dapo suggested he sleep from the bottom upwards and she from the top downwards. Still restless, he stilled all his senses and surrendered himself to a visitation from the spirit of the house.

Its most fecund presence was a sense of tears and a sickly self-pity. It bathed the place in an other worldly light, yet another waiting-room off real life that the children were agonising to start. Its chief possessee was their father. He felt his old man still could not quite believe that he had not become a Distinguished Gentleman residing in a lower numbered postcode. After supplementing his first degree with a second from London, his first relatively decent job in this country had been at the Post Office, junior manager level, in the days when the GPO was a bit of a haven for white-collar blacks and East African Asians. Now, in his time off from creeping around the lower rungs of the civil service, he stalked the house, a higher life-form, long bouts of brooding giving way to sudden flights of fury. Like some Late Great Black Man, now tossed around, desperate and dazed by his condition, clutching at the phoney straws and trampled roots, dizzy from the decay of his inheritance.

All that history, all those casualties. Quiet as it's kept. Weighs a ton. Dele felt himself at the bottom of this pile in limboland, gravely charged with fashioning some tool for empowerment and agency. Hadn't they spirited him, post-GCSEs, to Enfield for this very purpose? His school had been the low-level, direct grant kind – full of boxers' sons – but they'd saved their last to send him to class, it was true. Only he felt to pass on all that and skulk across the border to hook up with the fallen angels, Coltrane, Miles Davis and the dub-heads, and rap about stimulants and music . . .

Baba Dele had pressurised him heavily from hanging out with Caribbeans as a youth, even monitoring his comings, goings and company from the sitting-room window. That was all the encouragement he needed. And anyway, where he was living most everybody – Africans or Small Islanders – spent at least part of the time as a kid acting Jamaican. Life was a lot easier that way. There were a lot of Jamaicans around.

The situation had got a little distressed at school when some Jamos used to dish out abuse about dark, ugly Africans and bubuheads, and even gave him grief for taking piano lessons – as if real black pupils should be busy raping the teachers instead. But that was just sticks and stones and you ignored it. And even then the siblings had checked for their cussedness and the music. Then later, they had learnt how it had been Jamaicans who had gone to the aid of the St Lucians, when their dating of Teddy girls had sparked the original Notting Hill riots, and they had been first to the breach for them all ever since.

Concrete, to be fair, had been one Jamaican who had never given him grief. Maybe that's why they started. Dele remembered being sorry when Concrete's family had moved south and settled on Brixton's Angell Town when that sink estate was at its roughest. At first Concrete had been a little lonely and scared of all these Real Deal Holyfield outlaws around him, and had been the keener to preserve his link with Dele. Then he had gradually got absorbed into some of the runnings of his area, albeit at the fringes, and now their friendship struck an odd note to some observers. But, really, it suited them fine in different ways, and was in any case too old a thing for either of them to worry about. He thought that his spar was basically a regular guy who just suffered from the love of money. He'd hoped Concrete's stint at South Bank University, where he was doing a foundation year HND course in electronics, might see the end of much of that. But he was spending most of his time chilling around the Students' Union on Wandsworth Road, with his feckless people from Brixton and the Junction crews. Others who weren't going to graduate, whichever way you looked at it.

Dele got up and made his way down the landing to Dapo's room, where he pictured the house's spectral air waging grim war with her mantras and holy man charms. Their Mum had tidied up some of her clothes and stashed them in drawers, but some of her debris was still around. On the bed, slips and tops covered her kente rucksack, with brooches and hair bric-a-brac lying atop. Even the things that had been put away were slightly out of kilter; tops of skin care jammed awkwardly instead of rolled on smoothly, pens with the wrong tops, sundry tasks left unfulfilled and chafing. Dele made a quick, superstitious tour before shutting the door firmly.

He crept outside for a final cigarette, where the familiar periodic screech of dogs in the night from the poor white trash estate across the road, for once, calmed his spirits.

'Will those attending our service as visitors please make themselves known,' announced the pastor the following morning, as the guest minister concluded and stepped off the pulpit. His Dad threw him a commanding glance and Dele reluctantly eased himself up from his seat between his Mum and cousin Toyin, and exposed himself. The ageing pastor from the Tottenham Adventist church dubbed as 'visitors' anyone who didn't attend services on the regular, be they people based out of town, slackers or whoever. And Dele perspired pungently under his Saturday best as the congregation scoped him closely. Even the kids, huddled on the front stage to hear their abridged Old Testament tale, craned forward for a peek.

But today the looks were fairly neutral, even friendly. As they all broke into smaller groups for Bible reasoning classes with Sabbath school teachers, an acquaintance, Gladys Maynard, approached Dele's father and beamed. 'You must feel so proud to have such a sensible, hard-working son!' she said, her hands full with noisy grandchildren.

'Yes, we have been blessed,' returned the old man, before playing with one of her young'un's cheeks. Mrs Maynard was Bajan, but the old man didn't mind exchanging pleasantries with Caribbeans in church. It was just outside that the problems started.

Dele's mother sidled up to him by the entrance and put her hand on his shoulder. 'Now that you are finishing your studies you should soon start thinking about a girl, you understand my meaning?'

Dele laughed. 'Oh Mommy, you're so sweet!'

'Now tell me, Dele, what did you think of Mama Lara's daughter?'

'What, Faith?' He looked up to where Faith was standing, talking to his father and Mrs Maynard. So that was what it was about! He had come home one day last vacation to find this Faith sitting all comfy on the sofa. His Mum had introduced them and said that he should walk Faith home. Her looks were bleak. Like a pudding and, worse, she didn't have anything to say for herself. The only books she had read were the Bible and *The Highway Code* and she didn't even have anything to say about either of those. That fifteen-minute walk had been a serious struggle.

'Mommy, man, are you for real? Say it ain't so.' He laughed again and made a beeline for the exit. The old man would be looking for him shortly, so's he could parade him in front of pastor Henry and the visiting dignitaries, over coffee and biscuits. Presumably Faith would be invited along today. But there was just time to stretch his legs, have a few surreptitious puffs on a smoke, and cast his eyes over the young ladies.

Most of them he knew by sight. There was Lenora, in her black hat and lacy number. Her chest was stacked, but her breasts were long and pendulous. Gravity had not been kind to them. And Juliet and Debbie, those tremendously huge women known as The Weather Girls, there laughing with that six-feet four junior minister. What was his name, some unfortunate old school number – Augustus Hurlock? Or did he flip it to Kwame last year, when Nubianism had hit him on the head? All done up in that pale green designer suit, with the chunky gold rings 'n' tings on his fingers. Augustus must have worked his way through half the congregation by now.

Dele perched by the side of a Golf trying to earwig on the gossip. Then a girl he had clocked during the sermon came over. He had a closer look at her now: five-feet four, about his age, solidly, nearly generously built, his side of coffee-coloured, with straight extensions at the back of her head. She sported a pretty smile with chubby cheeks and a button nose. Homely. A home-maker rather than a butt-shaker.

'Hallo,' she said.

'Alright?' Lord have mercy! She had a northern accent. He had never heard a sister with a northern accent before.

'My name's Cheryl. You're Dapo's brother, aren't you?'

'Yup. You saw me stand up inside, right?'

'Right. I've met her a few times here and I wanted to visit her. Where is she?'

Dele fished in his pocket and gave her the details. They had a little chat about what she was doing, what he was doing. He said that, if she was passing by Dapo that afternoon, he might see her there. They shook hands. Dele felt a most proper and decent young man. Very strange. He made a mental note to talk to agreeable people more often.

At the hospital his sister was in no frame for fun and games. She was morose, too poorly to take a wander, and said the desferol was stinging her arms. She met his queries about this latest relapse with stubborn closed shutters. It was only when he ran her through recent events at college, and mentioned meeting this safe new guy called Gabriel that she got animated.

'Thank God you've got someone new to play with! Concrete's alright but a little goes a long way. That guy doesn't have nicknames, he has aliases,' she said. She had time for Concrete though, in her way.

She listened to the Helena story with a furrowed brow and a little smile. 'Historicise her, boy! Flinging down the Flower of England sounds well and good but you can't fuck an idea. Not *all* the time. Three long years – how many flowers do you need?'

Dele conceded the point.

With Cheryl's entrance and little pieces of gossip, Dapo perked up further. A guy had just hit on Cheryl outside, so Dapo started regaling her with a story about a friend, General Custer, whom the siblings had known from childhood days spent kicking around at the local library. They called him General Custer, with a logic that now seemed pretty confused, because of his penchant for Indian girls. He'd never got anywhere far but old Custer wasn't fazed. He repositioned himself and became your original Mr Smooth, playing cynically on female desperation at the shortfall of educated brothers, with his blagger's patter about a trailer-load of degrees from the LSE. It turned out he had chirpsed Dapo on the Piccadilly Line.

'All this "So why you never tell me you reach woman?", and ray, ray, ray. That Custer's got a nerve. Just blatant! I gave him the cold shoulder. By the time we got to Manor House, you could'a frozen a steak on his side. Not gonna let no damn fool fraud fling *me* down. Tch!'

Seeing the two of them so relaxed touched off a soothing something in Dele. He wanted to roll with it. Try a little tenderness, he thought. When they finally left, he invited Cheryl out for a drink.

They linked up the next day at a bar just by the central London YMCA off Oxford Street. It was early in the evening and the bar, neutral and comfortable in its deep reds and browns, was relatively quiet. The YMCA was the first refuge of the richer kind of transient: tourists and foreign students, office types, wealthy Africans of no fixed abode. Sometimes Dele came here to sightsee, and to pass off glamorous fictions about his life to unwary guinea pigs.

He smoked a hurried, nervous cigarette before Cheryl was due, then sucked a mint. It wasn't good enough. She had barely sat down before she started sniffing and looked around. 'Has someone been smoking in here?' she said, like as if this wasn't a public bar. He cursed silently and said that, if she found it a little stuffy, they could move to the Residents Lounge.

'Not to worry,' she said, and sniffed some more. He had ordered a bourbon. Cheryl wanted a coffee but they only served coffee at tea-time, so she opted for a Purdey's or, failing that, a still mineral water, or a still orange juice. All the bar was good for was a fizzy Britvic.

'I'm sorry, Cheryl. If you hang on a minute while I finish this, we'll go somewhere else.' He began belting the drink down, then suddenly realised he might be looking like a pisshead and slowed up.

Cheryl was staring at him. 'Do you drink as much as this every day?' she asked.

'Eh?'

'I said, do you drink like this every day?'

Dele looked at her. How do you respond to a question like this from a God-fearing woman on your first date? She might as well have asked 'When did you stop beating your wife?' It was probably already too late. Hesitation was surely worse than an admission. He mumbled, 'Not very often', and tried to look cute and disarming, but she only grimaced back.

'Shall we head?' asked Dele.

The walk took a little while. He didn't really know any coffee bars. Plus Cheryl, of solid St Kitts stock, sauntered with the stately shuffle of an African, her arms folded under a wool cardigan.

They found a cappucino joint off Euston Road, and Cheryl finally relaxed. She chatted volubly and Dele was content to listen. He didn't want to make any mistakes. Her old man had come over in the early sixties to Liverpool as a skilled mechanic. Only there wasn't any skilled work to be had so he had swallowed his pride and settled on the assembly line at Ford Plant like the others. On the weekend he and his friends would dress up, tilt their Fedoras on just so, and go raving. They used to step out with the Irish girls from the local nurses' hostel because they were the only ones who would go with the Silvery Moons. One evening his future wife, also a nurse, came along and he had begged her a dance.

'Why you always with those Irish girls?' she'd asked him.

'Because they are from a small island like me and they understand. They know what it is to be a small fish in a big pond,' he'd replied.

And Mum had thought that was sweet. Then they twigged they were both from St Kitts, and the rest was history, Cheryl and company.

Her Mum couldn't be dealing with bringing up the kids in a port city with all the big islanders and their nasty runnings, so they had upped and moved to Preston, where her Dad eventually found work as a mini-cab driver. But an irreligious temperament had driven him to drink and, when he started getting violent, Mum had left him and upped again to make the big move to the capital. Now Cheryl was partway through a course, en route to becoming a legal executive and one day, maybe, a lay preacher.

Dele took Cheryl to see *Jesus of Montreal*, a French-Canadian picture, for obvious reasons. Cheryl said she really enjoyed it, although it was a bit intellectual. But Dele knew he could do little wrong by coming overly cerebral with Cheryl. She said she'd never heard a brother so softly-spoken and polysyllabic before. At college he broke everything down with a little ragga blather. Now here he was buttering it up on the smoother side. Different strokes for different folks.

What she said. She said that Preston was light years behind London as regards a conscious community, like Afrocentricity hadn't happened. She said that black folk be going round saying 'Got a light, chuck?', 'Ta, cock!' and 'Our kid' as native as the natives. And as for romance, well Cheryl had never exactly been rushed, seeing as the brothers up there hadn't got beyond the white-girl-as-trophy trap. Dele countered that Cheryl shoudn't be so impressed with the London scene, because there was plenty of bogus brothery going down, and the fact that some proud Nubian couple named their kids Kwame and Nefertiti still didn't mean they could find Ethiopia on a map. Cheryl retorted maybe, but even if they were only paying lip-service, this would pay unforetold consequences for life, because the children would one day be intrigued at the origins of their names, and this would start them on a voyage of discovery. That Dele might be a smart guy but he shouldn't feel a way about how others tried to better themselves.

He saw her off at Finsbury Park and caught a bus back. A parting kiss? Are you crazy? Just the slightest peck on the cheek and he went his way. The original gentleman.

Next weekend he came up again and they went down to a Mexican bar in Camden for crêpes and tortilla. They rapped mainly about their backgrounds. Cheryl had a case of 'the brother syndrome'. Even in Preston she had known too many inconsiderate and roving black men, like her old man or kid brother, for her to want to get involved with them. But Dele was African and different to what she had seen around her, so Cheryl was prepared to give him the benefit of the doubt.

She told him about her one previous relationship; a white Anglican junior doctor called Graham. He was twenty and studying hard, she a sweet sixteen and they went out for five years.

'He was so kind and gentle and considerate. Ambitious as well, but very level-headed. One of the things I liked about him was that he never tried to pressure me, you know, push anything too far . . .'

Oh no, Dele thought, this can't work. He supposed he should have been ready for this, only most of the Adventists he knew had lapsed aeons ago. He did some careful probing and his findings were pretty grim. Four years and eleven months into their situation, they had neglected their own best natures and done the deed.

'Afterwards, things between us weren't the same, really. Probably we both felt bad about what had happened. I told my pastor about it and he said I should cut Graham out of my life. Anyway, it all fizzled out shortly after. I still see him, though, when I go back up there. He's got someone new now, and left our church.'

Dele was busy doing sums. Four years and eleven . . . worked out at 59 months. Even if she liked him ten times more than this Graham geezer, it would still take half a year to get his. One hundred and eighty days, or twenty-four visits to church. Thousands of minutes sipping Britvics and eschewing cigarettes. It was rare to find any decent sister giving it up with the alacrity of your average student, so he had been prepared for a longer haul. But *one hundred and eighty* days!

'So now I'm on the lookout for a good man again.'

She smiled winningly and he placed his hands, without thinking, over hers. It was sweet, not sexy, and before he could dwell on the arithmetic, he realised that it didn't matter all that much. Sure, he wanted to deal with her that way, but he almost had to remind himself to keep it near the front of his thoughts. Mainly, he just wanted to cuddle and see her across the main roads safely, like some knight in a courtly love fable.

Dele bought her a college scarf. He hunted high and low for a medium-sized Oxford University sweatshirt, the kind tourists or American graduate students wore. Cheryl ate it up. He said she should aim higher than being a legal executive and lent her law books he taxed from his college library. She said that one day he would be a solicitor and she his secretary, then after passing her exams the two would set up their own firm and truly be partners. He let that pass. She took out a subscription to *Ebony* magazine, and passed him a book by some Stateside corporate captain called *Mentors and Role Models: Forwards and Upwards*. He skimmed it and they discussed it. She was basically coming like one of those new breed black Republicans they were getting across the water. Why did none of this infuriate him?

Maybe, on some unregistered level, Dele was trying to impress Dapo. He wanted this decent Cheryl to kick-start him into thinking better of himself and, deeper down, he thought that dating her was in some way a vindication of his sister. Cheryl was a friend of Dapo's, after all. He wanted to show that men like him liked girls like her.

The answer, he eventually decided, was straightforward. Hitherto he had operated on the seedy, lower levels of relationship culture. All he had to do was be open-minded and accommodate her appeal by opening a new category, provisionally called 'The Cheryl Thing', and find out whether he was ready for this progression. The opportunity came sooner than expected. Cheryl invited him over to dinner.

'My Mum's going away, so I thought you could come over for the evening, if you've got any free time. Bring your overnight bag.' she added, laughing.

Her family were housed on the Elsinore estate off Seven Sisters Road. The residents there had made a nod to Shakespeare with their own brand of rhyming couplets. The 'Elsinore' sign had been tagged over with BLACK MAN RULE/ WHITE MAN FOOL. Dele, in his smart brown jacket, black polo-neck and chinos, wafts of *eau de toilette* trailing behind him, mounted stone steps, where lines of dried urine traced abstract shadows. Scrawled down a wall of the lift was a kind of block circular:

WARNING

    Bogus plumber
    Martin Denny
    Irish accent
    Spotty
    On no account open yore door to him.

Cheryl, in khaki shorts and bare legs, greeted him with a chaste peck on the cheek and, in disappointment, Dele forgot to wipe his shoes on the Welcome mat.

Inside was clean and respectable. Cheryl and her mother had moved into the council flat within a month or two of arriving, despite the two-year waiting-list, through a Greek landlord to whom they paid the fairly steep rent of £250 a month directly.

Cheryl was cooking up some oxtail, dumpling, spinach and sweet potatoes. He reached to aid her in the kitchen. As he prepared to steam the oxtail, Cheryl turned to him, her face hard, and said, 'Haven't you forgotten something? Your hands. You didn't wash your hands.'

'Oh yes,' he replied, walking to the sink. Fuck-up number two. Get it together.

Later they sat down, with a carafe of thick Guinness Punch, and ate. The atmosphere was muted. Dele felt nervous. Without his customary seduction accessories – a draw, a trunk of G-Funk – he was a mere shadow of the player he could be. Cheryl got up to slip on a tape, and he just prayed it wasn't the Winans. Luckily 'The Preacherman', Al Green in his rural blues seasoned with a little urban soul phase, piped through the door. 'Tired of Being Alone', 'Let's Stay Together' . . . very sweet.

'On a good day, Al Green makes me want to cry, to make love and to testify,' she said.

'Well, let's hope it's a good day,' he smiled.

She draped herself down on the sofa beside him. With the vibe mellow he softly kissed the back of her neck as she leant forwards. She did not resist for the first few seconds, then pulled her neck away, laid a hand on his thigh and whispered, 'No, Del. Don't do that now. That's not what tonight is for.'

He looked at her closely in her now slightly tense eye and, pulling her hand up, stroked and kissed it.

'Look, Del. If you think tonight is going to end in a mixture of juices, then I'm sorry to disappoint you!'

'Okay. Understood,' he muttered quickly and let her

hand drop. She got up and left the room.

Dele found himself staring up at the naked yellow light bulb. Not even a lamp! What good was this harsh, unyielding glow to a player weaned on the semi-secrets that soft-focus reds and blues allowed? The conditions had been utterly adverse, no one could say different. Even Concrete would nod sympathetically as Dele ran him through the first-night flop.

Cheryl returned, bearing two mugs of tea. She didn't look him in the eye, but curled up with her knees on the sofa. The Al Green tape played out cruelly. The rest was a sweaty silence until she piped up, 'You're not seeing anyone at Oxford, then?'

'Nah man, of course not,' he dissembled, surprised and genuinely indignant that she thought him capable of two-timing her.

'None of those intelligent, rich, glamorous girls attract you?'

Dele shrugged. 'Most of them are so dry-up, believe me. Anyway, I check for you and that's why I'm seeing you. Why are you asking me all that now, after all this time, for God's sake?'

'I was only asking. Even *I* know what most men are like,' she smiled warmly, the cheeks making a welcome re-appearance. 'I'm going upstairs now. Gonna take a bath and get into bed.'

She stood up, shaking her pile of hair. Dele reflected that everything with Cheryl was straight up. She was a church-girl determined to make the most after an indifferent start. There was no spin, no sweet tooth for scoundrels. She wanted a good man and a dinner was just a dinner.

'Shall I come up too?' he asked.

'Unless you want to sleep on the sofa.'

She finished in the bath, came out in a pink dressing-gown and heated the rod up for her curlers. Dele took his towel and went inside. The bathroom was tiny; barely an alcove banged into the side of the wall with a curtain draped around it. Soft'n'Free Curl Activator lotion and some skin care cream propped up on what passed for a cabinet. Above the wash basin hung a little thought for the day in Cheryl's hand:

> Nothing, absolutely nothing happens in the world by mistake. Unless I accept life completely on life's terms I cannot be happy. I need to concentrate not so much on what needs to change in the world, as on what needs to change in me.

Dele stepped in, then promptly out, of the bath: the water was freezing. He sat by the side and thrashed his feet inside intermittently, in case Cheryl could hear. Then he washed his hair, cleaned his teeth, and returned to the bedroom.

She had prepared some bedding for him on the floor. He was disappointed, but not surprised. He did not bat an eyelid. It was just another underwhelming moment.

They chatted for a short while, as she curled the front of her hair, about future plans. Cheryl was sparky, Dele perfunctory. His concentration had wandered to a trio of young honeys he had seen outside the tube that night. With their hair relaxed and pressed short with cow licks, they were dressed almost identically in little packages that popped style. One of them had been loudly carrying on to some guy on a mobile. He had tried to clock the youngest girl, but the sixteen-year-old looked through him and carried on chewing her gum. All that street theatre, the flair for the public parade . . . Man and woman seemed to be getting badder younger these days! Ah, but to be able to regulate that fire in the bedroom! Neighbourhood girls, around the way girls, hoochie booty . . . maybe that's what he needed?

As Cheryl prated he recalled the lines of an old reggae tune:

> Your body's still with me
> But your mind is on the other side of town
> Messing me around.

'Good night, Del! You know I'm not sore with you. It's been a real pleasant time,' she murmured finally.

As he fell asleep, with the episodes of the evening (the doormat, the oxtail) chugging along the mainline to the provinces of his mind, Dele suddenly hit upon the grand design for the whole exercise: an in-depth probe into his personal hygiene.

Whatever the test, he seemed to have passed, because things ran smoothly with her after that. Most weekends he made moves to see her. They waged wars on one another's musical tastes, trading tapes: Cheryl's Aaron Hall and Regina Belle for the eerie lushness of Dele's sounds. Her tunes bathed in the afterglow of quality adult loving, his strutted in a universe of flipped-over fairy-tales, where real niggas minded each others' backs, and sometimes went Rat-A-Tat-Tat Tat-A-Tat like that.

They went raving too. Cheryl was such a soul girl, but strictly soul venues were hard to find that early summer, certainly not locally, because even dances for the R & B posses were being affected by the first overground rumblings of drum and bass.

Dele stood entranced one night in the Ringside wine bar on Kingsland Road as the Chaka Khan standard they had been moving to was submerged under a crazy density of electro beats. He remembered the time a while back when Concrete had declared that, right now, he was listening to 'hardcore' and Dele had thought he meant gangsta hip-hop and he'd replied 'So what's new.' And Concrete had said 'Not *that*, padre. Me say *hardcore*. Like techno.'

Well, after Concrete had explained that he and a couple of his people went down to all these big greyback garage and hardcore raves across the motorways, and they were making just easy money selling puff and coloured paracetamols, Dele hadn't paid it much mind. He'd assumed that Concrete's interest in this new scene wasn't a music thing, just a hustling thing.

The sound had grown a bass since he'd heard it last, but

even so, he would never have thought a sound like that could carry the swing in a black heartland like this. The moody raggamatic crew, always the hardest to please, had rushed the stage as soon as the junglist tune had dropped. And while the lickshots and shouts of 'Tune! Tune! Tune!' signalled approval in approved ways, the punters were going loopy in a fashion that left the conservative standards of cool far behind. It was thrilling to see.

Cheryl stood with her arms folded on the side of the floor, hoping that the takeover was temporary. He pointed to the crowd.

'They're just shocking-out down there!'

She smiled barely and dug her fingers deeper into her elbows. Half an hour later, with the ragga heads still ruling the roost, she pressed him to leave.

In her bed, linking up tight, but still no joy. He didn't fret, though. He could spot momentum when it stared him in the face.

'Cheryl, what are you doing next weekend?' he said finally.

'Nothing especially. Church, but nothing much else.'

'Why don't you come up north and see me at college?'

'North! Oxford isn't north! It's west.'

'That's what it says on the map but, believe me, it gets like the Arctic up there. Cold and lonesome. Pure hot-water-bottle culture!'

She laughed.

'Come on, sweetie. Just to break things up a little. 'Cos I'm forever travelling down here and your chocolate baby gets so tired.'

Cheryl looked up. She knew the import.

She held and kissed him. 'I'd love to,' she replied.

Fired by Cheryl's imminent promise, Dele decided to knock Helena on the head once and for all. Juggling two girls and getting satisfaction from neither was a stressful and expensive pursuit. Better to get some from the one and at least Cheryl was part of a conceivable future. On his return to college he belled Helena, hoping to arrange a Checkpoint Charlie at the nearby Queen's Cafe, where he trusted her sense of public propriety would prevent her from going ballistic. But she said no, in a very quiet voice, and why didn't they meet at The Last Trump that Friday instead?

The Last Trump was a newish jazz bar and grill about half a mile away in an alley by the town centre. Dele had been invited there on its opening night in his capacity as number one Negro. The evening had been a flop and Dele had snapped a picture of an empty dance floor for a university magazine and ran the caption: THOUSANDS OF TRENDIES RAMMED AT THE LAST TRUMP underneath. But, after a little repositioning, business had clearly picked up. The owners had jettisoned the long-backed Gothic chairs, smoky lighting, and up-tempo jazz fusion in favour of something altogether more tasteful. Now pine reigned supreme. The walls were painted with a mural of some twenties upstate New York scene: white men in evening dress danced with bebobbed, boyish women. The sound from the PA was less jazz more forties big band, with every now and then, the brittle tones of some mediocre mid-century crooner floating over the dinner tables that filled the former dance floor.

A four-piece swing student band came on. They handled the trumpet and saxophone with their eyes half-closed, their heads shivering and swaying, like they were engaged in deep dialogue with their souls.

The waiter came up and, without so much as looking at Dele, asked Helena if he could take their order. And him the man at the table! That bloody lackey probably thought he was Helena's bit of rough.

'It's a nice place this, isn't it?' said Helena, between mouthfuls of nachos. 'Alex had a birthday dinner here a couple of months ago and I've been coming here ever since. It's so soothing to be able to sit down and relax and listen to nice music.'

Well, that just started him off. 'Why is it that some people find jazz a music they can eat to, a tasty little side dish? You'd still be munching nachos even if they were playing the blackest of the blues out there. At least you pay opera the respect of dining after it's finished.'

'Oh, God, not all this again! You've always got to chip in with something sniping or clever. You're so moody. You were on good form that first time we met, and now – '

'*I'm* moody? Boy, that's rich! Am I the one who doesn't know she wants, the one who . . .'

The evening had a turbulent, downhill momentum of its own. They abandoned their usual sly indirections and instead to reach straight for the jugular. Dele jumped into the convenient little rupture that had opened up between them, swiftly assembling a couple of other shells – on the time-honoured 'think in threes' principle. Helena, for her part, countered vigorously. It was Race this and Race that with him, when, in fact, when she looked at him, she didn't even see that he was black! He was colourless to her. Dele replied one, he didn't believe her, and two, why should he want that anyway? Being colourless was no good to him. God knows why she went out with him, she said. He had deceived her somehow. He said he hadn't deceived her, she was just a bad judge of character. She wondered why he was always looking to blame other people, when the ill-feeling started with him.

'I don't think that's true, actually. The issue gets started when people like Tabitha try to press-gang me into a slave auction. And don't think I didn't see you laughing as well that night.'

'Is *that* what this has been about, Del? I didn't even know you then! Sometimes you choose to get hyper-sensitive, and sometimes you act like you just don't care. You can't have it both ways. I just can't take you seriously because I don't know anyone who's profited as much from playing the black card at college as you have!'

'It's not as if I had a choice. I mean, I could have come here and sulked in a tent for three years. Or I could come and say "Well I'm here now, I may as well get set up and grab some of the pickings and the action."'

'Oh, here you go again! Why do you repel people from caring for you?' Helena puffed her cheeks and called the waiter back. 'Let's order another bottle. I feel like getting drunk. That's all this is good for.'

Dele looked round. There were a couple of greasy guys smoking roll-ups in the house but mainly the vibe was the richer set of students, the ones in Shetland jumpers, cords and brogues.

'You know, Del,' Helena smiled wryly, 'you speak as if you're fighting a war against everybody. I'm an innocent. I just wanted to have a nice time before finals. I just wanted a shag.'

'A shag!' He laughed. 'Well, why didn't you say so?'

'You didn't ask.' And she held up her hand when he started to protest. 'No, listen to me! By the time you did, I was so pissed off with you I wouldn't let it happen. To begin with, when I met you, I'd heard you were a bit of a shit and I thought, fine, he looks nice, anyway. We can just have a shag and we'll both be happy. And then I got to know you a bit, and I actually quite liked you! And you were nice and funny when you did those silly voices and dances. And I thought, oh, he seems interesting and different, let me get to know him a bit. Who knows. And it was then that you got so prickly – '

He tried to defend himself, although part of him conceded that her insights sounded on point. 'Maybe I let myself get pushed into a corner. Maybe I didn't see the wood for the trees. Probably all a mistake.' He clicked his teeth. 'Fuck it, I don't know, man.'

'I just don't think you were fair to me. As soon as it got difficult you ran away to London all the time. Don't tell me what you were doing up there – I don't want to know. It doesn't matter, anyway. While you've been burying your head in all your pressures, I've had some of my own.' She exhaled in pretty little wisps and a smirk played at the corner of her mouth, as if she was about to drop a master ace. 'But you just haven't had the time or inclination to notice what's been happening to me!'

Try as he might, there was no light he could shed on Helena's 'happening'. She certainly couldn't tell him she was pregnant.

'I am clinically depressed.'

'What?'

'Clinical depresssion. It's official!' she beamed.

The facts were that, what with her fretting on their relationship, and in a bit of a panic about finals, and some domestic dramas in Southampton, and her naturally delicate temperament, she simply hadn't been able to work and got into a bit of a state. So her old man had taken her to see a Harley Street specialist who had certified her 'depressed'. The physic was minor, Endsleigh League pills, counselling and general relaxation. Especially the latter. She had been given leave, and been granted a postponement of her degree exams. She would return in October, after a period spent dusting off her head in India.

Initially, Dele took her seriously and wondered what to make of it. On the one hand, he could see that Helena would be serious in how she felt. He must be partly to blame and he feared that these games he had played had claimed their first victim. And yet she was comfortably off, comfortably loved, with excellent prospects and he couldn't help but contrast her position with the deep shit that, say, Dapo, had to go through.

But as she continued, with that little smile still playing, he realised it couldn't be so bad. And finally she admitted that, yes, she had been as surprised as anyone to discover she was clinical but, what the hell, she had got the note and she might as well use it. She was flying off in a fortnight and was really looking forward to the trip. Another year here wouldn't be so bad.

He smiled broadly. Damn! Helena was a bit of a skanker, like his self. If only he had played it differently they could have had quite a funny little fling. 'Maybe I could get the same gig sorted with my GP?'

'Dele, you could have all the notes from all the consultants at Radcliffe Infirmary, and it still wouldn't do you any good with your tutors. That's the price you pay when no one takes you seriously!'

They both laughed deeply.

'Now that's better! You see how we can have a nice time

when you relax a bit. You look years younger when you smile. The Del of the silly voices.'

He nodded. 'I'm sorry, really! I've been acting in a certain dumb way with you, and really I was doing it to the wrong girl. I just needed a jolt.'

She leant forward and kissed him on the forehead. He said, Madam, why not repair to his rooms where, if she could do a little something for him, he could guarantee the attendance of Barry White, Teddy Pendergrass, and possibly other Superlovers Undercover? She giggled and replied that, notwithstanding everything she had said tonight, all of which stood, mind, the offer sounded eminently reasonable.

The small of Dele's back was pushed up against the side of his bed. Helena's knees were pressed against his chest as she licked the nape of his neck.

'She wants some dir-ty, stin-kin', frea-ky lurve!' he sang, in an overwrought Barry White growl. 'Did anyone tell you you've got serious Uma Thurman lips? She gonna give me some of that Uma Thurman full-lipped lovin' – ' he warbled as he got up to flip the tape over. 'It's good!'

Torn cigarette packets and music magazines littered the floor beside them. Atop were tomes of eighteenth-century English literature: *Joseph Andrews*, *Tom Jones*, *Clarissa*. They were working on a little excursion on the theme of Helena as a naive cooking-girl or wench, fresh of face and heart, with Dele as the rapacious, venal local squire. Dancehall is the soundtrack, but the time, the place is Shropshire, circa 1750. The script is straightforward enough but they've run up against a problem, with Dele struggling to find a suitable name for the lass he's just leapt on in the stables.

'Well, why not Clarissa?'

He shook his head. 'It sounds too posh. We need something more earthy, shy, naive, but sensual when roused. That should be the feel of it. How about Bethan?'

'That's a Welsh name!'

'Yeah, well Shropshire's just across the border, isn't it? That's sorted then!'

Their earlier rub up 'n' ting had sobered them up some

way. He grabbed some skins to build the spliff that he hoped would ease the path to the final frontier. Helena sidled over, took a puff and stared wide-eyed at him. 'What are you going to do, sire? Have your way with me?'

''Twill be my pleasure, wench. Just as soon as I unbuckle my garters.' Dele was having trouble with his belt.

'Zounds!' he exclaimed.

'Does this count as a rape fantasy? Because I don't really have them. I mean, not violent rape fantasies. Antiseptic maybe – '

'No, I don't think it does and Bethan, please stay in character, otherwise this can't work!'

The garters ungartered, Dele started tearing at Helena's long slip, then changed his mind, and pulled it up over her head and arms, swiftly tying them up; then he was licking and kissing her tummy, nibbling at the perky, fried eggs of breasts, and massaging her inner thighs. Now he had freed her arms, and she grabbed his head and steered it downtown, and gripping her arms tightly together on her midriff then her petite frame strained and surged and clawed at the pillows, warm and sticky with every little spasm, and reached back with her arms to the radiator for a hold, jerked his head up with pure pelvic action and moaned and –

There was a knock on the door. Their bodies collapsed in disbelief.

'For God's sake!' she gasped. 'Who on earth can that be?'

Dele looked at the big perspex maroon clock on the wall, shaped as a map of Africa. The small hand was dissecting sanction-bound Libya, and the big hand weaving through famined north-east Sudan. Quarter-past midnight.

'It's probably someone blagging a smoke.' He got up.

'Do you have to go?'

'Won't be a minute, H,' he said, slipping on some jogger bottoms. Smiling, he strode into the living-room and made his way to the front door.

It wasn't someone. It was Cheryl. Cheryl with some new Naomi Campbell bob-style wig, her lips in a dark, muted red, and a low-cut suede fitted jacket tapering at the waist, above figure-hugging blue jeans. She looked all-fruits ripe. She was grinning, an overnight bag on her shoulder.

'Easy, baby.' greeted Dele, his voice betraying nish. He gave her a hug, his mind working furiously, trying to focus but flailing. How can he swing this? No way to whisk Helena out of the place without her coming through the sitting-room. He needs must get Cheryl out of his rooms – maybe a tour of the college. But at half-past midnight? And would Helena co-operate? No way . . . You're fucked-up. Caught bang to rights, Rasta.

'I thought I'd surprise you. Once, just this once mind, I thought I'd skip church and come up tonight instead.' Cheryl put her bag down and sauntered around the sitting-room.

'The coach got delayed. Look at the state of you! Were you about to go to bed?'

Before he could reply, Helena shouted from next door, 'Del. Who's that?'

The light and warmth fled Cheryl's face, her cheeks dropped, and she looked at Dele searchingly.

'There's a friend of mine next door. Helena. We were just having a little drink,' he explained. He tried to sound casual but it just sounded weak.

Helena emerged, her face hot and flushed, clothed-ish, but her hair a touch raggedy, barefoot, smoking a cigarette. She saw Cheryl and froze.

Cheryl let out a stifled yelp, then erupted. Dele moved towards her. 'Hey, Cheryl! It's not what you think. We were just – '

'Don't touch me! Don't you *dare* come near me! You little fuck!' She struck out at his face. Momentarily shocked by the sound of Cheryl swearing, Dele was caught by the first lick, but swayed away from the second.

'Am I not good enough? You think I've been waiting all this time to take shit from you and your fuckries? Take me for some fool-girl – it's so mean!'

Helena, eyes wide, rooted to the spot, made some strangled response until Cheryl shot her a withering look.

Dele was struck by how fine Cheryl looked in the bob.

He suddenly felt really wasted, desperate to sit down. 'Come on, baby! We weren't doing anything. Helena was feeling a little down and – '

'Oh save it, Del. That's it. I'm not gonna let no blasted man just dog me!' She grabbed her bag, all composed: 'I'm just glad I found out in time. God, what was I thinking?' She gazed at him with a mix of disdain and pride, then made for the door. He followed her.

'Don't you *ever* touch me! Don't make me ask my family to come after you!' she said in a hard, even tone, before giving Helena one last, dismissive once-over, and heading out with a thud.

Helena bit her upper lip, her eyes closed briefly over and she flopped on to the sofa, staring straight ahead.

Dele had nothing to say. The music was finished. All he could hear was that the music has stopped.

'I have never been so humiliated in all my life,' Helena said. Then, 'Get my bag and call me a cab.'

He brought out her things, then belled the college porter and asked him to sort out Cheryl, probably now making her way to the college entrance, with a guest-room for the night. He felt light-headed and stayed in the bedroom until the minicab had come and Helena had gone.

After a bit, Dele got up and secured his front door. Just in case Cheryl was thinking of returning later on to burn him up in hot grits. Beside his bed, he built a final spliff to speed him to a dreamless sleep. He felt a little stunned, but mainly vexed that all this drama should happen over a relationship with Helena that was basically done and dusted anyway. Now he had hurt two people needlessly. He was especially sorry for Cheryl. True, they hadn't been fucking, but he'd confirmed her in all those suspicions of guys and, even if it didn't set her back too much, the guys out there would surely suffer on his account.

Now he came to think of it, in the harsh lights of bang to rights, it couldn't possibly have worked between them. Incompatible as lovers, really. If anything, they should just have been friends. Dele exhaled and shrugged, digging for a piece of bravado to cheer himself up. He had been canoeing through rapids and was now buffetted by the eye of the storm. Like Adlai Stevenson when he lost the American presidential election, it hurt too much to laugh, but not enough to cry about.

babylon gets rude

REALITY MUGGED Dele. It gave him six with its size twelves in his boat race. Reality boxed him several and left him wheezing and Cheyne-Stokes breathing, a doleful ringing in his limbs. It crowned him with a chopper and jumped on his rump.

Reality breezed through with a bunch of its crew – Sjambok, Boo-Ya and Babylon Blue – and dealt with him more than enough, and then some.

Reality was drumming it four track. First, of course, the snare, then the basest base in his face, topped off with the hi-hat. And the vocal?

> It's a sad song, that's the coup, it crooned, with a leer
> Your pain is great, but not too much to bear
> I'm a testy old geezer, I'm afraid (it said)
> Two million years old, and still banging heads
> As you're a fine youth now, with the future set fair
> We didn't want you to get the wrong idea . . .

'It's just up here. Other side of the block,' said Concrete.

He, Dapo and Dele were strolling up Brixton's Effra

Road and Tulse Hill, about seven in the morning, towards where Concrete's vaunted new wheels were parked. The three had been out on a bleach, checking different dances in the southside. It was Dele's first weekend out since finishing at college, so the night had really been for his benefit. Concrete was going to drop them off part-way home.

The ride was a nice second-hand VW Beetle convertible, which Concrete had assembled with a little help from his friends. A crew of white boys had ringed the car, he explained, and fitted it with a different engine.

'Hear it now!' said Concrete as he turned the key in the ignition. He sat, perched inside the driver's seat, with the car door open and one foot on the pavement. He toyed with a match in his ear. 'See how sweet and quiet it goes? You know how dem VW engines bang around, so you can't hear nothing in 'em? Well, my boys have sorted it just nice. I'll be creeping through town like a submarine.'

'Yeah, it's alright,' said Dapo. 'How much it set you back?'

'Ah, me nah need to worry about that!' Concrete smirked. 'The biggie is the insurance. Cost me near enough a grand to get it legal . . .'

Dapo threw a quick 'What are we getting into here?' kind of glance at Dele, but he had lost track of the extent of Concrete's runnings a while back. He knew that every now and then his friend got hassled by the Old Bill, and, one time, Concrete had said they were after him over some money he had and what should he do. And Dele had advised that he turn it over in trust to his mother, for her to set up a fund for him. But, that aside, Concrete was just another person in his life, like his parents, who didn't keep him fully abreast. And it wasn't the done thing to ask outright.

'It's your "Brinksmobile", isn't it?' laughed Dele, recalling some old reggae-inspired slang – stemming from the 'Brinks-Mat' Gold Bullion firm – for guys who lured girls into bed with largesse and sugardaddy ways.

'New name fe de man in Jamaica/ Brinks de women ah call them,' Dele sang teasingly.

'Now de women have no problem,' 'Cos Brinks came down this weekend,' Dapo continued.

A police car came along, slowing down as it passed them. 'Let's get some food to eat before we head, man,' said Dapo, 'I could cane something right now.'

An early morning sun was up although the air was a little dry. All three were feeling pretty bullish, for different reasons. Concrete had got his car and Dele's return would mean a respite from the unremittingly harsh world around him. Sometimes it seemed that everyone around him – with the exception of these two and, maybe, his mother – just wanted to take, take, take. Take liberties, take exception, take something for nothing. It was only with Dele that he could just hang, and not have to watch his back.

As for the other two, Dele had pulled out all the stops at college to come down with an honourable second-class degree. There was one more key battle to be fought over his future with his father, and then the rest of his life could begin. And Dapo, who had enjoyed a good five-week spell free of sickness, was relieved that Dele's presence gave her greater freedom to stay out late.

They were meandering back from the all-night take-away, flicking through all the flyers that had been wedged in the windscreens of cars along the road, when they turned the corner to see Concrete's Beetle being towed away upon the ramp of a truck, and a couple of policemen standing by conducting proceedings.

'Hey, what you doing with my car? Leave it the fuck alone!' Concrete shouted, running over to them.

'Oh, if it isn't Mr Avery! What a surprise it is to see you parked illegally,' replied the taller, faintly moustached policeman.

'Leave off out of it, Daniels,' said Concrete, breathing heavily now, and joined by his friends.

'You can't park here, Avery. Not today, not on any day of the week. Plus, you're bang outside an entrance anyway, or didn't you notice? And what's a little delinquent like you doing with a nice vehicle like this, eh?' PC Daniels sneered.

'Don't tell me you're a working man now. Do you wanna run a check on it?' he continued, turning to his colleague, a part-Chinese looking guy.

Then Concrete suddenly grunted, pushed past Daniels, and dashed up the ramp, pulling his car keys out.

Daniels began muttering into his radio, something about suspects, I/C3, two male, one female, asking for assistance. The truck driver got out of his seat, wondering about the commotion, then spotted Concrete on top, crazily trying to reverse his VW off the ramp.

'Hey! What do you think you're doing? Get off my truck!'

'Why do you radics always have to start something, for God's sake?' Dapo piped up. 'We were just going about our business.'

'Shut yer face, or I'll do you too.' snarled Daniels, sabre-rattling.

'You stop us the most and we have the least cars, isn't it?' She turned away disdainfully.

Daniels was beginning to lose it. His temples and fore-arms glistened beads of sweat. A small crowd, forming with that speed unique to these parts, only hyped him more.

The Chiny PC was gingerly climbing the truck, and Dapo strode towards it, until Daniels stopped her and hissed, 'I've told you once, haven't I? Don't your fucking sort ever learn?'

'Don't you try come and talk to me like that!' she said, fixing him a sub-zero stare.

'Best leave it, Dapo. I've got the numbers of these fools and we'll speak to their boss-man later,' Dele called out.

That seemed to press Daniels' buttons. He grabbed Dapo's arms, yanked them behind her, used his other elbow to dig into her neck, and pushed her hard towards the Rover. At that moment, an unmarked car and a white Transit van, sirens screeching, came firing up, and time, which until then had been behaving itself, started to bounce around errati-cally.

A trailer-load of police – there must have been six or seven – uniformed, rushed out, shouting out strangled instructions, then two bore down on Dele, arms akimbo, truncheons at the ready. Talk about a hammer to catch a nut. What did they expect to find? But Dele wasn't going anywhere, not with his sister stuffed in a Rover and Concrete Lord knows where. So he simply side-stepped one officer's grasp, and eased past the other, reaching for the Rover. Only the others were closing in, and someone thwacked him on the side of the head, stunning him, and there was a boot on his windpipe. How could this be going on? On the flippin' street! If they could do this that they're doing, they might do anything.

Dele's hands were wrenched behind him, then the most grunting from the Bill, and handcuffs that clicked behind his back, then he was forced up and desperately tried to keep upstanding as he was pushed to the van, so the locals could see he was a proud black man.

'Is wha' rubbish you call dis? Dem don't trouble you none!'

'Police hoo-li-gans!'

'Cho! De bumbaclaat! Watch wha' ouno do with de bredren, iyah! None o' dat raasclaat coarseness!'

There goes the neighbourhood.

Dele took time to throw the last spectator, a late thirties guy in a green 'As' baseball he recognised from the last party, a defiant smile. Time too to see three panting officers hauling their struggling catch, Concrete, into the van behind him. One was pressing a truncheon firmly under his neck. His breath came in short, sharp gasps, his tartan bobble hat all but flopping off his head. The muscles in his neck stood rigid, almost popping.

Concrete glanced hard at Dele. The look said 'Help me! If you're so very clever, do something!'

The look angled its fair share of derisory intent. Dele didn't understand how he'd messed up for Concrete to look at him so.

'Aren't you gonna tell us why you're arresting us, and give a caution, or don't you know the law?' Dele spoke up, as evenly as he could.

The policemen hesitated for a moment. Then one of

them put his hand on the side of his neck. 'Just get in!' he spat.

The van doors shut. Then they were off. Dele and Concrete lay on their backs on the floor. No sign of Dapo, only four officers. Dele scanned their faces and numbers and tried to store them away. He wished he wasn't so blunted and sketchy from the night before.

'Big up, padre,' he said to Concrete. Concrete turned to Dele, a rivulet of blood running down from his temple. It's funny what the first sight of their own blood can sometimes do to fighting men. For the first time Concrete looked broken. He bit his lip.

'My wrists are bleeding,' he croaked.

'Shut it, Avery!' Daniels bent over, then said calmly to Dele, 'I don't know what you're doing keeping company with this piece of garbage!' He kicked Concrete. He was clearly running the show.

'Do you like to play with knives too?' Daniels said, brandishing the three-inch Stanley blade that Dele recognised as Concrete's. 'Found this in the glove compartment. I wonder where it's been.' Daniels shook his head slowly. 'Oh boy, you really screwed up this time, 'cos you was fucking around in *my* patch, in *my* neighbourhood. It's not your patch, you black cunts, it's mine! So we was thinking, we'll take you around a little tour of my patch, see the sights. We call it the urban jungle. You been on this tour before, ain't you, Avery. Couldn't wait to get back on board, could you?'

That memory must have been too sharp for Concrete. Watch him start.

'You f-fuckin' bastards!'

'What? Come again?' Daniels rolled up his shirt-sleeves.

'I fucked your mother! I tongued her fuckin' pussy!' Concrete added.

Daniels cracked him across the cheeks with his knuckles. The heavy sound had Dele flinching, and the certain knowledge of their immediate futures emptied his insides.

'Get the blankets,' someone shouted.

'Where's my sister, my sister?'

'Shut it about your bleeding sister. You've got other problems mate,' warned one six-foot-plus brick-house.

YT384, Dele clocked, and mentally digested.

There's still plenty of time. Only been here but five minutes. Should be at the station by now. But they're not going to the station. They're going for a ride.

'And that's going for a start!' said YT384, tearing away at the T-shirt that a friend had customised for Dele from a New York original. Below a laser-print of a blown-up Magnum 45 ran the caption, *Brixton – It Sure Ain't Tonbridge Wells.*

'Oh, we've got a Ni-ger-i-an to keep us company.' Some sarky pig was rifling through Dele's wallet.

'Give me that,' said Daniels. He examined Dele's travel-card for a second, then kicked him in the jaw. 'You fuckin' Ni-gerians! You're all fuckin' crooks! You think you can get away with anything, don'cha?' He held Dele by his jaw and shook it firmly up and down. 'Who cut up Joseph in The Village, eh? Was it charlie? Was it charlie?'

Joseph was a young Nigerian who had been killed in a local club a week before, a possibly gang-related incident that Dele had only heard about that night.

'Talk to me, you cunt. Or I'll have you – '

'I don't know, I swear I don't know.' Dele's voice was too fearful to rise above a whisper. He could taste blood on his upper lip.

The officers covered their struggling bodies in dark blankets.

'Time for some bunny-bashin'!'

The first blows are always the worst. It was the same with Dele's old man. It's because they know what they're doing.

'Nothing to say, eh? Cat got ya tongues? Hold him down! Get his legs, Chris – '

What was Concrete doing? Something Dele should be? Chris, Chris, remember this. That rhymes, thought Dele. Chris, Chiny, Daniels and that number. 54–26, that's my number. What was a Toots tune doing in his head at a time like this? Where were they driving? Please don't let them kill him. Concrete is your man, not him. Thank God, a pause. Dele felt to shout out and plead, 'Okay, you've won, you've won!' but his throat was chockful of tears and he didn't trust himself to speak. They'd have loved that! Concentrate, Del, concentrate and release. Mantras, Dapo's mantras . . . Oh Lord, Dapo!

A further flurry. Lord, let him die. Let him be tomorrow's news. *That* would show 'em.

'That's enough. That's enough.'

Up came the blankets. Concrete lay completely still, eyes set, betraying nothing. Dele was still whimpering.

'Now,' a fevered Daniels peered over Dele, 'I understand you're in some doubt as to the reason for arrest. Does someone want to search these two sorry fucks?'

Two policemen dragged Dele's and Concrete's trousers and underwear down to their ankles.

'I thought you boys were supposed to have big dicks. What is it – Linford Christie's lunch-box? I don't think much of these. Sad, sad.' Daniels shook his head. A couple of his colleagues tittered and jerked Concrete's eyes open when he tried to close them.

They found two £10 bags of weed, one in Dele's front pocket, and one down Concrete's socks. Daniels clicked his tongue. 'Now is this to sell or for personal consumption, Mr Avery?' He kicked him in the stomach and Concrete coughed out globules of saliva and blood. 'Now what have we got? We got controlled substances, we got an offensive weapon. Maybe more when we check the prints. You're gonna do a nice fat bird at last, Avery. Scout's honour.'

He ambled over to Dele, pulled his head up and stuck a boot on his windpipe. 'I could snap your neck in a second,' he grinned, then turned to the driver, 'Station, Phil.'

A couple of constables pulled their trousers up and forced water down them. Dele glanced across at Concrete. The right side of his mouth was crushed in, compacted and swollen. The fringes of his hair were matted in blood. Dele could sense bumps and swellings all over his own body, but nothing – bones or skin – seemed broken. Lord knew what was going on inside. Never mind, he had survived. That was all he needed to know. Still cuffed and dazed, they were hustled in front of the duty sergeant.

'Stopped them on suspicion of possession and selling of a class B drug which was quickly confirmed by a search,' said Daniels, placing the draw on the table between him and the scribbling officers. 'They offered plenty of resistance. Mr Avery, as you know, has previous. So, assaulting a police officer . . .'

The constable nodded, the sergeant tsked and glared, and said Daniels was authorised to obtain further evidence. Officers removed the handcuffs, frisked the two and turned out their pockets, which led to renewed interest from the sergeant. The back of Dele's head had taken on a dull, discoloured hue and he gingerly touched it. He explained that the fact that some of his ID said 'Dele . . .' and others 'Aladele . . .' did not mean that he was involved in some fraudulent enterprise. The only time he lost his cool was when they threatened to go and search his family house for no good reason.

'Student by day, villain by night – you must have your hands full! What was it you gave to your sister, 'cos she's on some high-grade stuff, I'm sure! But I don't think she can handle it, you know. You should hear the trouble she's creating down the hall.'

'I want to see my sister and I want to ring a solicitor,' said Dele.

'All in good time, my son. Here's a phone. Maybe the two of you will get to go home-sweet-home together if you're a good boy and we see what she's hiding.'

Dele belled a Streatham solicitor that he had done some work for the previous summer, before being led across the way to the cells.

The freezing cell reeked of rank body odours, loose bowels and fear. The cream brick walls were splattered with graffiti. Atop the mattress on the bunk at the back sat a white and two black guys. They clocked him carefully as he came in, the metal door slamming behind with its thud of finality, but he blanked them and squatted down on a stone by the wall. It was funny. You could tell the others were all friends, but the brothers were subtly dissing the white guy. They were talking about what the police had said to each, only the bloods were chatting in a very fast, pure yard-patois, and the white guy kept on asking, 'What? What did you say?' The bloods had thick south London accents and the three probably rapped in their common tongue most times. Only here, they were raising the racial barricades. Something about police stations, Dele decided.

He breathed in deeply and felt again around his body. Try as he might to think about the fates of Dapo and Concrete, all that his mind would focus on was how to keep all these fucked-up runnings away from the ears of the old man. He would be wondering where they were; they should have touched base five hours ago.

His Dad had an implicit regard for authority. Authority strode suited and booted, with impeccable grammar and a smirking deference, decked in ties and bona fides. Preferably with a smattering of titles: Dr, FRS, Lady, PC. He would like policemen.

Concrete displayed exactly the opposite attitude. Where on earth was he anyway? How was he? Boy, those police really had it in for him. 'This is another fine mess you got me into,' Dele intoned.

But Concrete wasn't a bad boy, not really. He hadn't turned that corner. He still worked at the fringes, making little submarine raids in and out of the legal economy, committing unhistorical criminal acts. He was fond of saying how Man had to survive, but the words tripped too readily off his tongue for you to take them completely at face value.

There was a bang on the cell door and the grate was pushed aside for his friend's entrance. Concrete perched on the bunk, pulled his knees up and stared at the floor, not looking at his friend. After a while he muttered, 'I'm sorry, D. Believe! There was no need to stress the situation back there. I wasn't thinkin'. Sometimes I'm not thinkin', I'm just doin' it, you get me?'

He said that Daniels had been on his back from time, ever since he'd joined the division. Just on account of Concrete hanging around with certain guys that maybe had been involved in certain things. He thought Concrete was a lieutenant for some bigger operators. So Daniels was forever hotting Concrete on the street and taking him down the nick and trying to sweat him for information about activity in Peckham and Brixton. He hadn't done anything hardly, but there were grasses and words walked easy.

'You didn't have to get cheeky, though. And definitely not when my sister was around, you know.'

'True, I haven't been too clever.'

'Thank you!'

The cell door clanked open again and the Chinese cop led Dele out of the cell wing. For the briefest moment Dele considered appealing to him on people-of-colour lines, then he remembered the blows in the van and decided to forget it. They walked on in silence.

Gerry, the solicitor, was waiting for Dele in a small ante-room. Gerry was tall and gangly, with an engaging shabbiness that spread from his creased shirt-collar down to his temperamental zip and scuffed black shoes. Dele steadily regained his confidence as he filled Gerry in, showing the bruises, and only omitting the fact that they truly had been carrying a little puff on their persons.

Gerry spoke soothingly of Daniels being a notorious bandit in the local police's black-pack, of malicious prosecution and wrongful imprisonment, of civil suits and pure, punitive damages.

'First things first,' replied Dele. 'My sister. I haven't seen her since this whole fuckrey began, and methinks they're trying to stick some cocaine or something charge on her. She's not a healthy woman anyways. They won't let me see her. If you represent all of us, can you get to see her?'

'Sure, I'll do that straightaway. Then we'll get a photographer down here to look at these bruises and your nose. They'll probably want to question you soon and push for some charges. Don't say anything, you don't have to. Just make it clear to them that they've really overstepped the mark this time, and you're not going to let them get away with it. That should put some fear into them. And I'll be with you anyway. With any luck, you'll get bail and soon be on your way.'

Dele looked at him gratefully, before being taken back down.

He lay on the bunk. He was quite looking forward to the Q and A session to follow. Let them try to test him, Daniels would see he was no fool. Later, the tables would turn, the radics would be in the dock, and Dele would kick a rousing court performance, grinding the Met and Daniels into the dust. Then he would be carried out on the arms of his friends, a hero of the people . . . It would be nice. He could hear scurrying outside, then the door was flung open and a worried Gerry was beckoning him. 'You better come up. Your sister really isn't looking too well and she keeps asking for you.'

Dele jumped up, his heart thudding, and the two, with a PC leading the way, ran round the cell block, up the stairs, past the noticeboards and command orders, and the sounds of officers laughing, cussing and flirting in the doorways, ran what seemed an eternity, until he heard his sister's cries and they'd reached a bare, white-painted room.

Dapo was on the floor. Two officers pinned her arms back whilst a white-haired guy in a grey suit was trying to pour something steaming down her throat. Dapo, a big swelling on her cheek and bruises around her head, was gurgling and struggling. Stains darkened her white shirt and jeans. She was wild, wide-eyed and breathing heavily.

'Get this down you, love, you'll feel better. C'mon hold her, for Pete's sake!' ordered the older man.

'What are you doing, what are you doing?' Dele shouted.

'This is Dapo's brother,' said Gerry quickly.

'Hallo,' said the man, 'I'm a surgeon. There's nothing to worry about. She's just very dehydrated, I think. You can help by telling us what she's taken in the last twelve hours. The officer said – '

'What you talking about? She hasn't taken anything. She's ill, can't you see? She's got sickle cell,' Dele replied, rushing over to Dapo.

The surgeon looked extra-worried, the pigs shoved Dele away and carried on gripping the slumped Dapo like she was some Category A terrorist. They were looking at the surgeon, waiting for instructions.

'Leave her alone! You're fuckin' killing her! Where's her medicine? Her bag, her bag!'

The surgeon told one of the officers to go to locate the handbag and the other let the now howling Dapo fall into Dele's arms. She began thrashing on the stone floor, clutching her arms and hips. Dele was clawing against the terror, the paralysis, the drowning, because this was beyond his knowledge.

'Listen to me, Miss D, things are gonna be alright. Someone's getting your pethadine, then we'll go off to the hospital,' he said, pressing water to her lips from a jug.

'I can't breathe, I can't breathe. The pain!' She scrambled at her chest then gulped. 'They beat me! I didn't do nothing! I asked them. They wouldn't give me water – '

'How bad is it, D?'

'The worst. I've never felt like this. I'm gonna die, I know!'

'Come on! Don't you ever say that. The pethadine's coming in just a second. I'm here now, nothing can happen to you.' He was desperate now. He cradled her and turned to the surgeon.

Muttering about how they should have called him much earlier, the surgeon prepared a syringeful of something, and tried to get Dele and the constable to hold one of Dapo's arms up. But she was jerking too much, her movements spasmodic, involuntary, horribly exaggerated. Her breathing was all off, out of sync even with her shaking fits. Then she started frothing and spitting. She couldn't scream none now. Her eyes were glazed, but stared at Dele intently for one brief moment, then they rolled to the ceiling and went completely. One last shudder and she was utterly still.

Dele cried out, then reeled round and flailed ragingly at the officer, who shouted, 'Woman down!' and attempted to restrain him. But there was no need as Dele subsided, then fell faint to the floor.

welcome
to the
fold

EYES BLANK and devil-red through tears and strain, Dele dragged his steps to the junction of Seven Sisters and Hornsey Road. There he paused. Not waiting on cars, more for the next bad news. The heavens were giving it up in buckets now. He put his hood up and started off again, his look fixed dully on the puddles around him.

There was a wrenching sense of dislocation. One moment he had been operating in a relatively innocent sphere and the next thing he'd been catapulted into the bleakest territory imaginable: operating theatres and intensive-care wards; of police cells and parental despair, of probable death.

He would never forget the first time death was raised with regard to his own flesh and blood. The doctor hadn't actually said that word. He had come out of the theatre to where the three were waiting outside. His mother ran around in hysterics, ululating. His father sat head bowed, silent.

'The vital signs are okay and the brain-waves as good as can be expected, but I think we have to look at the possibility that Dapo may not come through,' was what he had actually said. That possibility had not yet eventuated, with his sister remaining in a coma caused by the crisis, then the fit, in her brain that night. But since then death had established its intimate connection, enveloping them all in its hug of gross obscenity.

All these rains have come to wash away your old, rancid skins, he thought, prepare you. He didn't know for what. But it was too late – this was the cruel thing! When this new stage occurred – and it already felt like it had – how would he ever be ready for anything again? It would be impossible, because the very person he needed to get his life together with wouldn't be there. He just couldn't get it together.

The first days had been spent between receiving the condolences of family and a few friends and beating himself to a shadow with regrets in his room, scrabbling for clues to a way out. He had been so crazily casual; about Dapo's health, about London, about life – where bad things happened to black people.

Who was it that had written that one must always live as though your favourite child is dying in the next room. 'He is always dying. And I am always dying . . .' It was almost too banal to call it a humbling experience. He had been coming unstuck and ignored the signs with a fine disregard. Now they had all been chastised. Maybe he had it coming. But Dapo!

Dele needed someone to say this was not his fault, but somebody else's. After five days Dapo's condition had not worsened, and he took this as an indication that he could somehow influence the course of events. He took a shot from a bottle of Hi-Wine (a demon drink that a friend had given him with the caveat, 'This stuff ain't for drinkers. It's for waking the dead!'), and reached into his back pocket for a cheaply printed card, its ink now running in the rain, which announced:

NO JUSTICE — NO PEACE

How Many More Of Our Sisters Must Fall?
You are invited to the first open meeting of the Dapo Defence Campaign.
Speakers include:
Distinguished American professor Horace Overton,

Chris Collins, SWP,
and Dele, brother of police-victim Dapo

6.00p.m. Monday, July 1st, The White Rose Social Club,
Seven Sisters Road, N7

X amount of people from various organisations had
turned up at Dele's door, but he had turned them away.
However, an SWP-affiliated group had had the fortune to
pass by the morning Dele's resolve had changed.

'Just recount the incident. Tell it like it was and say what
we can do for her now,' they had soothed, and Dele had
finally nodded wearily.

Now it came to it, he didn't really feel to talk today. But
at least he was out of the house, and Dapo would probably
have wanted him to do it.

The White Rose was a grimy red-brick Edwardian building with a cavernous, cold, central space. On his previous
visits there he'd been dragged, kicking and screaming, to
Nigerian community events: engagement and christening
dances, Businessman of the Year (import and export). And
what with the forty-something women in traditional dress and
tremendous, unapologetic, backsides bouncing up and down
to highlife, he had felt something of a generation gap.

So the omens weren't all that as he shuffled into the hall.
An SWP apparatchik gave him the once-over. He was tardy,
so she was testy, before she ushered him on to the podium.

Dele took a seat beside the speaker, an early thirties guy
in black NHS spectacles. He was exhorting the one hundred
and fifty-strong audience to trace the lines between the Dapo
tragedy, the rise in racial attacks in the capital, and the threats
posed to them all by a single Europe. This must be Chris
Collins, the SWP's great black hope.

The women shifted their buttocks periodically, and the
men sat, legs splayed, arms folded, stony-faced. They had
come for blood and fire, not Maastricht. Dele searched for
familiar faces, but got lost in a great sight of blackness. He felt
brutally exposed on the podium, a virgin in front of this black

gaze. Sure, he knew his way around certain flavours. But this was different. He had no crutch and this was such serious shit. He hadn't paid his dues here at all. His only legitimacy lay in his being the brother of an unconscious woman.

Collins was still banging on. Dele could sense the hackles rising at this Marxist mumbo-jumbo. Pray he wasn't next. That would make two brothers in a row who didn't know how to play this gallery. They wouldn't stand for that.

Ah-ha, there was Concrete, near the front. Thank God for that. Why wasn't he on the podium? Strange. And Roger, that hardy perennial whom he'd known from back in the days at the local library. Roger would come to the opening of an envelope if it was coloured black. And Jah Grizzly, the ancient artical Rastaman whom the mainstream media were forever hauling out to speak for the Tottenham community. But some local people spoke quietly on how he was just a grass who sold draw and rocks, courtesy of the police.

Collins must surely be winding down now. His spectacles were starting to steam.

Dele's old man held a special place for glasses in his simmering stew of comparative anthropology. Caribs didn't wear specs, he maintained, and this was the clue to what he saw as their general fecklessness. The TV presenters Trevor McDonald and Trevor Phillips were the exceptions, he maintained, that proved the rule. 'You see how we Africans all study in this country-oh! Years of thrift. Bad lights and so many difficulties. But the West Indians – you think you need glasses to stand on street corners? *Enh-henh!*' he would say, washing his hands at the joy of his irrefutable logic, eyes glinting behind his own pair of silver-rimmed specs.

Maybe he would approve of this Collins guy, but Dele doubted it. Certainly not the way he was using Dapo's name: 'I know that Dapo would want this/that . . .' The cheek – he didn't even know his sister, her spirit. Even her condition as a metaphor for the community's slumbering state was remorselessly invoked to cover the gaps, and stitch the political conspiracy up neatly.

The only thing to improve Dele's spirits was the sight of

a few white folk sitting on the side in an overcoated huddle. The organisers had promised press and had at least delivered that much.

As Collins stood down, there was a little buzz with the introduction of Horace Overton. The Professor had come fresh from New York where he had antagonised both liberals and Can't-We-All-Just-Get-Along black types with his attacks on the 'Wasp-Jewish hegemony'. Dele had read a piece about Overton somewhere, but was yet to form an opinion on him. 'Over-hyped, Over-the-Top, and Over Here!' the *Guardian*, no less, had headlined that morning. Well, 'Over here', in this corner of north London at any rate, was certainly ready.

Nudging his kufi cap and fingering the silk scarf draped around his neck, Overton began beguilingly with a tale about the origins of the United States' Statue of Liberty. He flitted between slides, colour transparencies and documents as he gave a rapt audience the lowdown on the lady's original Egyptian features: nappy head, flared nostrils, all the tell-tale signs. Its French sculptor had built it to commemorate the liberation of the slaves at the close of the American Civil War and wanted to hand it to the US as a present. Only they were so distressed when they saw the model they insisted it be changed.

'The lady in the harbour is a fraud in white face! For centuries Europeans have tried to conceal our history from us, but history began with Africa. Half of man's recorded history had passed before European man could read or write. We were there before the Greeks had a pot to pee in!'

The journalists at the back were acting impatient, playing with their stationery. They had come for Overton to shout 'Kike!' or 'Whites must fry!' Nothing else would do.

Dele, too, was fretful. The whole Dapo issue seemed to be being pushed way behind Overton's and Collins' manifestos. He was getting an ugly, sidelined feeling about this whole experience.

'European culture is based on greed,' the Professor continued, 'on ICE: Individualism, Competitiveness and Exploitation. Whereas the African culture historically springs from the three Cs: Communal, Cooperative and Collective. Caring and sharing, if you like. African and Caribbean countries are now mimicking the ICE men of Europe and are therefore doomed to failure. We must stop reacting but deal with our own problems, around our own values. Unless we can Africanise these Europeans,' he gloomily concluded, 'the whole world is doomed.'

Not the most amazing stuff you've heard, but the crowd nyammed it up. People looked the one to the other, grunted and nodded fiercely. Maybe the fact that this tenured American professor in a kris jacket was coming out with it, rather than some musty Rastalero in a youth club's Black History class made the difference. Even Jah Grizzly, his mind forever set in the old days – the greeting Haile Selassie in Kingston airport days – got up and shook his moody locks in acknowledgement of the new order. Dele got up too and crept to the mike, like a phantom.

'I saw my sister Dapo this morning,' he began. 'There's been no real change in her condition, I'm afraid. The only thing that, er, seem to grow fresh are the bouquets and messages that mount by her side everyday. I would have to say that the signs, the medical forecast, aren't wonderful. And obviously they say the longer there's no change in this comatose state, the less the chances are for her recovering fully.' He paused. 'But, boy, they've been looking for a cure for sickle cell from time and they're yet to make any progress. So what do *they* know anyway?'

People smiled and leant forward. They were urging him on, they liked him!

'She was, she is, also about self-assertion, about asserting her dignity as a second-generation Black Briton. "We are here because they were there," she would quote, and, in the end, it was this pride and dignity which led to her battery at the hands of what *they* call The Law.'

Some sporadic clapping, Overton smiled benignly. Bolstered by the sense that he had made a connection, Dele impulsively tried on a confession, a little vulnerability with attitude.

'This whole tragedy has been such a vicious shock to me, it's still difficult to comprehend. I suppose what is strange is that I should be so surprised when this kind of violence is inflicted every day in a thousand different ways. But, prior to this, I had spent three years as a protected, privileged student outside London. I mean, er, I think I had got out of touch, or kind of cocooned – '

Dele was beginning to stumble, as he clicked he hadn't got the tricks to turn this intimate realisation, only part mulled through, into the bonding declaration he craved. He was suddenly aware of how this tale could sound all wrong. The swift reminder of student unrealities was meant to prepare the ground for the enormity of the encounter with the police, then the story would segue seamlessly into a firing conclusion. Only, he felt, it sounded like he was asking for forgiveness.

Then a rangy young guy stood up, four rows down. To his discomfort, Dele recognised Chris Makanje, an old-time acquaintance of his family. An active, bright child, great things were expected of him and his school reports were approvingly bandied around in much the same way as Dele's own. Then, sometime around thirteen or fourteen, Chris had begun to ride off the rails: this thing and the next at school; disappearing for days from home, a hyper, hunter-glint in his eye. Leading unerringly to his first appearance on Newsroom South-East: 'Two youths have been remanded in custody for the apparently motiveless machete attack on a courting couple. Chris Makanje, of Wood Green, north London . . .'

Dele's old man forbade him from seeing any more of the family. (He needn't have bothered. Eager for anonymity, Chris's sister Hyacinth took to making tracks whenever Dele beckoned on the high street.) After serving his time at Feltham Young Offenders', the distraught Makanjes sent their son back to Nigeria for the traditional short, sharp, shock.

Two years later he had returned. Cowed, respectful, unnervingly quiet. 'Nigeria-oh! It tames you, you know,' he had admitted.

However, the last time Dele had seen Chris was at a

party six months back. He had distressed the most girls with his cries of 'Hey, lard-arse, I wanna bone you, I wanna bone you!' So even then you could see he was still not well. He had also condemned Dele wholesale with invective full of hip-hop hand-me-downs, for 'selling out' and going to Oxford. Eventually he had pressed on the wrong guy's woman, and the brother had boxed Chris down with the rhetorical 'So you wanna riot with me!' Chris Makanje, the living loose-cannon. What did he want?

'It's interesting that the speaker himself admits that his time at one of Anglo-Saxon England's great seats of learning taught him nothing at all about the real world outside,' he began ominously.

'White people will be shaking your hand while pissin' on your feet! Maybe if he and others of his sort paid more respect to those Afrikan warriors who cleared the way instead of dancing on their graves, all this would come as less of a shock! But what does he know of the situation facing the *urban black man in Britain today*?' If Makanje had even left it at that he might have got away with it. His attack had been so out of order that it caught people unawares, and the organisers looked too nervy to respond in any vigorous fashion. As it happened, Makanje took it one step too far.

'At the end of the day now, all you are is just a JACC.' Makanje grinned at his inventiveness and looked around. 'Just Another Confused Coon!'

They didn't like the 'C' word at all.

Jah Grizzly stood up first. 'Hey, hey, that's enough already! This young man has come here to speak, as he has movingly done, about what happened to his sister. He does not deserve to be shouted down like this.'

Grizzly's little speech was backed up with cries of 'G'wan!', 'You know dat!' and 'What the fuck do you know, Maudsley Makanje!'

But just as the podium thought the craziness was being repelled, some youths from around the way decided to bust the s on Jah Grizzly, 'Speak out if you nah like In-For-Mer – ' said one.

As Jah Grizzly stood confused, a couple more added, 'That's right, Grizzly Bear. Is you we ah talk to. You's a Grass!'

The place erupted in slanging and cursing. People stood up and snarled at each other, settling long-nursed scores. Jah Grizzly faced off with a couple of his critics and had to be restrained from throwing a fist. Meanwhile there were calls for peace from the podium. Collins dusted his glasses with a querulous look and said that as we were all brothers and sisters here, why didn't we act like it, and people who didn't have anything positive to contribute should leave. But the key parties weren't listening. Although most of the crowd were first-generation white-collar, respectful enough on these occasions, there was also a vocal sprinkling of street guys, used to settling disputes in more brutal ways. You couldn't quite tell whether things were turning farcical or dangerous when Concrete strode to the stage.

'Alright, alright. Listen we! This is Concrete, one of the three the police brok up, same time with my bredren here and his sistah. So mek we reason a while!' he commanded, and the noise began to subside. 'Dem radics try fi fit me up from time for ting 'n' ting, but me nevah entertain that, seen? Dem must tink we got sawdust for brains! A real joke ting dat, you know.

'Me no woman! Me born of woman and from that day I leave all that behind, so the world must ah deal wid me like a man! Only the police tell me it not so. Tink dem can come tes' me wit' dem batons still an' show we how the world run! So me say, "Alright, come now!" Serious. Me within two seconds of their asses nuff times but Man and Man were telling me just to cool it. Me nah wanna be another guy out there getting a life. But cho! All me ah seh, you know, me tired now. Now me done! Enough. Me digital! Me ready to freak. Let them come with their badness, their government 'n' army 'n' all that, and two-twos we'll go toe to toe, blow for blow. So who's badder than me? Badness is in the mind, y'unnerstan'? Hear me, when dem brok me up on the floor, directly now seh "make sure you can go the distance!" Y'unnerstan'! Cah what goes around comes around, as the good professor proved, we have fi let this anger in our hearts do the talking. Cah me ready to fix the whole of them in an instant!'

Concrete's rousing, rambling piece proved just the ticket. Spontaneous applause allowed Collins to close the meeting in pretty good order, apart from some spats still rumbling at the fringes.

Dele looked out for Concrete, but two admirers were already pumping hands with his man and taking him aside. Down below, a still-smiling Overton was rebuffing the hacks so they turned en masse to Jah Grizzly for his take on the evening. As Dele reached to enquire why they weren't asking him, he noticed the features of old college acquaintance Tamsin.

'Tamsin, what the fuck are you doing here?' he said, then remembered . . . Of course, the *Chronicle* bursary, old man on the board.

'Oh hello, Del. That was all pretty exciting!' Tamsin boomed familiarly, her unfeasibly posh Sophie-from-Surrey tones thudding off The White Rose's walls. Dele could feel the weight of a thousand black eyes boring on his back.

'Well, that wouldn't be quite my word for it,' he offered.

'Oh, I heard about your sister. I am sorry.'

Dele shrugged. 'Listen, Tamsin, you reckon you can get a write-up about what happened to Dapo or what?'

'I'll try, Dele, but it's difficult. It's a question of *news* values. Right now we're more interested in the *bigger* story. I mean, what do you think of this Overton? He's a real demagogue, isn't he? Do you think there'll be a riot? I'm putting together this feature on the terrible plight facing young blacks today. We should have a chat about it, now you've become quite a little radical in your old age – '

'Why don't you try that guy? Talk to him – ' replied Dele, mischievously pointing her in the direction of Chris Makanje. He had to get away from this flood of condescension. Then somebody caught his eye, beckoning him to the bar. He took in the little round glasses, the retro style . . . Gabriel!

'Welcome to the fold,' smiled Gabriel, embracing him.

'It's so good to see a friendly face. I was terrified back there, you know, with fucking Chris Makanje cursing my stink out of the place. I've never done something like that before,' said Del.

'Don't worry, you were fine. I was gonna give you a bell, you know, when I heard. I was so shocked. But then I saw you were appearing down here. What d'you wanna drink?' He explained that his brother Jonathan was away, working for the summer in a hotel in Switzerland, of all places, but had heard the news and sent his best.

The bar was chocka now – a few white faces with sculpted goatees, but you wouldn't call it mixed. People were reasoning with palms upturned and arms that jabbed, phone numbers were being exchanged, the odd petition was being signed. Dele was chuffed that he too had a part to play, had quasi-status in this hitherto secret, new world. He was the brother of the girl that had brought them all together. He thanked them all inwardly for this reassurance that what had happened to his sister was important and cradled his lager, attentive as Gabriel filled him in.

'Okay, right. See those two guys over there still in deep with your friend, Concrete? Okay, they're The Yardcore Agency. They run a sort of PR outfit, and they're always hunting for, like, protégés they can oversee and big-up and push through wherever. They see themselves as real Tribunes of the People and don't take too kindly to anyone with a different vision. Strictly hardline, Islam is the way forward, yawn, yawn.'

'Well, maybe they're lining up Concrete for something?' said Dele. ''Cos his speech just kicked it. I wish I had a flow like that.'

'You just got different styles, that's all.'

A shaven-headed twenty-year-old slipped a flyer on to the table. 'Sa-laam-e-le-kum, brothers. Come and find out what time it is – ' he said, pointing to a clock which adorned the promo, and which stood at two minutes to midnight.

Dele glanced up and smiled but the man only nodded sternly and wandered off.

'That's my problem with The Nation,' volunteered Dele, 'no sense of humour. They need to lighten up.'

'That's where you're wrong,' replied Gabriel. '*No one* wants to lighten up any more. Happy face, thumping bass, smiling race, one nation under a groove – that shit is played out! It won't fly in Dalston. Look at this –'

Dele picked up the flyer. At the top was a little Sankofa bird, which he assumed was the logo of The Yardcore Agency.

YARDCORE PROMOTIONS
Recycling the Black £

How do we get to keep the money that we spend?
Come and speak upon this vital issue with local business
leaders, and take part in other debates.

At: Carlton Vale Centre, NW6
This is a strictly AfriKan Family Occasion

There was more, but the rest of it was in Arabic, so Dele put it aside.

'You see how the Muslims have got things scoped! Ten years ago, something like tonight would have been a lefty breeding ground.'

Dele got up to go to the bar. He'd just caught a fly girl's eye and – with Gabriel stressing the politics of racial fixity around them – didn't want her to catch him quaffing a pint of lager, like some Queen Vic regular.

He was balancing two bottles of Guinness when a hand tapped his shoulder and there was Cheryl. Cheryl, last seen on that nasty evening that seemed like an eternity ago. Still with the sweetest of button noses but body language more guarded, not surprisingly, than he was used to.

'Hello,' she said evenly, and placed a hand on his shoulder. 'Don't be angry, don't be sore at the world. She'll come through. I know she will.'

'Thanks.'

She made to leave. 'Hey, Cheryl! Don't go. Let's have a chat. Please.'

'No, Dele. I've got nothing more to say to you. You had me when I was green and ready and you messed up big time! Why? Tell me that much. Because I wasn't easy like all that slackness you got up there?'

'You're all wrong, Cheryl. We had finished long time ago. Listen – '

'I listened to you too much before and look what good it did me! No, sir. Don't worry yourself, I'm not cursing your parts all over town. But you're somebody else's problem now. See you.' And she was off.

He fell back to Gabriel, annoyed that his own foolishness had prevented Cheryl from seeing the best of him, and he failed to perk up even when two women came to join them. One of them, Celia, was an old friend of Gabriel's. Turned out they'd studied photography together. Dawn, a social worker, was the one with the variegated lumber jacket that he has spied just earlier. Closer, she seemed older, around thirty maybe, and petite. She had a certain Caribbean ideal of prettiness: hooded eyelids and big round eyes. Celia was quite nice too, but her features were a litle bit bulky and mannish to get away with the little scowl that crossed her face periodically.

They were both well sociable. Whilst Dawn explained to Dele the journey of the jacket, purchased in Thailand on her holidays (safe – she must be a boho, he was thinking), Celia entertained with a story about how she had just sacked this guy. Her man had abandoned her on a date after a call on his mobile, leaving Celia for an hour while he sorted out his business.

'He just left me to cool my heels. I tell you I was screwing: I cut him off, dry! And normally I don't even call guys if they give me a mobile number. But cha! He was fierce to look at, but just derelict – '

'Gotta who?/ Gotta get a ruffneck!' Dawn and Celia chanted together.

'Nah, but serious though, I could have coped with his

no-good friends and even when he said that this girl had a baby for him a while back. Then I saw the pickney. The boy was lighter than the palm of my hand! Turned out he had been going with this blonde girl for ten years. Ten years! Can you imagine? How can a white woman bring up a black child now? You don't know what nasty habits Carl and his kid picked up in that time. I just had to say to him "Forget it, Rasta, I'll talk to you laters and goodbye, guy!"'

'You sacked him just for that?' Dele was surprised.

'Definitely. A full ten years with some killer bimbo, who has a kid for him! Nah man, the boy must be confused.'

'What is it about black men and blonde girls? You would think they wouldn't be so crude as to fall for all that, but they surely do every day,' Dawn chipped in. 'I always say if they haven't switched by twenty-five, then forget it. No hope.'

They laughed.

'So how old are you, Dele?'

'Me? I'm twenty-one,' he replied, although he felt about ten again – an infant in this hardline adult world where guys got historicised because of the race of their previous.

He fell quiet, whilst the women chatted amongst themselves and Gabriel exhorted him not to beat himself up about Dapo. He nodded but he was half-turned to the pair beside them. Celia and Dawn were whispering to each other and breaking into laughter. He could only catch the words 'Operation Run Down Man!', bounced about like the title of a game. Eventually the talk opened out and they all fell to conversating about relationships in a liquor-fuelled kind of way.

Celia and Dawn were emphasising how they were nineties women and really blatant about it. They exercised their right to have part-time lovers if the mood took them. Gabriel replied ah, but plenty of women were saying that now, and wasn't it just because this was the only thing they could say to the guys these days, what with most black guys running scared of commitment, frightened of Man Traps? Celia said no one was saying that they didn't know how to keep guys. It was whether you wanted to, that was the question.

'When a guy's in bed with me and we're getting it on,

me nah joke,' volunteered Dawn. 'I want him and I want him to want me, all of me! From my last hair root to my big toe. And stamina. Two- three-hour service. See, in bed I can tell. I can tell, like, if a man doesn't really *like* women. In an instant – '

Dawn shot Dele a discomforting, penetrating look and he was happy enough when a general move-out broke up the exchange.

Concrete was standing by the doors and introduced Dele to his people, Sol and Michael, from The Yardcore Agency. They were both in smart-casual jeans and jackets. Sol was the taller; his skin was rich mahogany and he looked distinguished in a faint goatee stubble, with two fat silver rings on his fingers. A two-inch scar ran just above his left brow ridge, as if someone had glassed him in a bar brawl, and at the back of his short hair he sported a single, twisted lock. Michael's memorable feature was a receding hair-line. They must have been in their late twenties, Michael possibly older. As Michael gave him their card, Sol's eyes darted over Dele's body, as if looking for his secrets to reveal themselves in a little gesture.

'Interesting,' said Dele, as they padded out along Seven Sisters.

'You gotta be careful with those guys,' said Gabriel, 'that's all I know.'

'Yeah, yeah,' said Dele. But he wasn't concentrating any more. His thoughts had turned to these two new female friends moving purposefully a few steps ahead.

'So what's the coup here, man? You reckon they're into us?'

'Maybe. Stranger things have happened. I've known Celia from those days and she doesn't hang around – '

'Change of plan. We're feeling a little lazy. Do you wanna come back to our place for a little nightcap and chat?' said Dawn, turning around.

'Nightcaps and chat with two beautiful sisters is my very favourite thing,' returned Gabriel, lightly enough to save him from sounding squirmy.

They piled on to the tube at Finsbury Park. Although the late night train was ram-up, the sight of the four of them, loud and maybe taking no prisoners, was too much for most. The greybacks swiftly buried their heads in their grey papers, and those without reading matter migrated to the other end of the carriage to be amongst decent people. Most times such a routine would set off a stifled, contrary response in Dele, but tonight this all seemed fit and proper. The white world increasingly seemed to represent a combination of indifference and hostility. It seemed right, as he settled securely into his seat, that your space should be guaranteed, one way or the other.

They changed at King's Cross. At Liverpool Street, one young woman, flying in the face of unanimous wisdom, strode into the carriage and sat opposite them. A white girl, dressed in a phat puffa jacket over a lined red and white T-shirt, jeans and a rucksack with a raveland design of a black guy crashed out, smoking a spliff and holding a Coke. She had moved with an easy litheness and now half-smiled at them, utterly unfazed.

Dele looked her up and down. She had olive skin and dark hair in a pudding-bowl cut: a boyish, gamine look. What was she? Jewish or something? The face wasn't flawless – was that a nascent pustule on her forehead? It didn't matter. The package was too fit.

'E-Di-Ble!' Dele muttered to Gabriel.

She fixed her eyes on the two of them and started playing games. She mimicked their every hand and facial gesture, leaning back, leaning forward. She must be crazy.

'To chirps or not to chirps?' debated Dele. 'Damn! Why now?'

He darted an eye at their friends. Dawn didn't seem to sense anything awry, but Celia was scoping the guys, to see what they made of their new neighbour. Dele suddenly noticed on Celia's upper lip a creeping hirsuteness that he could have sworn wasn't there before. And Dawn now, when she blithely laughed and her teeth spread, he spotted a clear protuberance in the upper denture area. A slight case of overbite. The original sweet scenario was beginning to lose its allure in the face of this mystery across the way.

As they pulled in to Stratford, the girl moved for the doors and threw the two what Dele could only describe as a 'Come Hither' look. Like the movies. Like as if she was throwing out a hoop for a sighter. Dele was ready to jump.

They lost sight of her down the subway. Then there she was again, standing by a post on Station Street. So knowing, arms folded behind her, framed by the streetlight above. What terrain were they in now – *The Third Man*, *The Asphalt Jungle*? She had penetrated Dele's dreamscape now. He *had* to go for it.

'Can you hang on just one second? I just want to ask that girl if she's got a draw. It'll be nice to have a smoke when we reach yours, yeah?'

Gabriel's face betrayed nothing, Dawn looked quizzical and Celia exploded, 'What? So you wanna go check that little scrubber? No – I got eyes to see! I saw her eyeing you and you getting all jumpy on the train. You guys, you're incredible.'

'Relax, Celia. Shit! All I want is a draw, not her sex.' Dele dissembled. 'Give me a minute and I'll be right with you, alright?'

Celia and Dawn didn't look happy and they looked less so when he returned and said, yes, she does have a nice smoke, but it's at her sister's house down the road. It was settled that the guys should sort that out and hook up with the women at their place soonest.

'So what's your name?' began Dele weakly, a little short of breath.

Their new companion didn't answer, or even register the query, but continued to stride at a lick down the Romford Road. They were pushed keeping up, but Dele didn't mind as he had a pleasant view of her batty as it jiggled up and down in her threads.

'Do you normally walk down this road by yourself at this time of night?' asked Gabriel.

'All the time. I like walking,' she said.

No use trying to romance her with that gentleman Mr Sensitivity business, Gabriel, thought Dele. She isn't interested. She's more on the *Last Tango in Paris* – just hard-core bumping, no questions asked – tip.

'Here we are,' she said finally, after half a mile. She told them to wait outside the house, asked for a score and said she'd be right back.

Gabriel hunched his shoulders, dug his hands in his pockets, and squatted on the steps. Dele walked up and down impatiently.

'Can we just forget this, Del? We should have stayed where we were wanted.'

'I'm sorry. Humour me just this one time. Boy,' he continued absently, 'she looks the kind of buckwild girl who'd wake you up by yanking your dick in the morning . . .'

He looked down the street at the parked-up cars. 'You know what would be nice? One of those rides with those booming suspensions that, you know, bounce and jump when you turn the ignition. Like the gangbangers have in their promos.'

'You mean those old Chevrolet Impalas? Those low-riders?'

'That's the one. Imagine one of those in London town. You reckon one of those would do it?' Dele pointed to a Ford Orion.

'Might do.'

'Alright!' Dele bent down under the car's hood, playing out the skit, but was no sooner down than he heard the woman coming out of the house. He tried to scramble up but bumped his head noisily on the belly of the vehicle. By the time he'd recovered and was upright, she'd gone again.

'She couldn't stop. Still no name,' said Gabriel, when he had done with wheezing at Dele's maladroitness. 'She said, "if your mate wants to get in touch, tell him I work in a restaurant on Warwick Road". Otherwise she'll see you at a rave someplace, maybe.'

'Warwick Road? Okay. Useful, if true.' Dele pondered: 'Which one?'

'She didn't say. That was a lot of bother for a sore head and very little, wasn't it?'

'No worries, my lieutenant. We know maybe where she works and where she, or her sister, or someone, anyway, lives. I'm almost snowed under with information.'

As they trudged back towards the station, Gabriel took Dele to task over his gross breach of etiquette. Fuck etiquette, it was common sense. You couldn't try and check one place when you'd already booked yourself someplace else. And with Dawn and Celia – was he mad? Every day they probably stormed around, feeling strong and independent and un-appreciated, just looking for some man behaving badly to make their day. It was a wonder they were still invited.

On the doorstep, Dele stubbed out a cigarette and popped a mint into his mouth as Gabriel pressed the bell.

Dawn answered in an intricately patterned sarong, reaching just above the knees. Dele didn't expect to see mat-ters so advanced and smiled as they obeyed her chirpy instructions to take off their shoes. Stepping into the living-room, he saw that Celia had opted for a less successful make-over. Her legs, which had the thick, enduring sturdiness of Californian Redwood bark, were now encased in a pair of baggy Indian pants – the ones that look as if you'd laid a turd that is stubbornly refusing to be dislodged in the seat. She grunted non-committedly at them as they eased themselves on to the rugs on the floor.

The place was cheerily messy; clay figurines of different mythic beasts dotted the room, and the walls were covered in framed photographs and prints of chiselled, chocolate bodies in a clutch of tinted, shadowy encounters. There was the famous shot of a handsomely-built naked prince being car-ried, legs straddling the neck of an equally mighty second man, in a village procession. But mainly it was Dawn, or bits of her, in the studies. What was nice was that the photos steered clear of the gritty social-realism that accounted for so many of the black images you saw around.

On the table were a series of monochrome slides of the two women side by side mirror-dancing, their moves one beat out of step with each other. Dele looked at Celia and Dawn's gyrating bodies rattling past through a stroboscope.

'That's bad, Celia. That really is. Gabriel didn't tell me you were so hot!'

Celia grunted again with a faint, sour smile. He put the sourness down to the fact that Celia was still upset with him from before and – while it was true that Celia was no longer giving this particular guest the benefit of any doubt – she was mainly sour because she was thinking 'True, I am a good photographer, so why the fuck do I have to work in a Video Shop to get my corn? I haven't been in a darkroom in twelve months.' She had almost forgotten how upset that made her.

'You got 'nuff films here!' said Gabriel.

'You know Celia works in a video store,' explained Dawn.

With this last remark Celia looked glummer still, so Dele, hoping to initiate a foreplay of free and frank discussion, began with an anecdote about his own local video store. How he'd had to step in the other day when he saw his friend Raj, who managed this store, flailing under an ugly tongue-lashing from a trio of black girls who didn't want to pay up on a fine. And how he'd seen a clutch of people giving racial shoutdowns to Asian shopkeepers recently, it made no sense, and north-east London had always been quite relaxed in those ways. He didn't know why it was, maybe the cheek-by-jowl housing policy. But growing up where he did, there were Asians, Africans, Caribs, Jews, pure Greeks up Palmers Green, Cypriots down Stokey, Orthodox Jews in Stamford Hill and Reformed down Crouch End, Irish most everywhere, and a guy could do most things with most people.

Gabriel piped up to say he would bet those associations didn't continue untroubled into the adult world. Everyone could afford to be nice to each other when they were young – there was fuck all riding on it. But he knew what Dele meant, and probably London was a bit more tribalistic than it used to be.

'The one thing that gets me is all these jokers on a

"Blacker than You" tip. It's like they're telling you there are only so many ways to stay true to the race. You know – wear long dresses and strictly no leather! On the one hand, we invented the atomic bomb 2000 years ago. Next thing now, it's all technology is the devil and keep it natural . . .'

They all chipped in with their favourite Nubianisms in extremis stories, until Dele tried to wrap things up with a comic flourish. 'There's this friend of mine, Samuel. Okay, he comes across a little bit camp. He wears neckerchiefs with waistcoats and his voice is kinda Ugandan Prince. On a scale of one to ten of masculinity where your "true black" man is ten, Samuel rates about one, okay. Now my man is straight but no sister will look at him 'cos he doesn't conform to – '

'What on earth are you talking about?' The others were smiling, but Celia was off again. 'Scale of one to ten and all that stuff! Do you *know* any black women? Yeah. Are you sure? 'Cos the way you run your mouth off, it's like you've swallowed up all those myths about black machismo and "threatening" black sexuality. Bwoy, I think you need to spend some time with your own people!'

Something in Dele's drooping shoulders must have alerted Gabriel to the fact that he was ready to throw in the towel. Gabriel's head got busy. He was keen to steer the conversation into an area where the potential for shells was minimal.

'What was that tune you and Celia were humming in the bar?' he asked.

'Oh, you mean that MC Lyte "Ruffneck"? It's the boom, innit? I've got the video somewhere,' said Dawn.

Dele got up and started kicking the rhymes, until Celia sneered, 'Oh, so our little Oxford boy is a ruffneck now, is he?' She lit a cigarette and turned to Dawn. 'He thinks it's about him. Only it ain't about him!'

At this point Dele was about to let rip on Celia with some ugly verbals of his own, then he remembered that they were supposed to be romancing these women. He demurred and made for the bathroom, wondering whether the evening had any legs left in it. What a night! He was ready to throw in the towel. They'd left him feeling as sexy as The Man with Two Heads.

Little new was happening on his return. Dawn had dug up some brandy, Celia had removed her Doc Martens to reveal a chunky pair of feet, and her face was set in its customary waspishness. He had ceased to be bothered by it. Now he just didn't think it was fair for Celia to look that way all the time. Dawn was idly toying with the fringe of her sarong. Dele built another smoke, thinking vengefully, 'Maybe I should make this short and stumpy, like California Redwood . . .'

The talk was more desultory than before, the false starts more frequent. It seemed clear to Dele that the girls – despite banging the strong women drum – weren't about to initiate anything. No one wanted to be responsible for either forcing the pace or reneging on the evening's promise.

The scene reminded him of any number at local clubs, circa two in the morning, during the era of the slow dance. Saturday night, and all the brothers would have reached in kris gear, spreading their legs and fretting about their trouser creases as the bouncers searched them up and down at the door. Inside, as other guys moved, in packs of four and studied surliness, from one wall to another and back again, Concrete would shoot his cuffs, press a drink to his lips, survey the gathering and pronounce, 'Nah, man. But Black Man is *elegant*. Fe real.'

Only, come the Wind-Down Zone, elegance was beaten down by panic as pure guys materialised from the shadows of the main floor, demanding a dance. No one wanted the ignominy of being spotted solitary on the way home, kicking cans.

Now, just like the Wind-Down Zone, Dele could sense something inelegant coming on. The source, finally, was an unexpected quarter. Dawn, breathing windily in frustration, asked if anyone felt like watching *9½ Weeks* and slipped it in, as Gabriel hummed and hawed and Dele wondered if this was some secret test.

With Dawn's hand on the scan button, the four gazed

dully at the screen, grateful for something to focus on. As she flicked fast-forward into instant oblivion, Dawn got up, twirled at her twisted mane and said decisively, 'It's four o'clock, you know. I'm whacked. I'm going to bed.' This was the Rubicon. Any sucker could see that.

'I'm going too,' Dele said swiftly and made to follow Dawn. At the door he turned to Gabriel and looked down apologetically, as if to say 'I'm sorry, G, but it was every man for himself!'

He tentatively opened the door to Dawn's boudoir to find her sitting, back to him, on the edge of a thick burgundy quilt, rolling her neck.

'Come and sort out my back for me, will you?' she said. 'I've got a serious crick in the neck region.'

'Sure.'

He sat down by her. Only he didn't know how to massage. Was he doing it too hard, too soft and where were those pressure points when you needed them anyway? 'Would you prefer some acupuncture?'

'You do acupuncture?'

'No, but that way I can work my hands over more of you,' he lyricked, dropping his hands down her back, and the voice an octave lower in his best Superlover Undercover style.

'Hey!' she replied, slapping his fingers.

'Sorry.' Dele carried on with the massage, a little fazed, wondering how best to make a graceful exit, when Dawn went, 'Kiss me!'

'What?'

'Kiss me – '

He planted a soft kiss on her lips and ran his lips lightly over her cheeks, thinking 'Let's start this slowly. Don't want Dawn thinking I'm some priapic yout' with my sacks full to burst after being in the country wilderness for three years.' Only Dawn suddenly pushed him away and snapped, 'I told you to kiss me, not peck me!'

She threw an arm around his neck and brought his mouth to hers, tugging them both down. All he could taste was the yielding pressure of full lips and ginger wine, before she let him go and smiled. 'I'm feeling kinda horny. What's wrong, you can't handle female African vigour? And you was so fast with yourself a moment ago. Come here – ' and she grabbed him again.

Ah-ha, she wants to rig me up. Just enjoy yourself, you've had a hard day, Dele was thinking. Dawn's fingers were now kneading the back of his head. Their mouths were still intertwined but his hands were free, just roaming . . .

As he lay there on his front, with Dawn running her fingers down his hair and deep spine gulley, straddling and massaging his back with plenty more verve than he had displayed, he could sense the spliff talking. It was like Dawn was working him over in triplicate, every sound he heard in quadrophony, and the warm muskiness of her body flowed into a dozen earthy fragrances.

'I love our hair. I love the resistance, the way it seems to fight back at you when you touch it . . . Ouch! Look at all these welts and bumps on your back!'

'It's a new line in Scarification!'

'The flippin' Bill! What a time you've had.' She kissed her teeth and began softly singing the chorus from that Gregory Isaacs hit over and over, 'Night Nurse/ Night Nur-ur-urse . . .' It was the gentlest thing.

'Enough!' she gasped finally. 'I'm not nursing nothing no more. I'm off duty now,' she said, slipping off and lying beside him. 'Feeling lazy.'

'Lazy and horny?'

'You know!'

She lay languidly, half-amused, as his hand hesitated over which breast to concentrate his attention on, finally selecting the right. Her skin was a lovely even dark brown. Sure, her tummy pouts there in full effect but that seems right and all true womanly. He thrilled once again at the contrast between the baby smoothness of her body and the bushy fecundity of the beef curtains, which he now parted. She sighed and up he stretched to assuage the tittie, keep it firm and primed, before descending again. This time he stayed for the full muff, licking Dawn's pussy 'til it was out there and pushing, teasing the clit from its flaps until it stood erect and fine. Her nostrils flared and her face approached a mask.

'Everything alright up there?' he asked, with his head bobbing between her legs, using the cover of her temporary blindness to wipe a rogue bit of beef from his cheek.

'Ummmmmh. Don't stop.'

He didn't stop. He worked it like there was no tomorrow. Duration and devoted service on the first tryst always made sense. One, as courtesy to your partner and two, it gave you the slack to act with unbridled selfishness at a later date. He worked it in and out and roundabout.

When she sensed she was all over bar the shouting, Dawn hooked her legs under Dele's shoulder blades, hauled him up and rolled them over, so she was on top. She clawed at his back, deeper and deeper scratches against his welts and there was some pain. She started thrusting until her fingers just tightened; he could hear a deep, extended rumble above him, and short, quiet gasps.

'Oh baby, oh baybee!' she said.

'Did you come?'

'Sure I did. I don't blow the walls of Jericho down, you know!'

They started up again, Dele on top, but as he tried to slip his in, casually an' ting, she grabbed it and yanked it away.

'You aren't sticking that thing in here.'

'Don't worry, Dawn. I got a rubber.'

'Uh-uh! Rubbers or no rubbers. Not if it isn't love. I know if I do that there'll be no turning back!'

'I need some sexing now, Dawn. So what am I gonna do?'

'Improvise – '

She took hold of his wood and stroked it all up. She was very fluent with it, but her rhythms were foreign to him. It just got sore. Eventually, she straddled him again and, with his wood pressed against her pussy in some dry-fucking routine, he busted his nuts. More a tired, deficient dribble than quality Yoruba jissom.

'What are you thinking?' asked Dawn, after a while.

Dele was momentarily luxuriating in the feeling of his first first-nighter with a black woman. He had known there were some out there. They had just been the devil to find. Makanje, eat your heart out!

'Nothing.' He paused. 'I'm thinking, "Will she want to see me again?"'

'If I like you.'

'Do you like me?'

She screwed her face. 'There are only three things I don't like. Men who lie, men who don't know how to give pleasure, and weak women.'

He lay there, her arms around him, with his head by her breast, nose upturned and pressed to her face and hair, breathing in all that muskiness as if it was the Holy Ghost which he could breathe over Dapo, for her for to take up her bed and walk.

A little while later, as they'd dozed off all misty, the bedroom door opened and the scarcely-clad figures of Gabriel and Celia jumped on to the quilt, hot for superfreaky frolics. Dele could just about see Celia's 'tash trembling in the draught. Dawn remonstrated with Celia: they're too tired and she has to be up for work in two hours. Dele turned over and feigned sleep until the other two took the hint and left.

wolves
and
leopards

IN THE night-time, the capital seemed a different town, as black London swarmed around it in wave after wave. The first thing you noticed was the radio. The twenty-four-seven pirates would be joined by their slumbering soundboys-in-arms during the small hours: PowerJam, Bassline ('Warm greetings without measure/, Bringing a lickle love and plea-sure/, You know the coup, you know the caper'), Skyline, Irie FM, Gals FM, Vibe FM, Rush FM, Kool FM. And most proba-bly even the legals would be playing something black at this time: Capital, Radio One, Kiss . . .

So you'd be sitting in your ride scanning the car radio through all this flavour, and suddenly you'd be joined at the traffic lights by black folk to right and left. Like a little convoy. The night-culture heads would be mainly a younger crowd, apart from the mini-cab drivers. You'd glance up and let on, before peeling away to attend your piece of business.

The third wave comes on foot, emerging in the darkest hour before the dawn. A clutch of Africans moved, stoic and set on the task ahead, to lonely bus stops. Because the race was not for the swift, nor the battle for the strong, but for those who endured to the end. They buckled up their coats against the chill. Only twenty-four hours in a day and who knew how many jobs to juggle. Cleaning the city's offices was a dirty job but somebody always had to do it.

It was this last group that Dele joined, on his way back from Dawn's. He passed a middle-aged pair of West African women and threw them as steady a look of solidarity as he could manage in his mashed-up state. But their response was a puzzled and slightly haughty stare. After all, he clearly wasn't on his way to work and most likely wasn't returning from anywhere decent at this time of the morning.

He picked up a newspaper from the communal garden space at the back of his parents' house. He wouldn't go round the front because – likely as not – the old man would be standing by the window looking out on to the road. There was no need for the subterfuge, for his father had spotted him already. Since the tragedy he had spent most of his day brooding by that window and this night he had stood there too. As he saw Dele scurrying down the back avenue, his mental register dimly stored this episode for a future confrontation. To impress upon Dele that he was his son, always his son, no matter how big or rich he got, and when he lived in his father's house he obeyed the rules. To come home at this time, at this time! And this boy who thought he was so clever and wise.

But he could not bear now to speak to his son, much less beat him. Even when Dele's mother told him of that foolish nonsense of Dele starting a march he had not raised his voice. It was all too much, too late for that. Let both his children hang by themselves. His mistake had been to be too lenient, simply that. He and their mother had spoiled them. Not come down hard enough when they saw them aping vulgar ways; their fooling around, and their music and their friends and their parties and their smoking! He knew much more than they thought he knew. When all he asked for them to do was to study. Be humble, study for a little while longer then play as much as they liked! How often had he told them that cousins their age back home walked miles in their bare feet, stitched sacks, carried and sold them at market, just to get to college? Truly, it was better they were in

Africa. But these children had thought they were so wise and clever!

Standing underneath the kitchen balcony, Dele could make out the form of his mother and whistled to her sharply. She opened the back door in a red apron covering her nightie.

'Aa-ah! Dele, eh! Where have you been now? All night!'

'I told you if I didn't ring by midnight I'd be back late.'

'How can you say that at a time like this? You being out on the streets all night will kill us all!'

'I'm sorry. Really. Is the old man around?'

'In the sitting-room. But he doesn't know you were still out – ' She said there had been no news from the hospital. Her hands rubbed gently across his cheek as if to check that Dele really was all here. 'You must stop all these politics and protests, you know. They only bring more shame on us. What is it good for, enh? Soon, everybody will know.'

'Who cares if everybody knows?' Dele exploded. 'Dapo's gonna die and you're talking about what everybody knows!' He perched down on the stairs and put his hand on his brow. 'I'm sorry, Mommy. Did he tell you to say that to me? I mean, don't tell me what he thinks, tell me what you really think.'

She didn't reply, but searched his face with pain etched on hers.

'Forget it. You know I've got all these people coming round soon to talk about, uh, Dapo and things?'

'Will you see her today?'

'Yuh. Later on.'

'I'll be there at lunchtime and after work. And then we must go to see the auntie, you remember?'

Dele nodded and crept up to his room. He lay crunched in a ball under the sheets, still clothed. He had been sleeping badly. Deeply, but badly. He would tumble into sleep severely blunted by whatever substance he could lay his hands on. That way, he did not have bad dreams. He did not have to cope with the Dapo voices and *déjà vu* that crept up and tugged him during the days. He could not remember his dreams these nights at all.

He felt as desperate as the day before, like last night's little relief had never happened. His eyes stared dumbly at the little hand on his clock as it struggled along Nigeria's east coast. Eight-nine-ten. Tick-tock, you don't stop. He reached under his pillow for a little brown wrap, unfurled and snorted a couple of lines of speed. He felt that he had become incalculably hardened, yet that his wounds were naked and open and that anybody could smell his funk.

If only there were clear-cut people out there to blame! If he could fashion a skein of cause and effect, from the old man's constant pressure to the gradual erosion of his sister's spirit and body. But that would have been too speculative, too harsh. The Bill were the obvious candidates but, again, they had crossed paths too briefly and strangely for it to seem right. He needed something he could make sense of in the fullness of his family's life.

Flicking through the paper, Dele couldn't see anything about yesterday's meeting until he spotted the headline THE ICEMAN COMETH and Tamsin's byline in the three columns the *Chronicle* reserved for humour amidst the oceans of dryness on its front pages.

'Meteorologists' gloomy forecasts of a new Ice Age were given a novel spin by controversial black rabble-rouser Horace Overton last night,' joshed Tamsin lamely. There was much mention of the Jah Grizzly contretemps, with Tamsin surmising that the old style of peaceful community leadership was surrendering to a younger generation of hot-headed nihilistic negroes. The piece juxtaposed a graphic picture of the carnage after a gun attack in a rich Johannesburg suburb, and the implicit spectre of a brood of bloods rampaging through the Home Counties, ripping tyres from Range Rovers and burning them round folks' necks, comrades-style, was tangible.

The only words on the actual reason for the meeting were relegated to a sub-clause in the final paragraph ('. . . nineteen-year-old girl, whose arrest on a drugs charge led to a deterioration of her sickle-cell anaemia that has left her in a coma . . .').

'Shit, you bitch! How many times did you make me frolic with you at the front of the stage, as the lights came up, to some tired-ass Motown classic? I thought we were tight enough. And you couldn't even honour her with a name!'

He could hear the bell ringing downstairs and loud greetings – no doubt, cousins and aunts arriving. Since this whole business had started, members of his extended family had ventured north-east from all outposts of the Jubilee Line: West Hampstead, Neasden, Stanmore. Some of them Dele hadn't seen in a while, and even then it had mostly been under muted circumstances, when Dele and Dapo would have been on waiting duty, fetching coats and cutlery, keeping their heads down. And this was the most muted of occasions yet, made stranger still by the fact that nobody had actually died. The proper observances to be maintained in this terrible, limboland situation were not clear but people paid their respects just the same.

It was always a little boost to see his young cousins. With their impeccable manners and impeccable ambitions – one eye turned towards home, the other to a part-time business future in America – they brought a classy air to the house. Peter, Enitan and Timi, in their light linen suits, polo necks and designer shades, were coming like mafiosi at a clan reception. And Toyin and Bunmi in their pink and black copied Chanel trouser-suits. Their folks had also come over here in the sixties to study. Only, unlike his own, theirs had taken their qualifications, and other necessaries, back, and now lived large in Lagos' desirable districts. They had sent their children here to do the same.

Dele went downstairs to take a peek. He could scope his Mum lamenting with his father's sister Bola, and Timi, her son, nodding to a speech from his Dad. Auntie Bola was very straightforward, even brutal, about these matters. She had taken Dele aside the second day, and told him, 'Not to worry, oh! It's just one of those things, do you understand my meaning?', in the manner of someone who has grown up with death all around her. And now, yet again, she was getting Dele's mother, amidst moaning and snatches of sad songs, to go step by step through the events from the moment she had opened the door to a distraught Dele that morning. No detail was too small for Auntie Bola. She really liked to feel the pain. His Dad was speaking forcefully in Yoruba, so Dele couldn't catch the whole drift, but he was using both his name and Timi's in a way, contrasting the latter, who conducted his affairs in the family tradition, with the errant ways of doing of 'this boy, this boy . . .'

Timi's eyes twinkled when he saw Dele. He mouthed 'Ja-mo' to him – his name for Dele on account of his 'Carib ways' – and he quietly divided his attention, until Dele retreated upstairs.

Daryl Scotland was the first to arrive. A chunky, gummy guy, in a jacket, tie and nasty slacks, Daryl clumped around the cramped bedroom. Clattering into bric-a-brac here, grazing pristine vinyl there, nervous as hell. Small talk was a sequence of tense negotiations, while Dele's suggestion that Daryl took off his jacket left the latter scrambling for hangers and the backs of chairs.

'I'll sort it,' volunteered Dele finally, as a chair fell crashing to the ground.

'Th-thanks,' said Daryl, addressing a point about thirty degrees north of Dele's shoulder.

It didn't help that Daryl, an emissary from Anti-Fascist Action, was making his pitch by indirections: a brief belt through the history of the organisation, famous hits against Springbok tourists of the sixties, outing neo-Nazis, a broad-based coalition, black and white/ unite and fight. Very old school. The only way Daryl was gonna get the booty was by boring Dele into submission. They were seeking his hand, so why did they send him this nerd with his whiff of failure?

'Listen, Daryl, you don't have to go through all that. You're preaching to the converted, believe me. Just tell me what you want me to do.'

'I'm coming to that. The first matter on the agenda is the march from Waterloo to Brixton on Saturday – '

'Yeah. Well, you know this guy Fitzroy someone from

Blacks Fight Back? Maybe the two of you can sort out the practicalities of this march together – '

'No. *No way* are we marching with BFB!'

'Why not?'

'Look, I don't have to give you a reason,' said Daryl sharply, in an unprecedented display of personality.

What the fuck is up with these people? Dele wondered. 'Anyway, he should be along in a minute, so maybe all three – '

'Fitzroy Lara? Is coming here?' Daryl spittled fiercely.

'That's right. Is there a problem?'

'When is he coming?'

The doorbell rang.

'That's probably him. Unless it's one of the others. Everyone wants to pay me a visit today,' said Dele, making for the door. He had a shock when he set eyes on the Dax-coiffed Lara. No one had told him it was *this* Fitzroy.

He had met the guy once before, at a French-Caribbean wine bar called Comme Il Faut!, a venue of choice for London's east-side cult-nat lites. If your core cult-nats had their domes deep in gnarled Nubian shibboleths, cult-nat lites wouldn't let Malcolm, Marcus and Marley come in the way of Mammon. They were your aspiring smart set: lawyers, public sector management, folks who worked in finance. Many had received their first leg-up courtesy of the race relations industry (funny how the council people always got to work in housing or social services, never in the prestige areas like borough architect or engineer), or else by corporate nods in the direction of equal opportunities – one negro per office – and were now branching out: setting up professional networking groups with names like Renaissance and Rapport. They had been brought up in the inner city but bought their first places in the suburbs: Norwood, Streatham, Crouch End, the white side of Enfield. They shook their heads at their less-deserving brethren as they peeled past in their Audis and Golfs. Their own promised land was Atlanta, a city where brothers and sisters with ambition could garner much corn, and folk in suits were too busy to hate.

Dele had only been at Comme Il Faut! that evening because a friend he was with, Carmen, fancied the trombone man in the house band. Four of them had been sitting there, sipping pricey Planters' Punches, when a waiter had brought them over glasses of champagne, courtesy of a gentleman in the brinksy party on the far table. A lean Fitzroy wandered over and explained that the largesse was due to the success- ful conclusion of a case he'd been fighting. The two got chatting about law, a conversation that left Dele in some doubt as to Fitzroy's real status. He surmised that Fitzroy was really just a clerk or paralegal whose expertise lay in directing minor east London villains to his firm when the need arose. Bread and butter criminal legal aid work. As the two groups sauntered out later on, Fitzroy had suddenly grabbed Dele, shoved him into an alley and slung his tongue down his throat. More strangely, he had began rubbing his body against Dele's in some kind of frenzy, muttering, 'Let the boys be boys!'

Dele had pushed him away and returned to the others, followed by a shameless Fitzroy. Further discreet enquiries had revealed the family-man Fitzroy to hold something of an underground reputation for compulsive frotting of both sexes.

Fitzroy, in his new hat as prime mover of the new jack Blacks Fight Back, didn't recognise Dele as they walked up the stairs. When he told Fitzroy of Daryl's presence upstairs, Fitzroy too was piqued and tugged at Dele's arm. For one grim moment, Dele braced himself for attempted frottage under his own roof, but Fitzroy only asked, 'He didn't get you to sign anything, did he?'

'Uh-uh. Should he?'

'Trust me, brother. These people are devious. You put your name to a piece of paper and, next thing now, so-called anti-imperialistic workers the world over will be writing you, asking for donations, or sponsorship for studying. It's not our struggle, it's theirs' he said, getting his retaliation in first.

The old adversaries grunted their greetings before Fitzroy perched uneasily on a beanbag.

If Dele had known beforehand about all the beefs he

would have taken steps to stagger the appointments more ruthlessly. As it was, the others were soon joined by Chris Collins, Beth, an English girl from a support group for families of folk who died in official custody, and Inder, a balaclava-clad Persian from a local vigilante group. On his hands were a pair of thin, stretchy gloves, the kind burglars wear when they drum your house. It took Dele quite a few words to persuade him to take the headgear off.

Once inside, Inder picked his way around the crowded room, flexing his gloved fingers as if he couldn't wait to get them around a pretty neck, before glancing conspiratorially around, casing the stereo, and finally easing himself beside Dele on the bed. Like he saw his future in a televisual world of pixillated images and shadowy quarter profiles.

The air was thick with pure hatchets resurrected and roaming. Open conversation was sporadic, as one after another they took Dele for 'a quiet word' outside. Some wanted him to sign his name on a blank sheet for them to fill out the rest, others just to fill in on the dotted line, underneath the aims and the statement of principle; Inder didn't have any paper 'cos it was thought better to keep everything in your head, but he was keen to get hold of some possession of Dapo's that he could use as a talisman. Everyone insisted on exclusive rights to the Dapo prize.

Dele finally lost it when Fitzroy, with breathtaking brothery, wondered if Dele's family might advance BFB some money 'To fight this campaign on a variety of fronts'. All around the cult-nat lites were busy inventing a canon, through their numerous promotions and events, for bourgy-bourgy blacks: telly celebrities, solid church ministers and gradualist activists, plus the usual slew of sports stars. And Dele suspected Fitzroy's interest in Dapo was a bid to propel himself into the hungry spaces of this canon.

'Listen everyone! I don't know all the ins and outs of this situation, but there's no way I can give my family's endorsement or whatever to one of you and not the other. I don't have that right. We don't know what we're letting ourselves in for. I mean, why can't you – leastways some of you – get your heads together and sort this out so's you can pool resources. I mean, I can't get my head round any of this. It's the last thing I want to be losing sleep over.'

'That's right,' said Fitzroy with one of his expansive, empty gestures, and even Daryl added 'OK'. Then there was a new difficult silence, so Dele flopped back on the bed, lost himself on the stereo's wall of sound, and tried to levitate.

The bell rung once more, and it was a somewhat agitated Dele who scrambled downstairs to answer it. It was one of The Yardcore Agency. The taller, more imposing one, his dome encased in a Fruits of Islam cap. In tow was a woman Dele hadn't seen before. His friend was a striking red twenty-something. She looked like she might have had a hint of Arab in her. She was smartly casual in a long, cream coat and tapered white jeans, her hair styled in corkscrew twists.

'Hi! Del,' They punched knuckles. 'If you remember me from last night. This is Genevieve. We were in the area and Concrete said you wouldn't feel a way if we dropped by.'

At first Dele's insides hardened in the face of a fresh bout of canvassing, but his mood lifted a little when he saw Sol was clutching a bag of records. 'Ah! You come bearing gifts . . . You got this! I've been hunting for this for the longest time. It's like rare groove to me.' After he had taken the pair inside, Dele gawped once again at the treasure in his hands: a copy of *The Further Adventures of Slick Rick*. Of all the tale-tellers in hip-hop, Slick Rick was his sentimental favourite. He gave you dark fairy-tales of the derelict city, but with a flow that was studded with whimsy. Crazy stage asides, a battery of arch English voices, nonsense rhymes – Slick would drop it all in the mix. Reportage laced with ludic love.

'Remember la-di-da-di/ I likes to party and all that –'

'Yeah, yeah. The man's bad! I just picked it up at this record auction way out north' said Sol, leaning over his shoulder.

The sleeve design was mid-eighties, and The Cool Ruler was crouched over a backdrop of Manhattan. The town was all skyscrapers jutting arrogantly, Manhattan as Gotham City with Slick as the Joker figure.

'Can I help you get everybody some tea or coffee?' Genevieve's tones broke Dele's spell.

Some progress had occurred by the time they had brought the tray and some extra cushions back up. Beth and Daryl had discovered school-mates in common, even Inder looked settled, and only Chris was making to leave.

Sol shook his head when Dele offered him some of the brandy he was pouring into his coffee, but stayed behind with his girl as the others gradually made their exits.

The three sat scanning a report about the Bosnian war on the TV screen, with Dele wondering when this suitor was going to up the ante. If you've come to talk music, talk music, Dele was thinking. If you've come to talk Dapo, talk Dapo, but don't sit there with your bassist in a dub band cool, saying nish, 'cos I've got moves to make.

'Bwoy! Seems that everyone wants a war these days, wherever you look. People not asking for shit, just taking it,' Sol threw out finally. 'The football gangs mashing up the place every Saturday! War in Bosnia, they're chatting war on the records, there's a war out there in the cities in the States – only no one's declared it official yet.' He chuckled, 'Nuff man ah dead nuff skull ah bore', you don't think?'

'S'pose so – '

'Even the British are getting hip to it. It's getting deep! People are done with chatty-chatty politricks, isn't it?'

'I don't know,' Dele pondered. 'I mean, a lot of the wars out there are about petty nationalisms. You wouldn't catch me fighting over whether I'm Azerbaijan or Armenian or whatever the fuck it is! You gotta have a serious, serious cause.'

'Seen, seen. And African-Americans – do they qualify?'

'Do they fuck!' Dele laughed. 'I mean, if they want a state – I hear Texas is being talked about – sure, they should get a state. But it's gonna have to come from free and frank discussions! They can't burn the place down, Rasta! For what?'

'But they're gonna fight, you watch! Uprising won't be the word, you understand? Within two generations – '

'You been there?'

'Yeah, yeah. I seen it.' Sol rubbed his hand across the silver ring on his finger.

'So what can you guys do me for, anyway?' asked Dele eventually, sitting up and wondering why Genevieve was being so meek in a corner of the room. 'What's The Yardcore Agency about? You know, just so we're on a level – '

'Well,' said Sol, after a long pause, 'we're a management and promotions agency. We manage, we facilitate. We make interventions.'

'And where does the Nation fit in? 'Cos you're part of them, aren't you?'

'No, sir! We're not part of them or affiliated to them like that. We just have dealings sometimes. Think of it like this,' Sol explained, 'you know how people say gangsta rap is like the virus on Black Nationalism? Well, we see the Nation's thinking as its steroids. It's like a booster, gives you energy. It's the steroids of this whole project.'

'You think so? I just think they're, you know, full of foolishness. Like our equivalent of flat-earthers.'

Sol nodded, like a tolerant uncle. 'That too. But viruses, steroids, they've all got their uses.'

'In small doses.'

'Exactly. Anyway, about all this with Dapo. Let's see . . . the demo drops on Saturday, right?'

'Ah-hah.'

'Safe. You seem to be getting everything taped. I mean, we've got ideas but obviously it depends on what you want. Why don't you give us a ring before the weekend, if you want, and we'll talk properly?'

'Alright. Will do.' And he meant it too. Sol left Dele with a book called *Cataclysm* which he thought he might find interesting and, very nicely, his Slick Rick record for Dele to tape.

After he'd shown the two out, Dele stepped into Dapo's place at the end of the landing. He moved quickly around the room, never looking back at parts he passed, picking up bits and pieces once again for the hospital. He chided her for her inability to mark up her tapes properly ('Dapo's tape #3 –

Various' . . . What good is that?). As he left the house, his Dad spied him from the window.

'Alright, Gerry. So you've got some news for me?'

The two were sitting in Gerry's Streatham office. He was opening out the thin 'Dapo' file and played with the micro-cassette recorder in front of him. Brixton police station's chief had told Gerry that he was waiting for a formal complaint from Dele and Concrete, so he could then start to examine the matter, pending a Police Complaints Authority inquiry. Gerry advised Dele against this route, saying only one in fifty of PCA complaints ended in any action being taken against officers, plus any statements he made might be used against him later if the police tried to go for him in a future action, and recommended he should sue instead.

'What are my chances?'

'Difficult to say. The pictures we took are pretty strong and support our case, as will the doctor's report, hopefully. But the police will fight this every which way, starting with you both, of course.'

After Dapo had collapsed that night, the police had pro-ceeded to charge Dele with possession of a quarter ounce of cannabis, and assaulting a police officer. Concrete had also got done for assault and possession of three-quarters of an ounce with intent to supply. The Bill had bumped up the quantity, presumably to get Concrete on a supply charge, but that was to be expected. They were both on police bail, with no date yet for the trial, but luckily Dele only had to report every couple of weeks.

'Not just that, I'm sorry to say, but, with what happened to your sister, the police have been holding a couple of off-the-record briefings with the Press, telling them the arrests were part of some larger Drugs and Robbery operation, that Concrete was a key mover in the network, though yours and Dapo's connections are as yet unclear. They've also been stressing that Dapo was a very ill woman, similar to someone with a serious heart condition who then has a stroke. That, basically, it was an unfortunate accident waiting to happen. I haven't seen much in the papers. You got those press releases sent out, didn't you?'

Dele nodded.

'It's such a shame. All these things make it harder for us. One other thing. Concrete said he didn't want me to represent him. If you can find out who else he's got, then we can start co-ordinating our cases.'

'Okay. I'll see to it.'

Dele was screwing. It was like he'd crossed a line inside. He'd never felt so hard, so set before. Digital and impotent in the face of these calumnies. He brushed past and bumped into fellow pasengers on the tube, but no one troubled him. They could see that he was in a scary way.

Middlesex Hospital engloomed him even more than ever. Nurses and fellow sicklers avoided his eyes or lowered their conversations and nodded to him in respect as he walked past. He reached straight for the Intensive Therapy Unit off the main ward, set aside for Dapo. Was she quick or had she passed? No, she's quick, but still still. His sole witness, his most dearly loved. Nineteen but looking younger than her age – a sickler's thing. Her sleeping figure seems too tiny and helpless, set against either the foes ranged against her or this great tenderness radiating from the cards and bouquets.

The tubes and needles were different these days. One ventilator through the nose, then up the back of her mouth, and a drip that pierced her left forearm to feed her. And the ECG and dialysis machines that bleeped fitfully.

He kissed her, then flicked through some of the messages: friends from her college; church; a lovely dedication from FTP Radio's Blaize, a DJ she was sweet on; any number of local worthy organisations. Even the Tottenham police station.

'Miss D, I never knew you'd been so busy!'

Maerag, one of the round-the-clock nurses, stepped in and shook her head when he asked if there was anything new to report. 'Not really, Del. Dr Ferguson was looking for signs of conscious reaction today – on the soles of her feet and below her knees – but all she got was an involuntary spasm. Which is something, I suppose.'

'Have they got any idea yet how it happened?'

'No. They just keep on saying it's so unique. They think she had a sudden grand mal fit in the brain. But we're continuing with all the foods and antibiotics, and there's been no adverse reaction. We're monitoring all signs very carefully. The blood count hasn't deteriorated anyway.'

Maerag fiddled around the room while Dele pulled out the tunes he had brought for Dapo's delectation. She would want something spiritual and life-affirming, and classical reggae was her best vibe for that. She had looked for clues as to why this should feel holy to her all the time. Something in the combination of the choppy rhythm and the fractionally slowed Nyabinghe beats, the rhythm coming at you at the same tempo as the heartbeat; or all those 'Time is longer than rope' and 'Sensimilia was found on King Solomon's grave' rumours from Dreadology that Dapo pored over. She still wasn't sure why, but she loved it off.

Dele laid out a batch of tapes; some righteous seventies culture and silky, modern-day singers. He played bootlegs of sound-system clashes, with their specials and dub plates; Stone Love Saxon, some conscious Shabba . . .

> Memories live like people do
> Don't you know I remember you?
> To every singer respeck due
> We're gonna big up the DJ crew
> Alcapone, U-Roy, I-Roy . . .

His head was down and far away, so he didn't notice his mother's entrance until the tune suddenly stopped. She watered the flowers in the room, leant by the bed and said two prayers, the first silently. Then she held her daughter's head firmly, shaking it softly and peering at it as if she thought Dapo could tell them something. She talked on in two insistent, low tones, a one-woman call and response routine. The same mysterious half-smile, half-smirk teased her mouth that had replaced the wailing from the second day and had so affected him the first time he saw it.

It was early evening when she finally said 'Okay, Dele,' and he led her out, with one final admonition to Maerag to keep the tapes rotating. The two boarded the bus for the trip to the special 'auntie', visited only in times of dread. Tonight, his father's dinner would have to wait.

His mother rocked back and forth in her spirit world as Dele anxiously scanned the streets through the steamed windows. This auntie, the medicine woman, lived in Plaistow, off Silvertown Way, and the far east side always made him fretful. The was a sprinkling of Africans down there, but it was the one place in London that gave him the same fear he experienced when he stepped outside it, into the small-town white republics. Here seemed one endless sprawl of concrete flyovers, where the light and brickwork were bleak, and many of the locals' faces seemed set in bull-like masks of hate. They didn't give one the impression they liked you very much at all, and it was only in this part of town they could actually do something about it.

Outside, Dele paced up and down, looking for potential sources of cover, while his mother tried to remember how she had last gained entry to the small estate. It was Dele's first time to the medicine woman's home. Until now, his Mum had simply brought him back talismans and symbols on certain occasions – when he had public exams and twice when Dapo had been seriously ill. A large crucifix, hanging above a chipped mirror, greeted them as they entered the hall. By the window, facing back on to the street, was a picture of a blue-eyed Christ, complete with halo and the words 'Jesus – My Personal Saviour' stitched in.

Hymns to 'Je-su' were the theme, too, of the tinny music coming from little twin speakers placed on the mantelpiece in the front room. Four or five family people sat around, respectable but poor, waiting to be seen. Two of the women, full-figured and forty-something, whispered to one another, beside a man whose shiny, furrowed forehead betrayed his nerves. He clutched his Bible closely and shifted in his tatty old suit.

Dele pitched his hand in his mother's lap. He felt very protective somehow. Everyone else looked of his mother's age and first-generation background. He, with his Oxford papers, should be the one to bring the necessary reason to stop any slaughter of the innocents. The corner of one eye was turned to any movement behind the door leading to the main room, the forbidden zone, as he concentrated on voiding himself of negative thoughts. He was up for this whole experience completely, if only it could be shown to be true.

When their turn came, it took a moment to adjust to the baleful light and musty smell of the room, then Dele's gaze settled upon the munchkin woman scrutinising him from behind the table. She was short, with a big Afro, and you couldn't quite tell her age as her skin bore the blotchy after-effects of ravishment by some kind of skin cream. Bleaching, quite possibly. She looked like something from *Star Wars*. Could the Good Lord really have invested quality powers in this creature?

Dele and his mother stood by the low seats in front of her. Pride of place on the centre of the desk, surrounded by candles and more crucifixes and pictures of Christ, was a money bowl.

'Mammy, this is my only son, Dele. Dele, pay your respects to Mammy.'

Dele got down on one knee and lowered his head, while Mammy said a few words in Yoruba, and added that she had worked hard for his success. When they were seated, peering up at her, Mammy asked Dele's mother if her husband had enemies back in Nigeria. She said yes, there were jealous men who envied the fact they had moved to England, and the family's success, but that her husband was a good, Christian man, and had never given these men cause. And Mammy nodded and turned to Dele, and said that these enemies had been practising evil and casting spells on his sister and that they would try to kill him, and that he must never journey to Nigeria without he and his mother coming for a consultation with her first.

Then Mammy wrote down a heap of phrases and references from the Bible for the two to read and say regularly, and two bottles of mineral water for Dapo and his mother to drink. Dele waited outside whilst the pressing money bowl matters were negotiated.

He wondered what the damage was for his mother's visits to Mammy Munchkin. Presumably, Dapo's condition demanded premium rates. He knew his Mum had little space to manoeuvre, seeing she had to account for all the money spent out of the family budget to his father every Sunday. He very much doubted she had sought his permission before making these Plaistow forays.

On the bus back, he became more and more exercised with the situation. The thought of his family at prey, to doctors and chance and this Mammy who was most likely skanking them out of sterling and hope – both in short supply. And this legal shit would take forever.

The first thing Dele did when they got back was to bell Dawn. He'd been wanting to do it all day but had checked himself. He had allowed his mind to race ahead and imagine all sorts of short- to mid-term pleasures with her. They could maybe model together in some studies for Celia, if Celia could get over last night's rancour. They could go to clubs, movies. She seemed literate and broad-minded, and obviously mature. What part of social work did she say she was in? Residential care? He would have to find an interesting angle on it to chat about.

Celia answered with an ugly 'Oh, it's you!' in her voice, and, after a long pause, Dawn's tone seemed similarly underwhelmed. He rattled off a couple of remarks about his day then quizzed Dawn about hers. She mumbled a few one-line answers so he went back to his day, trying to convey this impotency that he had been feeling. Then he started thinking it wasn't done to get so personal so soon with someone, and changed tack and asked about her plans for the weekend. She said she was busy and no, she couldn't really hook up this day, or that evening, or even next week, really.

'No? Not at all? Well, that's a shame.'

He tried to sound unfazed but something must have given him away. Enough for her to say, 'Don't even bother trying that tone with me, suh! Just because I let you come to my house one night and whatever whatever, it don't mean you can start pressuring me!'

'Dawn, no way was I trying to pressure you! I just thought it would be nice to meet up maybe – '

''Cos I won't wear it, you know. Look, I was thinking maybe we could have a little ting. But you can't be on the phone and be laying all this stuff on me, and me hardly knowing you.'

'I wasn't being heavy. I was just, you know, wanted a chat with you – '

'Right,' she paused. 'So when I've got some time we should talk. Give me a ring.'

'Alright .'

'Alright. So I'll speak with you?'

'Alright.'

'Bye.'

'Bye.'

His head was reeling as he replaced the receiver. What had he done wrong? When had he done wrong? How could Dawn bale out on him at a time like this, when he so needed it, needed a cuddle? He knew she owed him nothing but, still, it seemed very hard of her. He got to feeling angry with her, then angry with himself at his ludicrous misreading of their situation. Maybe she was one of those Maoists, seeking permanent revolution in her relationships. Or maybe she just hadn't liked his fuck. His performance had hardly been quality. He'd been drunk and mashed-up. True, he'd shown stamina, but the vigour wasn't there, his traction had been poor . . . You can't come to a thirty-year-old woman like that! And her a good decade into the game. And even before then, the battles with Celia (had he rowed with Dawn too?). He trying to be clever-clever in the chatting – oh shit, that girl on the tube too! He had forgotten about her. He felt that his whole record had been weighed in the scales and found wanting.

What with brooding on this, and the bigger thing (he bitterly regretted, still could not quite believe, that when it had come to it, he could not save his sister), and his head hot and his thighs cold-sweating, and his gut churning with the speed and fatigue, he just gave up and broke down and cried. He mumbled every self-pitying thing he could think of for about ten minutes, then shook his head and said 'Mista D, Mista D, Mista D! Listen to you. Pathetic.'

He took the unprecedented step, this early in the evening in his room, of lighting a cigarette. He smoked it furiously, before going downstairs to place a final call. It was time to get busy. A female voice answered.

'Hi. Is Sol around?'

'Who's calling?'

'A friend of his. Dele. We hooked up earlier today.'

'Oh *Dele*, hallo! It's Genevieve here.' She sounded well-perky. 'You've got a cute voice on the phone, haven't you? Hang on a minute, I'll get him . . .'

'Sol, alright?'

'Yes, Dele.'

He was a little nervous. He fingered the *Cataclysm* book that Sol had left behind.

'I've been looking at your book. Yeah, it's interesting!' It was a lie, but he couldn't think of anything to say.

There was a slight pause, before Sol came in with 'So, yuh ready for me now?'

'That's right.'

'Good to hear. I can't chat now. I don't give phone. Come over. Is tomorrow alright?'

'Sounds good to me.'

a man
died

CONCRETE LOOKED at his watch again. 11.10a.m. That was
the problem with Del, he was always late. He went over the
plans for the day with his two friends once again. The two
threes razored in at the backs of their heads marked them out
as soldiers in the 33 Posse, a local crew of hardcore young
hooligans. After the briefing, he felt to take a stroll around the
neighbourhood and let off some of this nervous energy, but
Babylon was still on his case. And the police would get real
jumpy with these three walking around.

The Saturday had dawned muggy and clear in Brixton,
but the early morning moisture had all but dissipated, and
Concrete's throat was dry. His man, Troy, went to fetch some
tins of Nutrament while Concrete pushed his hands deeper in
his pockets and scanned the middle distance for Dele's shuffling figure.

Dele was only half a mile away, but eight hundred
yards was a long distance in Brixton. It was as he swept
through the newly automated ticket barriers, shaking his
head at the myriad grotesques who descended, yelling
'Travelcard! Travelcard!', ready to buy or sell, that the first
flush of foreign hit him. Nowhere else in London gave him
that feeling of crossing a border the way Brixton did.

Peckham or Dalston felt more Jamaican, certainly, but nowhere else had quite this flavour. Two policemen clocked him closely as he came out the exit, but let him pass. He thought of turning round to see if the unfortunate had it written on his face, but thought better of it. Do not ask for whom the bells toll.

A flower seller thrust him a copy of a new freebie magazine, *The Brixton Village*. On the cover was a snap of the town hall prettied up to resemble Buckingham Palace. Inside ran thirty pages of community positivity: arts and crafts, letters and views, ads for restaurants, and a firm declaration from the editor that he 'Always backed Brixton'. His boasts made the place sound like a horse.

By the public phones outside the station, a busted old white woman hobbled along, then suddenly set aside her bulging bags, dropped her skirt, sat back on her haunches, and urinated right there. Dele drew a wide berth around the scene, where some onlookers were rather recklessly staring at the woman – as if she looked like someone who could be stared into shame. When the woman, preoccupied with wiping herself, noticed her public, she drew up her hands from her thighs, and pounded them savagely at her breasts, exclaiming, 'I am a *Maori*! *Know* me!'

Dele creased up as he walked down. No amount of fronting as a village is going to convince anyone. As if this place was Hampstead or Barnes.

He'd got an important package for Concrete, and he was late already. He moved at a trot past the guys with tics and crazy eyes, and the trendy insurgents, recognisable by the unfeasible optimism of their smiles. In a side street off Effra Parade he bumped into a blast from the past.

'Delboy! I don't believe it. How are you? You remember me? How are you? It's great to see you!'

Nick was suited, with his tie pulled down, holding a bag of bachelor grocery goods. It struck Dele that Nick was only the second person, including the brief exchange with Tamsin, that he had spoken to from his student days since this whole bleakness began. Those days just seemed like ages ago. He had two abiding memories of the man. The first was of Nick, the cool Jewish guy – little goatee, home in Hampstead, all the trimmings – who played keyboards in a multi-culti groove band and imported classy black women from London. The girls were nappy-headed and strong-featured and Dele had thought, 'Yeah. You really do like them unreconstructed.' It had been the first evidence he had seen of that Black Wives' Tale that white men liked their sisters 'African', whereas some black guys wished they weren't. The second was of a night at the one black club in Cowley that students frequented, and these three bullies had picked a beef out of thin air with Nick and beaten him down with savage, clubbing blows. His face had been all bashed up, a real sight.

Running his fingers through a flop of dark hair, Nick explained that he'd just come from a half-day at the office. He was in some sort of financial futures and Saturday was a productive time.

'And you?'

'Not really doing much at the moment.'

'Oh. Never mind.' Nick looked at him with pity in his eyes. 'So you live around here, do you? I've been here quite a while.'

'Actually I – '

'You must go to Fabrizzio's. You know the Pizza place in the market?'

'Pizza isn't really my bag, you know.'

'*Everyone* goes there for lunch. How about the Queen's Head, or the Ark?'

He reeled off a host of local eateries and pubs, none of which Dele had ever seen any black people in, apart from your full-on Europhiles. But anyway, Dele was already looking behind Nick to a blue-black babe in an unbuttoned long coat and micro-skirt, smiling and moving inexplicably their way. She had a centre-parting in a soft bob running down to her neck. But the smile was too fixed and, when Dele returned it, she scowled at him before beaming again at Nick. Something was up, for sure.

'Friend of yours?' asked Dele.

'Well, I get around,' replied Nick, standing up straight and grinning.

'I'll leave you to it, my man. I've gotta cut.'

The babe reached. She had eyes only for Nick.

'Do I know you?' asked Nick smoothly.

'I'm sure we've met before,' she replied, far too readily. Her widest smile yet revealed a gap two inches across, where her front teeth should be.

Dele shook his head as he strolled away. He had visions of old Nick, sacks fit to burst, getting it on, whilst the girl's pimp made off with the twenty-eight-inch Nicam stereo telly and Lord knows what else from the lounge. He hoped Nick would be alright, but really he shouldn't leave himself wide-open like that.

Dele's destination was just down at the bottom of the road: the William Hill bookies. This was where Concrete sold his pretty green most Saturday daytimes, to meet his expenses for the night to follow. He waded through the ranks of low-level guys (it always surprised him how much he disliked this squalid space), looking for him. But no joy. Only another youth whom he recognised from the perennial sociology text-book beside him. The youth was loosely measuring out a draw on to a betting slip held out by the punter, explaining to the latter, as he did to anyone who'd listen, how he was a serious student.

'But me no herbman. No, suh. This year a man haf fi have ambition . . . Concrete? I ain't seen the brother, you know. Try his Mum's?'

And sure enough, there he was. Outside, with a couple of friends. His people are wearing Dance-hall fatigues: bullet-holed blue denim jeans with plenty of green and yellow patches, and matching shirts. But Concrete was different today. His sculpted patterns had given way to a shaven dome, and he sported a blue cotton shirt, pressed black trousers and loafers on his feet.

'Is what time you call this?'

Dele held up a hand. 'Local madness. I see you changed your style.'

'You know! The new fashion. Ragga but employed!' Concrete patted his head. 'Sweet, nuh?'

'Yeah. Nice. I thought you'd be at the bookies.'

'Nah, boss. Me nah deal with dem tings deh no more. So wha', Sol give you someting for me now?'

Dele handed over a wad of notes in a brown envelope. Sol had explained it was something to help Concrete organise the little side-show they had planned.

'So what's the coup with this?'

Concrete's eyes narrowed imperceptibly and he muttered, detecting some spin on Dele's query.

'Me haf to get a little change. Nuff times me nah haf two ha'pennies to rub together!'

'Okay. So they're paying you now? Full-time or freelance or what?'

'Listen, Del, no disrespect, y'hear,' Concrete continued, 'but now you's troubling my business and dat cyaant run so. Bredren still an' all that, y'unnerstan'?'

Rebuffed, Dele tried another tack. 'So how are things anyway? I've hardly seen you since, you know – '

'Copaset, copaset.'

'And Gerry, my lawyer guy, he tells me you sacked him.'

'Yes, Del,' Concrete kissed his teeth. 'Me nah check for that geezer too tough. Him too, you know, speaky-spoky. Plus I didn't like the set-up. I'm fixed up now with someone more on a level. Local people – you get me?'

Concrete didn't furnish any more details. As one of his people leant forward, Dele spotted the 33 pattern on the head, and the stories he had heard about the teenage posse – ripping off clothes stores, street robberies, black-on-white, black-on-black, they didn't care – whistled through his head. It was funny to actually see them. Like meeting somebody famous.

The group soon parted. Concrete would stay and chat, but he'd got to prepare to deliver a speech. It was the first Dele had heard of it. But he didn't enquire further. There was no talking to Concrete in one of these moods. You could always tell by when the patois started getting thicker. He didn't know why his friend was acting all big and bad when there was no need for it. Must be in aid of impressing his homeboys.

Dele found his way back to the high road, barred by the police setting up positions and cordoning off neighbouring streets. It was just one poxy march, it wasn't all that.

Or two marches, in fact. The AFA/SWP on one side, and the BFB on the other hadn't been able to agree on salient points, so there would be two, with Dele supposed to take his place at each. But the key for today, Sol had counselled, was anonymity. Dele shouldn't be giving the authorities any further opportunities to lick him down, nor the politicos a chance to bounce him between them like a plaything. Keep a low profile and keep your distance, and Sol would let the others know he couldn't make it nearer the time.

Dele's forehead was starting to sting a little with sweat. It must be the sun, or a few nerves. He made his way down the side roads behind Coldharbour Lane, en route to a rendezvous with Gabriel and Celia at a local sandwich shop.

The sun had done the day such service that there were untold people out, styling a little extra in appreciation. The Boy Racers in their cars – Jeeps, Astras, Golf convertibles, any manner of customised business – boomed their basses fearlessly, taking brazenly illegal liberties on the road. On the street the guys preened with no particular place to go, and women languidly walked the gauntlet, braced for the long dog-days of community chirpsing to come. Even now, a little posse was assailing two ladies up ahead. One of them was pushing a couple of kids in a pram while her friend, dressed in a one-piece Lycra body suit with a hooped micro-skirt, had the latter blown up by a sudden gust of wind.

'Hey, sweetness,' shouted out one onlooker quickly, 'me see wha' you have, and every-ting al-right!'

The Lycra girl responded, 'Ah, mi haf a man who loves me already!' but her lyricker, unabashed, was ready for this.

'Honey, ouno haf too much loving for one man!'

The girls smiled and walked on.

Another woman, quite stush, paused in a puzzled fashion outside the grilled-up Bradley's off-licence, as if she was wondering why it was shut. She must have been from outside these parts. Even Dele knew that old Bradley tended to shut from about March, when the taxman sent him letters, until mid-July, year-in year-out. As she walked away she was pestered by a man who wanted to give her a lift. She finally turned round irritably, pulled out some car keys and waggled them in his face. As she strode away the guy hurled petulant abuse after her.

'Look at the state of you, man! You think you're too nice! Weave hair, fake eyelash. Nah, I want straight-up sisters. The real deal!' he shouted, looking around for support.

Dele cut across, past the gathering crowd, past the ranks of police officers, and headed into the sandwich shop. It was the first time he'd seen Gabriel or Celia since their encounter a few nights back. Celia threw him the most crocodilian of smiles but Gabriel, who was taking pictures of the event for a local paper, was happy to be getting paid for an event he would have come down to anyway. However, his face clouded over when Dele told him about his meeting up with Sol.

'Are you sure you know what you're doing? I told you already. They're bad news.'

'Come on, Gabriel. You talk as if Sol's the beast in the cellar. They're just helping me out. He talks a lot of sense. He's not so bad. He's into Slick Rick.'

'You just hear all these things about them. I don't know. Maybe people are jealous of their success.'

Celia, of course, had to haul her oar in. In addition to the usual shells over his sex life not being homogeneous in earlier incarnations, came the bizarre piece of rumour that Sol was quietly involved with a pop meets hip-hop outfit called Backstreets. Their act, all flaxen-haired pretty-boy dancers and blatant homeboy posturings, had landed them an unprecedented major-label deal worth a nice million. Not surprisingly, people were furious. Dele didn't believe it. Their conversation was drowned out by some commotion starting up outside.

They could hear a few hoots but plenty of cheers, and got up to check proceedings. Concrete was up there on a soapbox in the square, speechifying in the heart of what looked like a mini Nubian convention. One insistent young man, yelling 'Awakening Our Nation!' and flogging the *Alarm* magazine, jostled for attention with the two guys Dele had seen Concrete with before. They were doing shout-outs for *The Lives of Osiris*, a glossy comic, embossed with the Sankofa bird logo that signalled Yardcore Promotions. It promised to be 'A ten-part graphic novel series celebrating the adventures f Egypt's great man-god and father to us all. The comic is a great medium for sharing vital information with the people, but one frowned upon by "intellectuals". Fortunately, we are no "intellectuals"!' On the back, a little confusingly given the editorial, was a gushing endorsement from Professor Horace Overton.

It was a real trip to see Concrete centre-stage of all this. They had come in midway through, so the drift was difficult to discern, but it was harsh for sure. He was berating his listeners for sins of omission and ignorance. The lack of unity, the lack of self-love, and all that silly business. For shame. He said that we had certainly had our fill of sinners and possibly of saints too, but what were needed now were men of action.

His performance today was a hundred per cent more polished than the one at The White Rose. This felt scripted, not just spirited. With a little lump in his throat Dele realised that he was witnessing the birth of a new cool. Part of him felt like standing up, like the complainant at a wedding ceremony, and shouting 'Fraud! Fraud!' And part of him tingled and was just a little envious.

'Isn't that your mate? He's got a bit of a following, hasn't he?' said Celia.

'Well, he's playing in front of a home crowd,' said Dele.

But it was difficult to see how much of the crowd were actually tuned in. Most were talking about or sampling the product on sale, which seemed to be the central point of the exercise. Others had succumbed to the *Alarm* man. The numbers were swelled by mainly black defectors on their way to the march proper.

A woman emerged from the crowd and tapped Dele on the shoulder. It took him a moment to recognise Genevieve, as she had styled her hair differently. Her twists were piled high on her dome, and curled round in ovals, like an elaborate wedding cake.

'The lovely and sensual Genevieve,' he said, which produced a giggle. 'What are you doing down here? Overseeing your charge?' Dele looked across at Concrete on stage. 'That's if Sol put him up to this?'

'Me you asking!' she said. 'What are you doing here, more to the point? I thought you were gonna disappear for us today, eh?' She played across his chest with her hand. He wanted to reach across, grab her breasts and do the same.

'Yeah, I know. I'm about to. Listen, Genevieve, I'm a bit worried that if everybody is standing around here, then there'll be less people actually going on the march.'

She assured him that, at least so far as Sol's input into the little scene around them was concerned, things would soon be wrapped up.

He took his leave of the others but – there was so often a but in this neck of the woods – thought he'd just grab himself a quick bite to eat from the mobile food stands set up by the side of the square.

As he handed over the coins for a cup of nutmeggy punch, he spotted an unmistakable figure at the back of the stall, in a grey hooded Tunisian jacket and white jeans, fiddling with pots and pans. It was that feisty thing who gave him the runaround on the tube that night with Gabriel and the others. She'd burnt in and out of his life so fast he'd all but stopped believing she truly existed. He thought she'd dropped in from another galaxy.

'Alright?' he said, slipping off his shades. 'How are you? Remember me?'

She turned round. Her dark hair was tied back and her forehead was high and glowing with hot honest toil. The little spot had been despatched. Beside her were a Mediterranean woman and a Caribbean girl who might be the stallholder's daughter.

'You was with that geezer the other evening on Romford Road.'

'That's right. You disappeared without even telling me your name.'

He grinned at her. She wiped her hands on a cloth and pondered him for an instant.

'I told your mate where I worked, didn't I?'

'A-ha. Something precise like a restaurant on Warwick Road!' Dele paused and leant forward. 'I tried all the restaurants in Warwick Road and I couldn't find you.'

'What day did you look then?'

'What is this? A police station!'

She smiled. At last an unambiguous, human response.

'I help out my Mum's friend doing some cooking sometimes,' she said.

'Watch it. You're being positively reckless with your information today.'

'You talk funny, you do!'

'Only if all the black guys you know are rudebwoys and roughnecks. I'm an educated Nigerian. There are loads of us around. Ask your friends about their briefs, and they'll tell you I speak the truth.'

'Nigerian, yeah? You can't say nothing to me about Nigerians. I know what you're like!'

'Good. That's good.' He couldn't think of anything witty to say on the Nigerian question, so he smiled disarmingly instead.

'So, do you live round here?'

'Uh-uh. I've just reached for, well, kinda for the march. What time do you finish anyway?'

'I'm done soon. Ten minutes. Its only a half-day for me, as it goes. Let me ask Mrs Walms – '

'Wicked. I'll wait for you then. Watch you cook.'

'Alright. But I'm not going on no march. I haven't got my stomping boots on.'

Dele returned to the fringes of the crowds which were filling the streets behind the police and the metal barriers. He could hear a group of demonstrators moving their way, not more than half a kilometre away. The event for Dapo was turning out far bigger than he had expected. He was impressed, and chided himself for having mentally written off Daryl and Fitzroy beforehand. But what with it being a Saturday in summer, the mixed crowds, the guys around sipping lagers or the sickly sweet Cisco, and the women knocking back juices, there was a strange carnival culture to the day. This conspired with his incognito role to give him a sense of being lifted out of the frame. He felt a little overwhelmed, and impotent again, an abstract but intimately connected observer of this scene panning out all around. Almost like he was attending his own funeral, and fretting about whether it was being conducted in the appropriate tone. Just as well he was making himself scarce soon. Things were starting to do his head in.

His Fanny Craddock was moving nimbly at the back of the van. He couldn't get a fix on her background. The accent was mostly a familiar east London one, but with a tinge of somewhere else that he couldn't pinpoint. The strangest thing was when she had talked about getting permission from her boss, she had pronounced 'ask Mrs Walms' as 'aaaks . . .', the way Jamaicans did. Very peculiar for an English girl. Might she be one of those trashy 'Black Man Whore' types you saw encumbered by pure mixed-race pickney, pushing prams on council estates? He didn't feel so, really. There was a chic to her manner which didn't come from those places.

He speculated eventually that maybe her folks were skilled working-class, who had moved to London when she was still young enough for her peers to make the crucial interventions which had changed her inflections and landed her with 'aaaks' instead of 'ask'.

When she was done she strode off. Dele had to catch up with her just like on the Romford Road.

'So what are you doing now?' she said, staring ahead when he struggled alongside her.

'I don't know. I don't have any plans. Fancy a drink?'

'Nah, I haven't got time for a drink. I've got my run up and down to do.' She suddenly turned to him. 'Do you wanna come for a little drive, just up the motorway?'

'Sure,' he laughed. 'You're crazy, you know, you really are.'

'Do you drive?'

'Yup. But I haven't got wheels.'

'That's alright. I've got a ride. I'll drive up, you drive back.'

'It's De-le, by the way.'

'Andria. That's with an i not an e . . . This is it, this is my baby.' She stood beaming in front of an antique black vehicle that resembled a police car in those fifties Ealing films, with plenty of chrome on the bumper and boot. Inside was all lived-in leather and wood – no plastics in sight – and one of those outsize steering-wheels with the gear shifts attached. You could drive it slouching back with one elbow out of the window.

'That's a vintage Wolsey, that is. 'Aven't seen no one else in London with it. Only set me back five ton, and the guy ticked half of it 'til the end of the month. I'm in love with her. And these are my deliveries –' she added, opening the back to reveal five demijohns of Malvern Spring Water.

'You're going up and down in this graveyard number to deliver this?' he asked.

'That's right. Here, have a little tipple – ' She poured a short into a paper cup. He took a gulp and nearly spat the mouthful out on the street.

'Aaaargh! God! It tastes like sea water or something.'

'GBH – innit. Haven't you tried it before?'

'Call me old-fashioned but – '

'Sixty notes for ten hits you can flog it for. Money for next to nothing. You're just laughing.'

'What's it do for you then?'

She shrugged. 'Dunno, really. It kinda gets you pissed, without having to drink lots and lots. Some people say it's like liquid spliff but I can't see that. Are you sure you're okay?' She was concerned as Dele continued to splutter. 'I hope I didn't give you the animal tranqs by mistake. No, I couldn't have. That's in the other bottle.'

'Animal tranqs?'

'Yeah. You know – tranquilisers. The tonic they give to horses to put them down for a while. If you can shift a bit of tranqs as well it doubles your profit. Don't give me them eyes! It's only like the way you black guys pull a flanker with your liquorice allsorts to all the green kids out there. Do you wanna get another hit and get your scuzzy ass in the passenger seat?'

The front seats were one long bench of leather. Dele had to sit right up. By the button on the dashboard Andria pressed to set the motor into motion were two flyers declaring JUNGLEFEVER, one with a crayon drawing of a Roman in a tôga and laurel crown, the other with a snarling tiger.

He looked straight ahead as she busted a sharp right on Streatham Hill and headed for the South Circular. He would turn to look at her more only he worried that if he moved his head a fraction it would fall off. The GBH was like a jackhammer, like amyl poppers, the high fuzzy-edged rather than sharp, deadening his perceptions not shifting them sideways. All the dull pains and dizziness of being drunk. He had hoped GBH might provide him with further ammuniton for his work in progress on narcotics and sonic savants. But it looked as if he'd be disappointed. This stuff felt more like an accessory to white boys' drinking culture, only a few rungs up from glue or lighter fuel. A sleazy thing you slung down your throat in your provincial housing estate before you staggered out to someone else's car for a spot of joyriding. This stuff most definitely wouldn't fly in Dalston.

143

'I'm never short of guys, you know. It's just the calibre,' Andria suddenly said, apropos of nothing at all. 'The men down here are really rank. The sort who'd ask you for a dance and then break your back! Ninety per cent of the time it's just bad news. I just got no time for it, you know. If I was a guy, I wouldn't be the kind. So I don't let them get to me. No way.'

The Wolsey slowed as it rumbled right to slip on to the A23. Dele inclined his head, as quickly as he dared.

'Where are we headed by the way?'

'Brighton. Well, Brighton and a couple of places on the way. It'll be great. Clean, fresh air. Guys who aren't trying to press you. You been there before?'

'Uh-uh. I've never been outside London as it happens. Apart from some time in Oxford.'

'Oh well, it'll be a treat for you then. Sit back and enjoy,' she said briskly.

The mid-afternoon sun beat down. It was such a lovely day! Dele looked for a radio so he could catch any news report on the march, but there was only a tape-deck in the car.

'Slip this in – Andria grinned, thrusting him a tape marked 'Global Explosion'. 'I'm a junglehead. I fiend for it!'

The yearning, three-part harmonies of an old Jones Girls' standard was ripped up into a thousand freaky fragments on the boombox. The evil doll's refrain from the horror film, *Child's Play Two*, notorious for supposedly provoking two kids to kill, punctured the tune repeatedly. 'I'm Chucky. Wanna play? I'm Chucky. Wanna play?'

'Yeah? Are you sure?' he replied as this mutant discharge of deep house and hip-hop with R & B licks snarled around him. He was yet to be totally enamoured of this new programme. He used to be thinking the jungle sound was just a layby that wouldn't take you anywhere far, although that theory was being blown out of the window, judging by Andria's trailer-load of tapes. Maybe it was its crazily accelerated electro beats, or its dank science laboratory aroma, only the sound had just seemed to lack soul. But five minutes in the jungleverse now and he was hooked.

The strangest thing about the sound was its lack of a middle range. It was all tops and lows, trembly trebles and thick deep basses mixed at hypervelocity. Only the basses weren't seamless, finite and localised the way they were in hip-hop, but rippled into waves, emitting vapour trails like dub. Something of dub's talent for liberating sound into space, but none of its capacity for serenity. Whatever space these junglists frequented was clearly between a rock and a hard place.

'Listen to the rhythm. It's just wild. So buzzy-buzzy! You can feel it crawling and tingling on your skin.' Andria took her left hand off the steering-wheel to stab home her pleasure, as the languorous ride of an old Jah Shaka tune was dismembered to the ghoulish shrieks of an MC: 'Oh my gosh! It's firin', it's hurtin'! What-a-rush, what-a-rush! And London town, we love you bad!'

The tunes had become darker, more soaked in psychosis than he recalled. The insolence of dance-hall and the edginess of gangsta rap on cold turkey had all but buried the happy-happy utopias of acid. With the London DJs cannibalising their parents with such gusto, this culture could run and run.

Andria told stories of the east-side jungle assassins and the faces at the monthly West End dances, of pure dollars slipping through the fingers in a night's bleaching, to be recouped the next week through GBH for the white boys and Es all round. Her catering skills and local knowledge had given her the entrée, and now she wasn't looking any other place.

'I just like the set-up. See, I used to do the rave scene quite a bit. Recently, it got to be just geezers all leery and messing with Mace and knives. No way you could just hang out 'cos you didn't know what was gonna happen. But on the junglist tip, some of the heads are still a bit extra, but it's mainly safe.'

He scrutinised this drum and bass connoiseur closely for

signs of 'feel seh dem black' dom but, really, she had converted before him. This was her territory, part of her rights of residence. Why should she know any different?

She shot him an enquiring look.

'Ah-hah. I see it now. GBH mash-up my head, and jungle mashing up my bones. Andria, you got plenty to answer for!'

A new tune made tracks across twenty years of big-assed breaks and riddims but still it could get no satisfaction, and wouldn't rest. And, all the while, yet another disturbed girl's plaint flying above the beats: 'I felt that I was in a long, dark, tunnel.' Andria shaped sub-bacchanalian, arms and neck creating, shaking her shoulders, handling the steering-wheel with the occasional fat flourish, while Dele flexed with some slow motion raggamatic moves, feigning some order in the chaos. He flicked his lighter from side to side across his chest; the joy of it was lost out there in the daylight, with no strobes or darkness to throw the flame in relief, but it helped to keep him on a level.

'Those mad girls' voices – just like Pinky and Perky, don't you reckon?' said Andria.

'Yeah, you're right. Pinky and Perky is good.'

He began building a spliff to stabilise things, prepare them for the next aural assault. And between sorting the blunt, and singing along and shocking out as best they could, they lost purchase on one critical part of the whole package: the fact that they were doing 80 on the A3. So the moment was extremely harsh when Andria glanced up at the road signs – straight for Brighton, and the left lane for its satellites. She screamed, 'Oh shit!' braked hard and swung the car left. But as she tried to right it, with the oncoming traffic neighing and braking behind them, the wheels got locked and they skidded all over, tumbling towards the hard shoulder.

From that first half-second of grasping the situation Dele thought, 'Alright. We're gonna die', and felt quite calm as an awful lot of his life flashed past. It was amazing that it actually did and that it did it so quickly. Though everything seemed to be happening in slow motion now, as the car suddenly reared up and the tyres screeched and squealed for their missing undertow of concrete. The tubby Wolsey bounced about on two, then three, wheels and the others were almost upon them. But there could still be time if Jill be nimble, Jill be quick. The giant steering-wheel that Andria had been grappling with continued to look an extremely poor investment, but somehow his girl finally managed to right the vehicle and race successfully for the safety of the verge borders. She stopped the car, snapped off her belt and pounded the wheel before falling forward against it and letting out a mighty sigh.

'Je-sus! I only got the belts fitted a week ago. One week ago.' She spaced out this last sentence, just turning the fact round.

Dele took his hand from his face and they shared the grateful smile of the reprieved.

Gabriel was fidgeting with the shutter on his camera in a second-floor conference room in Lambeth Town Hall. The council had hired it out to Anti-Fascist Action for the day and it now functioned as the hub of the media operation. The thinking had been that the Press would be more likely to come down to these parts if they could take the temperature from the comfort of this eyrie, and a score of hacks now chatted amiably to each other. They ate canapés and sandwiches, backs to the window, whilst AFA footmen moved amongst them, soothing egos and fighting boredom. A council official and Police Liasion Officer floated in to the chamber intermittently, providing updates. Gabriel wanted to go outside, but he was only the second-string photographer. His brief was to stay at the base and pick up any action that might happen away from the main event. But the chamber's stuffiness had all the lousy atmosphere of a phoney war.

'How do you spell "goeffel"?' said Celia.

She was idly compiling a list for bi-racial people in different countries. They were one of her issues.

'What?'

'*Goeffel.* It means mulatto in a Zimbabwean language. Did you know that in the States you only need to show you've got one-sixteenth of a minority background to get a Federal Grant? It's like we're the dustbin race. Anybody can get in!'

'What is it with you? How should I know how to spell "goeffel"? I've never even heard the word.'

Gabriel sighed. He and Celia had begun so promisingly that other night, after Dawn and Dele had disappeared. She had been a surprisingly vigorous bedroom-worker. He had expected her to protest that she wasn't up for this or that because it wasn't cultural. But no, they had got on very well under covers. She had said that all she was interested in was this kind of freelance service every now and again. So he had thought fine, freelance is fine for a time. But these little obsessions of hers reminded him of why he had originally kept his distance at college.

'God, I'm bored,' she grumped, looking around icily at the crowd and ambling to the window. 'I want some colour in my day. No way we can go outside?'

'You can. I can't.'

'You're sure your boss wouldn't want you to use your initiative? There's something going on out, you know – '

Gabriel ran up to join her at the window. Outside, behind the square and the church, behind the AFA banners and SWP tags, plumes of smoke were wafting thickly in the east. Grey at the fringes, but the kernel was as black as a funeral.

'That looks serious,' said Gabriel. He turned round to the group inside but they were chatting on other matters and the policeman was nowhere to be found. 'I'm going down. Will you page me if you get any news up here?'

He reached the square, tingling with adrenalin but cursing at his camera gear, as tumult began to break. The smoke had taken a little time to blow over on this windless afternoon, but the sight of fire behind the podium had started people off. If the heavyweights on the platform hadn't been waiting vainly for Dele to turn up, the stewards might have already begun to disperse the five thousand assembled. They were anxious to avoid any possible unseemliness with the

BFB whose rival rally was scheduled to take them within fifty yards of the square, down Brixton Hill and Brixton Road, en route to the police station. They initially took the sudden surge in the crowd in front of them for impatience, and it was only the booming tones of a police megaphone urging the crowd to keep calm that told them different.

The plea shifted events into third gear. Ugly rumours circulated of fire bombs, death traps and frying in the summertime. The stewards tried to move the crowd on, but still clung to the original plan of diverting it from the BFB troop, even now approaching the town hall. Fitzroy, in a freshly laundered, white pleated shirt, was angrily consulting with a colleague as his mobile belled Dele's house bootlessly. Already sore that the AFA was sharing his limelight, he was in no mood to be tested. Then two things happened: as the panicking crowd finally broke through the barriers and ran every which way but east, a couple of cocktails and petrol bombs landed and exploded behind the few hundred strong BFB, further up the hill. Nothing too serious, but people didn't know that.

'What was *that*? A bomb. My God! A bomb!' shouted one.

'Ricky! My baby, my baby!' shrieked another headscarved woman. As she turned round to go back she was knocked down in a flurry of arms and limbs.

'Keep them moving. North, north,' a radio voice crackled to a policeman.

'Them cunts got guns, you know?' said a guy, dressed in joggers, hurtling away with a friend.

'Carl, darling – '

'D'you wanna die today? You obviously do. Move your bumbaclaat!'

'Who, who's got guns?'

'The BNP boys. Came down in vans is what I hear – ' hazarded another, bringing a new variable into the equation.

The woman's scarf was knocked off and a foot trampled her hand in the grit, leaving it a bloody mess of raw, dangling skin.

'Hey, hey! Thief! Man just thiefed my wallet!'

'What?'

'It's a stitch-up. The wankers are all over. Gonna be some licks out there,' confided a BFB soldier to a bewildered Fitzroy.

The first fist flew. Then another, then another. Fire vehicles screeched noisily down the back streets and a police helicopter hovered above.

'Look at that baby. Look at that poor thing – ' A woman picked up the toddler.

'It's that blasted 33 Posse. Rob an' steal their own.'

'Ah, let it alone, Gary. Let's get out of here.'

'What are you gonna do with the flipping kid? We can't take it with us.'

'Just wait for the mother.'

'And get us killed. No thanks.'

'Michael?'

'Don't "Michael" me!'

Gabriel moved nimbly in the armshouse, amidst the shoving and fighting, and the desperate official response. He was doing his best now to find some way round the crowd, some aerial vantage point where he could frame the key picture to sum up the drama. He was slowly inching down a side road when he felt a vicious tug on his arm. The youth assaulting him was already in the first steps of sprinting away, his trailing hand tugging the shoulder support of Gabriel's leather camera bag. But the support held and, as the bag's contents tumbled on the ground, the youth scooped up what he could and tore away, followed a few moments later by Gabriel. The youth, wearing an American football shirt numbered 33, scarpered down an alley and through the back of a house, and Gabriel was just cursing Brixton's stink when he spotted the same guy running down Dalberg Road, a hundred yards ahead. As he chased again – managing to take a quick picture as he ran because it seemed a vaguely good idea – the youth shouted out some garbled words to a spar in shades who was being hailed at and falteringly pursued by a middle-aged man. Or maybe this man, in a blue Hawaiian shirt and BFB armband, was hailing down one of the others swarming around. Suddenly, and Gabriel would tell you the man was always in his field of vision, although he couldn't say he had actually been focussing on him, the older guy staggered and screamed and fell on his front. As Gabriel reached him, he saw thick red blood staining the pavement, pumping out in spasms from the man's chest. The man kicked his legs involuntarily for a few ghostly seconds and then fell still.

Gabriel looked up, but the youths had disappeared. There were a few other people around, but most were running blindly, keen to put some distance between them and the main flow around the corner. The first woman he called out to didn't want to hear, but he got a second to stay with the body, and do what she could, whilst he rushed away to find an ambulance.

With one hand covering Dele's eyes and the other on the steering-wheel, Andria continued his sentimental education.

'Okay,' she said, 'Now open your eyes slowly and, one-two-three, tell me what you see – '

'What I can only call rolling countryside. Trees, crop-fields and not a satanic mill in miles,' replied Dele.

'Welcome to Sussex,' those grey-green eyes shone. 'I used to come up here, when I was a kid in Brighton, an' pick rosemary and fresh herbs an' that! The mornings here get so fresh and sunny, the light's just different, you know. I can feel like a hothouse flower! Are you alright, love?' she said, in mock concern. 'You can hack it? No withdrawal pains?'

'Uh-uh! I feel like I was to the manor born.'

But he spoke too soon, as they soon rolled into a small market town. The place was the living advert for an age he thought had done. The little roads were dotted with old-school butchers' shops, passed by women in fitted blouses, white minis and white stilettos. Elsewhere, clutches of young white adults, lank of hair and limb, stalked the streets. Despite the warmth of the early evening, they wore drainpipe jeans and black leather jackets covering T-shirts with death heads and diabolic symbols. The bigest contingent chilled in the main square, in front of a flint museum and the war memorial. Here five local dons on motorbikes raced each other in front of a largely female crowd. The coup was to start up your 500cc Triumph, pick up as many screaming girls as you could on the back, and then ride round the square before the church bells chimed such and such. Horrible, horrible. Rockers eking out the last of English before the sun set.

'Boy, I don't think this place is quite my speed,' said Dele weakly as he sank into his seat and wound his window up.

'Don't worry – they won't bite,' reassured Andria, despite them receiving a host of very interested looks from the crowd.

They made stop-offs at a couple of flats, unloading the GBH. The second place was occupied by two Gothy sisters, 'Done In' Diana and Maxine, dressed in long black dresses and bangles. All four knocked back a Bless This House libation of sea water then the sisters insisted they visit the smallest pub in the south for a drink. Dele cracked his head on the ceiling, and whilst he rubbed it, Diana took his other hand and read his palm. 'Times have been very hard,' she said, 'but love, comfort and release are just round the corner.' Dele offered to buy her a drink.

'Cheers. Mine'll be a lager and black. I always get a lager and black – I like the colours it makes when you throw up,' Diana explained. 'That's why they call me "Done In Di".'

With the victors of the Great Bike Race and their partners throwing hostile glances Dele's way at the other table, he didn't check for the vibe at all, only their looks triggered a stubborn bravado in him. But finally Di said she wasn't feeling too good, and they moved out.

As they walked the narrow, quiet, street to the Wolsey, they were followed at some distance by around ten of the Grebos who taunted him with 'you fuc-kin' nig-ger!' and 'jungle bunny!' and other out-of-date verbals. It was the first racial public challenge he had had in the longest time but, after weighing up the numbers, and the fact that Diana was barfing noisily behind them, Dele urged them to hurry to the car. Just in time, as the pack suddenly ran at them and beer bottles rushed in the air past them and smashed against the ground and wall, to the sounds of 'niggerlovers!'. To his surprise, many of the shouts were female voices. It was only as they dashed inside the car, Diana groaning uneasily into their wake, that they kicked off. Andria and Dele picked up a couple of the shards of glass and bottles and hurled them back, before Andria started the car and steered it straight at the Grebos. There was a stunned realisation on their faces as they clocked that she wasn't joking before they hurled themselves out of the way. Then the chase was on. Their foes piled on to their Triumphs and Kawasakis and they exchanged insults vociferously before Andria slammed her hand on the gearstick and bumped the ride into their main man's bike, leaving him busted up and writhing on the street. They dropped off the sisters and floored it to Brighton.

Three paramedics and one burly policeman, courtesy of the still-whirring helicopter, vainly pumped the poor man's heart. Behind a hastily strung-up cordon, another officer did his best to extract information from a largely unco-operative crowd. There were a few raised voices, and one old woman from a house across the road was wailing piteously, but the hundred or so who had gathered along the road were just staring on. Gabriel, still in shock, gave a cautious tuppence worth.

'I was just running down the street, trying, you know, to get away from the crush. There were a few others around but, you know, I wasn't really focussing on anything. Or anyone. I think I may have heard a scream or something but it all happened so quickly you know, you're not really concentrating. Then I saw this guy running towards me and he just dropped down in front of me. It was only when I saw the blood that I realised that, you know, what happened – '

'So what exactly did happen, sir?'

'I don't know. He just fell down there is what I'm saying – '

Fitzroy and two of his colleagues, all with BFB armbands, arrived on the scene. Fitzroy slid under the cordon tape, rushed to the corpse and threw a hand across the blood-ied Hawaiian shirt before an angry officer hauled him off. Three young guys were breaking the habits of a lifetime and chatted eagerly to a policewoman, causing Gabriel's ears to prick up.

They were explaining to her that they all saw a white youth, his forehead wrapped in a red scarf, accost the dead man and then run down a side road like lightning. A woman came up and confirmed their point of view when a second officer arrived.

A white guy, they were saying. Gabriel didn't see one, he didn't think. Mind you, it had all happened so quickly and his head was just set on the other guys. Maybe the old guy had been done in by a white kid even before he reached the street. Gabriel braved some vicious looks to take some final photos of the scene as the medics wrapped and strapped the body up in a white sheet and bundled it into an ambulance.

A bunch of punters lined the wall of Brighton's Easy Duz It like barracudas on the case. With plenty of the guys black and nearly all the women white, it could have been a scene from one of London's crossover West End nightspots. Where did the sisters go out to play down here? Dele scoped the floor, but there were only two, and they had just sidled up to an English ex-pop star whom he recognised from the man's three minutes of fame on Top of the Pops a decade ago. They were all over him, like bees to the honeypot. His jacket sleeves were rolled up, exposing the track lines on his arms, and he threw his hands around both girls, tapping their booty to giggles.

The DJ played a string of eighties soul/club classics. The guys started to swarm, making the advance and hoping for a some trim from the ladies. Andria, all pouty and frisky and fresh to these parts, got rushed periodically but she shouted in their ears and pointed out Dele. The guys turned to him, grinned and threw their hands up in a 'No disrespect, seen? More grease to your elbow,' gesture. One of her rejected suit-ors walked up to Dele, and they puffed on a no-hard-feelings spliff together.

When a mighty anthem tune dropped Dele returned to the floor and shook a leg while Andria threw her arms up above him and yelled 'Go, Dele, go!' and he returned the compliment as Andria took centre-stage with some nifty extempore moves of her own. That girl, she was really something else.

He asked the DJ to play a few jungle tunes, but the DJ said they got a nice crowd down here, and they wanted to keep it that way. So he prevailed on Andria to leave. She'd done her business and he too was a busy man. Best they head.

They took a little stroll along the pier before returning to the car. Andria was as charmingly tangential as ever and Dele had to rein in a desperate desire for intimacy. He wanted to tell her that the march she cooked food for was on account of his sister, and such and such, but he fought it off.

'At night, my baby really comes into its own,' she said, pressing the ignition and 'play' on the stereo, and curling her feet up on the long leather seat. 'See, this could be a sofa in a living-room.'

Two wicked pieces of tune filtered through, which scuppered the stillness around them, but gave Dele a different sense of sanctuary. The second tune intercut the guttural tones of a DJ with one of those accelerated young-girl voices covering this pretty melody he had first adored from Lovers Rock:

Your Lo-o-ove, keep it new.
Why doesn't love stay new
then we could too / (we could too)
See the world through coloured glasses.
Your Lo-o-ove, keep it new.

'Ah, that's just awesome. Pure butter. I've never heard drum 'n' bass put together like that before,' he said.

'Have a look at my pictures,' said Andria, reaching into the glove compartment for her photo album. There was Andria at work, Andria at play, Andria shooting pool in a

Kangol beret and a grey Waffen SS-style trenchcoat, a suede-head Andria in dungarees as the original tomboy, and a podgy puppy Andria with a grown-out bob looking like a seventies sub at an unfashionable soccer club. But he didn't reach the end of the album because Andria grabbed a blanket from the back, threw it over them, and giggled about how she used to play 'tents' as a kid. She and her kid brother, in the house on their own, turning a little corner of it into a new world with their chairs and blankets, making believe they were stranded in the jungle, or a nuclear fall-out shelter, spending the afternoons preparing rations.

'Guess that's where I got into the cooking,' she said, fidgeting under the cover as she nattered.

With something approaching resignation, Dele realised that now was the time to make the play. He tried to fix his mind on savage thoughts, rewinding Britain's glorious pantheon – the way he had once with Helena. He thought of the thugs from earlier that evening, and pictured Andria in undignified, wanton positions, her on all fours and him grabbing her by the legs like a wheeelbarrow, balancing her frame on his big-lion haunches, running his dick deep up her ass . . . But he was finding it hard. He didn't want to do that shit an more. Not with these sounds. Not with her.

'Andria,' he broke in, 'you know it's twice you nearly got me killed today? I think you owe me. You can start by giving us a cuddle and resting us up in this tent you're so keen on!'

'Don't wait for the best bit, will ya?' she smiled and slid her arms around him.

Sol rolled back to his flat in Westbourne Park in his black BMW. He got in and went straight to play the video recording he had set of the evening's news. He has seen it once already, but now he could look at it at his leisure.

Over pictures of the fire, the stampede and chaos, the spitting, shoving and fighting, a dry BBC voice intoned that 'The innocent victim of the fatal stabbing is Derek Dalton, a Blacks Fight Back steward, of Forest Hill, south London.

Police are anxious to trace a white youth, wearing a red head-scarf, seen running away from the scene . . .'

He slipped off his Timberlands and padded to the kitchen. He poured four measures of overproof white rum in to a jug, added half a carton of orange juice, then neatly cut up slices of lime and lemon and dumped them inside with a spoon of brown sugar and a dash of honey. He poured the mix into a glass, took a deep draught and kicked back on the sofa. Today had been a long day.

ego-tripping

ONE MIGHT have to agree that, although Derek Dalton's murder was clearly a terrible matter, it did have its fringe benefits. Gabriel, for one. For nearly a decade he had pursued a passion for pictures, on a mainly hand-to-mouth basis. There had been a brief interlude of bliss in the late, great days of the Greater London Council, when dollars walked freely, and the young Gabriel was fixing abiding memories at black arts events around town, but the GLC was guillotined, the subsidies for the groups dried up, and Gabriel was forced to go knock-knock-knocking on photo agencies' doors. They looked at this locksed-up boho and handed him the boxing beat. He didn't check for boxing – from ringside it seemed a circus, too much blacks beating up on blacks for whites – but Man had to pay the bills, so he spent his evenings in insalubrious East End halls, and his Saturdays snapping away at community weddings. Now his' exclusive pictures of Dalton's time of dying had upped his stock dramatically. It was so rare that picture editors got material this hot – still with the choking temperature of real death. They belled him, cheques at the ready, and were relieved when he said he only wanted a hundred pounds as his fee, and a month's work experience. A deal was swiftly concluded with one and Gabriel, delirious with joy, pumped up the sounds as far as his Vauxhall co-op flat could reach. Four weeks and he'd show 'em what he'd got.

Fitzroy was large too. The killing had bump-started the BFB from marginal to mainstream overnight. Once again, race relations had sorted him out. He carefully adjusted his tie in the mirror, patted down his greased-up hair, and cursed the relaxer he'd indulged in over the years for hastening the thinning of his hairline. His brow furrowed as his thoughts turned to The Yardcore Agency, the BFB's new PR team. They'd forced his hand really. He'd had no other option. Still, he'd have to admit they were coming up with the goods. He glanced at his watch and scanned out the window of his South Norwood pad into the summer's twilight; a BBC cab was due to arrive to take him to his first interview on Radio Four.

Across town, on the west side, Sol looked on with an avuncular smirk. Genevieve was downstairs changing, Michael was drifting in and out of the sitting-room, his cousin Sam was doing his books, and Concrete was demonstrating to Dele the science of the headbutt: '. . . Always remember, okay, a couple of quick jabs straight off. And from you set him up, then butt him on the nose, y'unnerstan'? Greyback's nose goes west every time, with a quickness – '

'Each one teach one,' Sol said, as the others started chuckling, and sipped on his juice.

Michael beckoned him into the kitchen. There was the small matter of X-Cess, a new Anglo-Polish owned club that had opened locally, on Goldhawk Road. The pair of them as seductive as all hell, had gone to see Mr Kyscinki and offered him the services of their security affiliate to run the door. Kyscinki had less politely declined, so they had sent in some local hooligans to distress the place on its first Saturday night. Michael thought it was now time to return to the Pole, but Sol wasn't having it.

'Uh-uh! What we should do is send the guys – maybe some other people – send them down one more time, don't you reckon? That way, we'll have no more trouble from him down the road. What's wrong, bro? You look all touchy. Look, everything's coming together sweetly for us, BFB, new clients all the time – we just need the flow to treat them right, that's all. Like we say, no pause in the cause and show me a cause that doesn't need money.'

When it came to persuading Michael of something Sol knew the best way was to wrap his words in tidy little slogans that he culled largely from videos rented from the local store – action films and documentaries on Muhammad Ali, Richard Pryor and the Cosa Nostra. This particular bite he had borrowed from a martial arts movie where a revolutionary Hong Kong Chinese gang kidnapped a group of American athletes.

Michael began nodding quickly enough. He had longtime been too overrun by Sol to argue with him. Michael couldn't tell you when the shift started, but somewhere down the line. It was Michael's business originally, after all. He had been flogging clothes, copied designer gear mainly, and promoting clubs from a Harrrow Road basement when old school spar Sol had dropped by with a proposition for expansion. Quiet and self-effacing, and happy enough with the status granted by success, Michael had gradually lost the upper, even an equal hand. He was keen to retrieve the situation. Sometimes, he didn't even know who he was dealing with anymore. He was waiting for Sol to slip.

'Okay, I'm ready,' said Genevieve finally, poking her head round the door.

Sol and Dele, in jackets and ties, and Genevieve, in a blue cashmere coat and high heels, made for the car. They were eventually reaching for an engagement party at a West End wine bar: Dinah Bevan, a TV reporter, and Roger Bradshaw, who did something in diamonds, were getting hitched and celebrating in style. Sol had invited Dele along to make friends and influence people, prior to their own big benefit night which was to form the centrepiece of the Dapo campaign.

'It's a Black Tax vibe from our point of view, you get me? But you don't need to bash them around the head with *that* bit.' Sol took his eye off the road a moment to turn to

Dele in the back seat, 'Just tell them about the big benefit we're having, boost it up, about how we look forward to them attending, and all profits going to your legal fund and the BFB. If anything, just slip in softly that donations are welcome, yeah?'

'Cool,' replied Dele.

'So, Del, you're getting in deep now?' enquired Genevieve.

'Yeah, man. He's down with the programme,' said Sol.

Dele settled back comfily in his seat (his family had never had transport and he remained, he would admit, too easily impressed by car culture), as Sol offered him some notes on his life story. Sol didn't strike one as being an open or spontaneous kind of guy, so you had to wonder why he was sharing all this privileged information. But then again, it was his Beemer, so let the man talk.

Maybe it was ego-tripping, but Sol had known all along he was gonna do alright. As a youth growing up in Wembley, he was tall and fit, quick in his head and on his feet, good with his fists and neat with his hands. He got into Chelsea School of Arts to study graphic design, the first in his family to reach college. Success followed in a quality graphic design company. Life was sweet for the twenty-three-year-old young gun. Company car, a place in the white end of the Grove in one of the mews, the works. Until he got fresh and started using his employer as a base for other pursuits, drawing flyers for raves, proposals for comic-book ventures. They slung him out: misuse of company premises, time and, possibly, funds. No thorough investigation, no written warning, they just got rid. They said there was no 'black mark' on his record, but it had taken him a good while to get another gig in some dibby-dibby outfit. It irked him greatly that he had not been given a chance to answer the charges, so much so that he all but erased the memory of the original sin. His work was already suffering with all the brooding by the time a barely tolerated colleague began humming the Fagin tune from *Oliver*, 'You've got to pick a pocket or two', around his desk. At first Sol thought nothing of it, but after a week of this he reckoned that news of the business at his previous employer must have been leaked through the grapevine. After two weeks he conked his singing colleague's head and laid him out on the office floor. And, seeing how the guy was the owner's son, Sol was shortly out on his ear.

Dele looked at Genevieve's profile and thought how pretty it was, even when she was staring out of the window in a bored fashion. He wondered whether she was in love with Sol, how well she knew him, what she thought of him, or anything else for that matter. She was a bit of a closed book. All he knew was that she was a singer and Sol was supposed to be sorting a record deal for her, but it hadn't yet happened.

Sol was saying that he'd spent two years underground. Two years of thwarted ambition, finally touching base with old acquaintances and planning guerrilla PR campaigns. He had re-emerged with The Yardcore Agency when he judged the time was right.

'I didn't get the breaks that were due me. Or, I got the breaks but they didn't last. But I wasn't gonna be broken up by it. No, Rasta. Big Man nuh cry! But you, you're a true insider – '

Dele snorted. 'That's not how I feel, especially not now. I don't want to be part of that vibe.' He explained to Sol how his last few months at college had been an increasingly bitter period for him. The more he thought on it now – all the incidents, all the people – the more his time there largely resembled a series of grotesque cameos. And he didn't quite understand why he should have behaved like that – maybe some reaction to the strictest of upbringings, and then that sense of release at college. But it hadn't been minstrelsy, more some toxic problem of self-presentation.

And Sol nodded and said it had been the same for him at the firms he had worked, and there was no doubt about it, but you lose something when you're all but the only black person around in an environment. ''Cos whatever your relationships in such places, they can't help you deal with dat essence dere, you know,' Sol prodded at his chest. 'But still, Dele, you have to stay in. You with your book smarts and your papers, it's gold-dust what you've got.'

'Is that the score with that band Backstreets you're pro-moting? Trying to get on the inside?'

'Who said anything about that?' Sol lost it slightly, for the first time Dele had seen. He pressed Dele hard for the source.

'Celia? Do I know her? It don't ring any bells. But yeah, we've done a few things for them. It's no biggie,' he said, before falling silent.

Their first port of call was the Carlton Vale Centre, in Kilburn, where The Yardcore Agency was based. Reconstructed out of a striking, eighteenth-century church fallen into disrepair, the building – its iron gates, stone drive and little park – had been Brent Council property for some time, and been finally reinvented as a spanking two-million-pound community centre eight years ago. Only the other communities that had been part of the original deal – the Irish, the Asians, the pensioners – had been informally ousted, and now all you got were black businesses, black folk in the table-tennis and weights rooms, and the continuous brrr-brrr and 'Who dis? What's the move?' of men and mobiles.

Sol asked Dele to do him a little favour. Dele laughed as he explained, and was still smiling when he was introduced to these young Americans waiting for Sol in his office. The two brothers were very slick, homeboy executives at Flatbush Records, a young label that boasted a stable of brand-name hip-hop and R 'n' B. They were negotiating a licence deal for one of their acts with Sol's agency.

'This is Dele. We're working on a project together.'

It was a trip to be sitting in with the famous Flatbush – the kind of thing he would have looked forward to gossiping about with Dapo. Sol was waxing frothily about the history of Yardcore or rather the YCA as Sol was constantly calling it – as if Yardcore sounded too militant to be said in front of money-men.

Every now and again an office hand, a dark-haired white guy in jogger pants and a Chicago Bulls jacket, popped his head round the door to pass on messages. Dele tried to catch Genevieve's eyes but she was flicking through magazines. He watched as Sol picked up a soft ball from his desk, squeezed and juggled with it, then bounced it repeatedly as he listened. What the hell was that about? Executive stress relief? Behind him stood two striking pieces of decor. He had a blown-up still from the NWA video for 'Express Yourself', where the band members burst through a white sheet covered in Martin Luther King's head and his 'I Have A Dream' speech. It was a stunning image. The other was a mounted, poster-sized version of the Ice-T cover of his *Home Invasion* album. Here the suburban whitekid was mainlining Ice-T through the headphones on his Walkman, and his parents were standing by the door, really fretting because they couldn't stop it, and Ice-T was hovering over in one of those comic-book bubbles, leering triumphantly. On the original you had Ice-T actually burglarising the place.

At the pre-arranged time, Dele got up and quietly left the office. He sauntered down to a nearby corridor, and smoked a cigarette, earwigging on two young women, one clasping a baby, conversating by the reception area below. What caught his attention was something about the 33s. He listened closely.

'I feel seh dem must do fat birds some time soon!'

'Dem just bullies. See dem cut up dat Derek on the 'line, you know – '

'You could see it coming, ehnnit though? But radics dem still hold the body – '

'Why don't they just bury him and done?'

'Hear what, though. Forensic man gonna pay a visit and directly now, and see what he can see!'

'Someone haf fe deal wid dat Archer man coarse. It was only when Archer come down to Vauxhall College that him get his, you know. Him get brok one time bad and, true, him a Hackney man, but still dem cut him. Only the cousin right, when him get released, and two-twos come down with a gun . . '

They moved out of earshot, as Dele pondered what he'd heard. Was Archer one of the 33s? Was it the same Derek they were talking about, the steward on the march? It didn't seem likely. They had talked about him as if he was a mate, or a local man, whereas this thing had happened down south. Which 'line were they referring to? Brixton's or a local variety? He could have misheard them, they were chatting very fast. But what also struck him was the way these neighbourhood girls – they couldn't have been more than seventeen spoke in an everyday way of so much blood. He finished his cigarette and went back inside.

'Sol, you've got a call. You can take it in the manager's office. I think it's overseas – ' said Dele.

Sol nodded and turned to his table guests.

'We're talking to the Japanese,' he explained, in an off-hand, but confidential fashion, and got up.

Dele sat down to hold the fort, pouring himself a glass of orange juice from the carafe on the table as Sol pretended to field the call. He floated a few long-nurtured thoughts on breakbeats and his favouite bands, but unfortunately these homeboy executives displayed all the laid-backness of musodom. No one took him up other than to say X or Y was firing or still the lick to long nod ya head pauses. In the end, the sum of what they said was that the East Coast rocked, which he knew already.

They seemed more interested in talking to Genevieve anyway so he let them get on with it and took a peep around Sol's desk. In the local paper was a piece headlined: CRISIS AT CARLTON VALE, saying that the council were calling in their own accountants to look at the centre after more than five hundred thousand pounds had gone persistently unaccounted for. He was just poring over the details, chuckling to himself and thinking, not another public-sector skank, when Sol came back and wrapped the meeting up.

In the car Dele flicked through that fraying paperback, *Cataclysm*, which Sol had lent him. The book was a real countdown to Apocalypse trip. Its big idea was that a third force, a black diasporic coalition, would undermine the West; that the large settled immigrant communities, such as those that originated in Lagos and Kingston, would knit together in the urban centres of the new world and infect the state and its infrastructure from so many directions – from gunman crime to white-collar fraud – before linking together to effect new types of crime, that the hull of the ship would be fatally holed.

But he couldn't really concentrate on it, with his mind troubling again on Dalton's death. That all of a sudden he should have this tragic link with this poor man he had never met! Both their families had been turned upside down from nowhere. He had sent a letter to Dalton's family but he should go and visit them, really. No one had yet been charged with the killing, although two young white men, with far-right leanings, had been arrested then released. The BNP said talk of their involvement was preposterous and Dele was pre-pared to believe them. It made no sense for them to do it. But you couldn't discount the possibility of some white national-ist renegades having done this shit. After all, there had been witnesses.

The supertrebley sounds of soca greeted them as they stepped into the basement of the Circa Bar in Soho. Sol and Genevieve were accosted by acquaintances within a few sec-onds, so Dele strolled over to the drinks table to grab some mixes.

Little clusters of guys chatted and swayed slowly, hands clasped in front of them. Others, in jackets and waistcoats, stood by the bar, folded ten pound notes in their outstretched hands, demanding service. Starfuckers muttered excitedly about micro-celebrities walking past, and what the grapevine was saying they had said about love, life or the community. It seemed that all you needed to do was to appear on TV and you were a role-model these days. Couples, led by Roger and Dinah, held each other closely on the dancefloor, but more eyes were turned to its edge where a crew of three young women in bobs, ruffled dresses and sin heels, swayed softly in perfect time. They were the best movers in the house, which was why they were standing where everyone could see them.

Mostly, though, guests were standing around network-ing, making happy noises about the welcome rise in black power couples. Chatting to a few, Dele noticed how many –

if they weren't working for themselves – had got their heavy duty gigs through word of mouth. Not your ordinary, say, friend in the council housing department who gets you sorted-type deal. No, these people had *serious* friends of friends, the way students did at Oxford.

Like this woman Carole, a young solicitor whom Genevieve introduced him to. Carole sported a royal blue tailored suit with blue stockings. The single-breasted jacket was buttoned low to reveal a lacy black bra underneath. The two-piece reminded him of what Islington councillor Lurline Champagnie had worn when she stood in front of the cameras at a party conference and announced 'I'm black, British, a Tory, and proud of all three.' Carole worked in entertainment law, she said. She'd been sitting around firing off applications to do articles when a friend heard about the vacancy at a firm and put in a good word for her. It only turned out her friend was Rab Edwards, a variety star who had mined the Cheeky Cockney territory to the tune of half a dozen TV series. Dele, a little laterally, replied that he too had friends, but only Sol had any money. She gave him her card, he gave her a flyer for the upcoming gig of all benefit gigs, and told her she wouldn't find a better cause. Sol worked the crowd, every inch the man whose star was rising. He told the waiter to take a bucket of pink champagne down to his American friends and told anyone of importance how he was going to hire out this space and the Roof Gardens this New Year's Eve, so the Afristocracy massive could wander from one to the other through the night. Everyone agreed that it would be an unprecedented coup.

A greased-up head bobbing amongst others by the table alerted Sol to the fact that Fitzroy has made his entrance, fresh from Radio Four. He'd let that foolish frotter have his moment's pleasure. The people that mattered knew who was truly in charge. He scoped the room for Dele and noted approvingly that his man was reasoning with that Nigerian sculptor, what's-his-name, the one who had just won that big-time Art Prize. What was he doing here? Probably looking for buyers. It was good. He didn't have much hope for sculpture carrying much with the people out there, but getting a man with such credentials on board could only be a plus.

The thirty-something Tayo Adeniran, kindly, elegant creator of 'King Ja-Ja Meets His Destiny', had opened with an 'I knew your father,' when Dele had introduced himself, but then backed up this well-worn countryman's gambit with genuine, lovingly rendered anecdotes, about how their families had grown in the same part of town, and how his Dad had been a frequent house-guest and a brilliant young man, if a little wild. Tayo's eyes lit up as he recalled the famous occasion when Dele's Dad, just recently married, had arrived with chauffeur and baby nephew at a rich man's house to pursue his liaison with the wife. Only the husband had returned unexpectedly and chased Dele's Dad out of the place with a machete. Baba Dele then realised he had left without the baby and had had to sneak back in, clad only in underpants and armed with his trouser belt, grab the boy from a cot and flee into the night. Dele was chuckling, thinking of his own bang to rights night with Cheryl and Helena, when Tayo looked serious and said that their town could still remember the grave injustice done to his father by this expatriate teacher, who had somehow forgotten to pass on his Schools Certificate results in time to the Cambridge colleges that were waiting for them. It was an old story and he didn't know if it was just the first time he had truly thought upon it, or because Tayo's was the first independent testimony to his father's deeds that he had heard, but Dele felt shamed. That in some way he had probably always doubted his father's contribution. Maybe he had been too harsh.

'But you must have strong memories about the country too?'

'No. I've never managed to get there, you know!' He was about to add 'But I miss it' but realised it would sound strange to miss a place he'd never visited. He had what somebody once called nostalgia without memory.

Tayo was insistent that he must come by soon and visit Dele's family. Dele said that it was an exceptionally tense time. He didn't elaborate. Tayo said if there were domestic problems then Dele must talk to his father. Dele replied Tayo didn't know his Dad like he did, and Tayo said that was precisely his point, the why he could say that Dele must be big and talk to him. He spoke like he understood. It was a shame when he took his leave. It had been the nicest part of the evening.

Concrete barely looked up when they returned to Sol's place. He was busy with one of his Streetfighter games, plugged into the telly in the sitting-room. He was racking up points – he knew all these secret moves for his soldiers. Dele relit a half-smoked blunt from the ashtray. Sol made some tea for him in the kitchen.

It had become a bit of a fixture this past fortnight – late-night culture at Sol's yard. After a bit, Genevieve would retire, and then the action would kick up.

Rich burgundy sofas, thick, fluffy carpets and a huge lion stitched into a rug covering one wall. The lion was leaning languidly forward on its paws, jaw ajar, ready for dinner. Mind you, apart from that the furnishings were a little spartan. The framed black and white photos on the wall – a cool sax player with his hat slightly askew, and a slush courting couple exchanging a kiss in an ode to buppie-love – were tastefully intentioned but felt more like kitsch. No books, he noticed. Maybe they were down the short steps, in their bedroom. The sitting-room needed filling up but it was a good size, with a lovely high ceiling. He vaguely tried to work out how much Sol must be pulling in to afford all this – this place would go for what, a hundred Gs? And the L-reg Beemer and the champagne. But this man was clearly dipping into so many pies it could easily be possible.

Dele hassled Concrete to quit playing with his toys. He had little love for all this Nintendo stuff anyway. The old-school Space Invaders had tested him plenty enough. And anyway, he wanted to have a peek at Sol's multi-channel surround-sound cable service. Cable was new in town, he didn't even think it had got to north London. He had never known such visual joy.

He knew where he was headed, but he liked to warm up first. On Channel Four it was *The Word* and some grinning stripper was thudding his dick across the screen for a good three seconds. His wood was tremendously thick and and you could see the guy was thinking, 'Sorted, sorted'. He knew his dick was top. But then the presenters came on and the whole thing got too embarassing. BBC2 had a politics show and Michael Portillo's Mediterranean features and serious lips were filling the screen.

'Look, it's The Moor!' laughed Sol, bearing Dele's tea and a bottle of Martell.

It was *EastEnders* on UK Gold and Jules, the peaceable old Trini and paterfamilias, was still seated improbably in The Queen Vic drinking his improbable drink and talking his improbable script to that nagging pensioner. Auntie Nellie, that was her name. Were they really destined to get it together in the most unlikely bout of prime-time miscegenation yet? That might be enough to tempt the YCA boys to riot.

Genevieve finally said her goodnights and Dele slid out a wrap from his pocket, unfurled the precious half-piece of crushed-up washrock, sprinkled it over his weed and built a super-slim mix. Now he could relax.

He stretched out on the sofa and began zapping between The Box and IDTV, ready for a concentrated fix of the magical country of the music promo. In this absolute state, where rules and dress-codes were strict and set, the proletariat were most definitely the video hos. These women were the worker-bees, shaking their pneumatic bits in your face most anywhere you looked, but especially in the films representing Los Angeles, Miami and Kingston, Jamaica. You could actually track a couple of them from promo to promo. There she was, springing out of the car boot at the end of Coolio's 'Fantastic Journey', then washing Big Daddy Kane's feet in the bath, then she's been stuffed and laid out as part of a sumptous feast, for 'Two Live Crew's delectation . . .

That pungent smell, like something burning that shouldn't be, darting across the room indicated that Concrete must have fired up too. Sol was explaining something to him at the table – from this distance it sounded like macro-economic theory – using salt cellars and the fruit bowl. Concrete was saying 'Is it?' periodically behind little curlicues of smoke. What with Concrete's shaven dome, it could have been a scene from a Nubian remake of that old Kung-Fu series. Dele walked up to them, like a supplicant, his hands clasped in a prayer position: 'Master Grasshopper, sir? Please to beg a moment of Master Avery's time?' he asked, in a cod-Oriental accent.

Sol smiled with barely-repressed irritation, the way he did if he thought you were taking the piss.

'Can I get a pull from that?'

Concrete kissed his teeth lightly.

'You done finished yours already? You always licking hits off me, man. Enough already.'

Concrete passed the smoke over and returned to Sol's table-top jugglings. From what Dele could work out, the salt and pepper were Africa's raw materials – zinc, copper, coffee and gold, which should have been kept at home to feed the people, instead of going west. And the same applied to the apples and oranges, which were stand-ins for real apples and oranges. And the brandy bottle, which was the oil deposits, could then have been sent and sold for value and wealth, and Africa would have been fine. But that didn't make sense. Dele was sure there was something missing. Shouldn't the salt and pepper, or at least one of them, have got going too?

'. . . Now the Jews, and correct me if I'm wrong because I haven't really read the Bible cover to cover, y'unerstan'? But weren't the Jews asked by Caesar Augustus to pay him a tax, yeah, in Jesus's time? So they asked Jesus what to do. And Jesus said: Pay unto Caesar what is due to Caesar and give unto God what is due to God. Am I right, yeah?'

Dele winced. Oh God, they've started on the Jews already. Now he knew they were in trouble.

'. . . So now they'd manoeuvred themselves into a position where Caesar comes to *them* for the tax, you get me? They lend him the money still! Stockmarkets and everyting.

And true, them clever those ways, you know, always been a money-minded people – '

'If it don't make dollars/ It don't make sense,' sang Concrete.

'That's right. But, you know, I've got nothing against the Jews. They're tight together still. They don't ramp with our girls, they don't run around with gun an' that. More time now, they just go about their business, quietly 'n' ting.'

Concrete really had Dele going. Shutting him out, and hotting him about sharing the smoke and the money! He'd ruined his enjoyment of the smoke just when he could feel a really nice whoosh coming on. Listening to Sol's street-corner economics when he'd had twenty bloody years to get an education, but had spent them sitting around common-rooms across south London when he could have been in the library. And where was his money coming from anyway? Running errands for Sol. Time and again, Concrete had taken to putting him down in front of Sol, and no ways would he have done that if Sol hadn't gone on with his subtle flatteries. But Sol was just a . . . well, he was smooth. A black man's black man. But definitely a hustler. Otherwise what was all that rubbish about the Japanese about? And when was *he* gonna get some pissin' money? He was the one who deserved it.

The two seemed oblivious to his presence. He couldn't see what Sol saw so much in Concrete. Concrete was Dele's spe, to be fair, but even Dele wouldn't say Concrete was exactly your leader-of-men material.

Ah! First that sudden numbing of the throat, as if you've been sucking on a Strepsil and then that aroma around you. Before, when he'd occasionally had a pipe he'd thought it had something to do with plastic and glass burning, but no, this sweetness, this strange fruitiness was part of the thing itself. But he preferred sprinkling the rock on tobacco. It didn't get so hot this way, more manageable all round. It was giddily good!

Dele returned to the sofa and the comforts of The Box. It was one of those dial-a-video channels, but for reasons presumably connected to the fact that one in three of the youth was unemployed, and another good proportion self-employed, they nearly always showed black videos. The only dodgy period was around three to five in the afternoon, when schoolkids were coming home and you got fizzles of pop. At night, though, you could hope to get a clear run.

It was clearly the era of the ass. X amount of tunes were shameless odes to the high, round, packed butt: 'Booti Call', 'Boo-tee Bounce', 'Move Something!' As the weather was always hot and young Americans seemed to spend their days either at a basketball court or a block party, or else driving to one of those, there wasn't much need for clothes. Just a crop-top and anything that ended at the top of the thigh. You had women stretched out on the pavement shaking it down there, dancing on tables with a guy's head wedged happily under their buns, or strutting in swimsuits with the straps disappearing up their cracks, trick-assed hos touching their toes all the better to waggle to the camera, butts wining it slow, wining it quick, butts that seemed to have a mind of their own. When you muted the sound, it got truly surreal.

'The US of A. I'm gonna get me a nice crib out there,' said Sol, glancing at the TV over Dele's shoulder.

'Yeah,' he said, his mind far away. 'Listen, Concrete, can we get any more of this tonight?'

'I think so.' Concrete looked queringly at Sol. Lee, the rocksman, was Sol's contact. Sol was fine about it. The only thing he wouldn't cater for, he had earlier established, was freebasing in his flat.

'Sure. Give him a call. He can make a pit-stop if he wants.'

Lee did half a gram for forty pounds if your custom was regular. Dele didn't have a red cent on him, and there was no chance of getting the gear on tick, so Sol lent him twenty pounds.

'That makes a one-er you owe me,' said Sol.

'Alright.' He was in trouble. His Mum had lent him money too, money she didn't have, plus he had dipped liberally into Dapo's bank account with her cashpoint card. What could he do? He would sort it out when all this shit was over.

Lee came over. Early thirties, a big man, with a huge

head. His head looked like it had been fitted with extra skull plates. He distributed his goodies two ways and settled down.

Dele got busy scratching off and crushing bits from his piece. If he wasted not he could make five or six from this. Sol may be a bit of a joker, but the man did talk some sense. He was pretty much in the man's debt.

Dele was getting bored. He needed something more nourishing than the big booty girls. The West Coast made hip-hop for that ass and those jeeps, the East Coast for the head and the subway – it was true. Surely, he should be an East Coast man, if anything. Their stuff was a good deal more left-field, the wordplays more trippy and dense, just right for the Walkman in a mad town like this. He zapped in hope to IDTV. It was an ad-break. The ads were pure Central Office of Information output: public health warnings, don't drink and drive, buy a smoke alarm, keep Britain tidy – that kind of thing.They were shot in drab browns and serpentine greens – seventies colours, cheap and nasty.

'Raas! Look at that!' Sol gestured in disgust at the TV. 'Our one station and who's propping it up? The Government. Doesn't it embarrass you to look at? How we gonna fight the Power when it's the Power that's funding us?'

Nas, the East Coast's latest great hope, had reared his head to save IDTV from further shelling. The tune was 'Life's a Bitch'. Close-ups on the anguished eyes of ghetto youth had replaced tit 'n' bum – all in treated monochrome. You defi-nitely wouldn't catch the video hos in black and white.

> Life's a bitch
> And then you die
> That's why I get high
> 'Cos you never know
> When you're gonna go!
> Life's a bitch
> And then you die . . .

Word! Dele hummed the tune. Things were so rough, he was within a step of losing it completely. He needed support.

And Sol was the man. Not a man for all seasons, by any means. Truth say, Sol made him a little nervous, the way Concrete did these days. He definitely wouldn't make it to Dele's ideal comfort zone. There would be room for Andria and Gabriel maybe, and Dapo, of course, within arm's reach, and Tayo Adeniran was looking a dark horse. Not Sol. But Sol . . . Sol was the instant future. He had the contacts and the independent sources of power and the will. He was like his prince in dark times. Like the Chinese warlord had said: If we go backwards we die, if we go forwards we die. Let us go forward and die.

'Life's a bitch/ And then you die,' Dele sang, getting up and dancing around the table, before placing a hand on Sol's shoulder.

'Alright, brother?' said Sol.

'Yeah, man. We're going down but we're leading a top life.'

'So what's happening with you and Carole? You get her number?' Sol explained how Genevieve had introduced this young, single lawyer to Dele that evening.

'Nah, Supes.' Concrete shook his head and snorted. 'You wasting your time with this one. Him just preps grey gyaal on the regular. Innit, Del?' he goaded.

That's too cheeky, Dele was thinking. The number of times you and I have sacked a neighbourhood party 'cos the girls were hardback, and burnt up to the West End to get easy European pickings before Bar Rumba shuts . . . But he didn't want to get heavy now he was in a hundred per cent better mood.

He would have liked to tell Sol about Andria and entertain the three with some of their stories. But he didn't think that would drop too well somehow. So Dele just smiled and patted his groin: 'My heart is Nubian, but my dick is international!' He had adapted the line from somewhere but they all creased up anyway. 'Anyway, she wouldn't be interested in me. She's three, four years older.'

'I don't know, Del. You're an eligible young man. They're few and far between.' said Sol.

'Why is everyone trying to fix me up with the Law? You, my Dad! Damn!' Dele laughed, trying to steer this subject into a blind alley and kill it.

'Fuck the Law, though!' Sol was warming to a theme. 'We need a better class of criminal out there. Check it. Two-twos Lee come over to my yard, right? But isn't this the smart way to do it! See the fools standing on the 'line, selling our whatever, where every man can see and point! What rubbish is that, after all this time? Everyone else sits in their mansion in St John's Wood or Essex an run deh tings deh!

'. . . White man rob bank. Gets away with fifty thousand pounds. No one hurt. Black Man rob Seven-Eleven. Maybe grabs a monkey if him lucky. Out with him ratchet! Two Asians haf fi dead! But from we just get the humanistic level going between us, street man as well as what they call superior types, right . . .'

Maybe he was being set up to become the lawyer to the underworld? The badman's brief? Like Robert Duvall in *The Godfather*.

Lee was caning the brandy and supplementing with his own little glosses. His refrain was 'When I was travelling . . .' or 'When I was away . . .' It took a little while for Dele to figure out he was talking about prison.

The three others were finally agreed that south London was the baddest. The things they did made vaunted veterans from crews on other sides – shopbreakers, housebreakers and baseball batters all – weep at their particular brand of viciousness. Concrete was revelling in his own rock rush so he re-positioned himself from chorus member to main player in half of south London's action. How his people would go north, west, east, they were real blatant about it, and trouble any situation. Sometimes different factions would meet on neutral ground like The Trocadero and blood must run that day! He himself had got cut up yahso, yahso, and dere so. Or else wait for the summer and wait for your enemies to come down to a reggae festival in Brockwell Park, and fuck them on home turf! Rip their phones and their dollars off, settle whatever score, real or perceived, it was . . .

Dele hovered between an edgy impatience with Concrete's fronting and an absurd feeling of inadequacy, of being the gooseberry in the bunch. He returned in hazy fashion to the screen. The first Jungle videos were coming through and he was pleased to note that they were closer to the East Coast's take on representation. Cramped, cluttered cityscapes, and dangling street names pursued by steadicxm giving a version of London in all its grime and rush. The British street soul-singers had aped the nasty-as-they-wannabe West Coast, only it came over all flat. The cars over here just weren't the same grand size they were Stateside, the pool of video hos' shallower. It was as if these artists were embarrassed at their difference, and were instead worshipping at the American empire's feet.

At least being excommunicated now Dele didn't have to worry so much about what time he reached home. Some of the space he had craved in this town had finally come, only naturally there had been a catch in it. And why had he set himself thinking down this road, just when he was getting sleepy? He tried not to think about Dapo at night, because she would dog his dreams. Better in the mornings.

At the last he found himself in dispute with Concrete over a rubber of blackjack (it being west London, they could not agree over whether north or southside rules applied) and then some crazy chat with Lee about, of all things, English public schools. It turned out that Lee was ferociously keen on education, and was set on giving his various children the private opportunities he had been denied. Dele took him through all the grades, starting from the grant-maintained neither this- or that-style establishment that he had finished in, all the way up. He could remember thinking what a trip it was, smoking rocks and discussing the pros and cons of Eton college with this gold tooth glinting graduate of Feltham and the Scrubs, and then he must have crashed out.

When Concrete and Lee had gone their ways, Sol began clearing up the ash-trays and the glasses and depositing them in the kitchen. He wiped up little flecks of coke with his finger and licked them. Dele lay across the sofa, mouth open, dribbling slightly, shaking quite violently from time to time.

Sol was reasonably satisfied. He'd got a new street shock-trooper, an establishment insider who'd turned – both coming through. The one worry was this looming Carlton Vale inquiry. But if his fellow directors managed to keep their nerve, that should go gently enough. He removed Dele's shoes and draped a blanket over him.

'Did you get the tapes?'

'Surely.'

'You're a star. You can hold my hand. I'm coming right over – '

'Not today, Andria, please. It's not a good time – '

It's never a good time with you, is it? But when I come it looks like you need me!'

'Look, if anything, maybe tomorrow – '

'I'm coming right now. I've got a little something for you, as it happens.'

'Alright, alright.'

179

There was no saying no to her, really. She just wouldn't hear it. These past three or four weeks she had devoted a lot of time to her new man, in that free-wheeling way of hers. Sometimes she'd call first. Or else, she'd just drive round from her mother's in Bethnal Green or her sister's on Romford Road, and Dele would be interrupted from his abstractions by the deep belly rumble of a car horn that sounded like no other. Once, when he wasn't around, she had rung the door-bell, got his mother, and presented her with a big pot of chicken stew and black-eyed beans, already cooked. Andria said there was no way mama should be cooking at a time like this, and would she please accept this? And she needn't worry seeing Andria was a very good cook. Satisfaction guaranteed!

When Dele got in a little later he had been staggered to see Andria vibing with his Mum and Auntie Bola in the sitting-room, with his Dad staring out of the window. He wondered what they would make of her. She was all but the first white presence in the home since the police had fucked their lives up, and it wasn't as if friends of his had ever come knocking at the door much anyway down the years. But he needn't have worried. True, Auntie was squinting at her as if she were a Martian, but that was more to do with the fact that Auntie was trying to work out how this young woman could make a stew that looked legit and who, moreover, knew a smattering of Yoruba which she delivered without embarrassment. His aunt and Mum slammed the floor with the palms of their hands as Andria rolled through the greetings and the names of a clutch of Home-country dishes.

'Oh, but she is good-oh! Heh!' they laughed, with tears in their eyes. They thought it was the funniest thing.

Mum had said there must be some Nigerian line in her family, but Andria replied no, unless Naples counted for something. It was her ex-boyfriend, Wale, who had taught her to cook certain things. Auntie wondered aloud 'Wale, Wale . . . what is his family name?' but it was a vain attempt to trace a connection. Chic, import-export Auntie only knew Nigerians resident off the Jubilee Line, whereas Andria knew Nigerians coming like Yardmen in Hackney.

So Andria – you couldn't really faze her. Even when Dele explained to her the bones of the Dapo situation, she kept on nodding in her brisk fashion, as if she were urging him to hurry up and done. She never asked to visit Dapo in hospital. It wasn't that she was hard-hearted, she simply moved in a crowd where people saw a lot of fate's vagaries. People got work as and when they could – in between having children, hiding from the Home Office Man or DTI Man, or your small business started up then shut down, or your cousin was getting into trouble and going inside, or maybe you didn't want to work at all. You didn't probe much as you might be told something you didn't want to hear. So she didn't ask questions. She just brought food.

After the first few pots of rice and stew, Dele thanked her, but said no more. They already had enough relatives cooking for them and taking the presure off his Mum in that way. So instead she had begun bringing around these exquisite savouries and cakes: little cylinders of caviar, muffins and goat cheese; portions of French chocolate and orange cake. Some she had taxed from the restaurant where she worked. Others she crafted herself. Today it was something new: Banoffi pie. She laid it carefully down on the table in his room, tapped her cheek to demand her 'Welcome' kiss and slid off the paper wrapper. 'Banana, toffee, all sorts on a cheesecake base,' she said, proudly. 'That's pukka, that is!'

'Sounds a bit rich, you know – '

'Look at me,' she said. She was holding his face in her hand, peering intently. 'Your pupils are gonna disappear, I reckon, if you keep on going how you're going. You've got that low-cal feeling all over – you dirty-stop-out! What am I gonna do with you?' she said, with mock exasperation but real concern, and fell on to the bed.

Dele went downstairs for some cutlery. He returned to find her at work cabling up his little telly to her video, in preparation for the grand moment: a three-episode chunk of their favourite American soap, Knots Landing. They had discovered a mutual fondness for the show and since then Dele had been taping fat chunks of it from UK Gold on Sol's cable service. He just thought it was the best-written of its type, the characters were rich but relatively real, plus he checked for a couple of the women on it. But Andria was truly caught up with the series; she was on first-name terms with everyone on it, and now sat rapt, only moving her head to flick the spliff in the ash-tray or deal with another slice of Banoffi pie. And she was right – the pie truly was the lick.

She played with his clothes and horizontal body from time to time. Her semi-detachment and his anticipation that soon she might rise to full throttle warmed him up just nicely. He wondered whether it was worth consuming his last lines' worth depending on what was going to happen next, and quickly decided that it was. He sat up and cut up two little lizards and pressed one to her. Dele knew Andria didn't like the frequency of his intake but she was not averse to a little snort herself at times like this, which enfeebled her stance.

After a bit, it was he who was playing with her halter top and pecking at her neck. But it was not until the final episode of Knot's Landing was done and dusted that she surrendered completely.

When they had sex she shook him around and clung to him with this desperate ferocity whilst he tended to be more low-key, quietly attending to little bits of business about her body. 'I'm "Big Hugs!" and you're "Little Kisses!"' she had once laughed and they had agreed that that was right. But when they were asleep together, the position changed. She would lie slightly across him, her face and cheek on his breast, while he wrapped his arms around her, clutching her in a grip that tightened as the night progressed. It didn't help that his body was like a convector heater, sweating pools and radiating much heat. She said one day he'd wake up to find her frazzled to a cinder. She fitted very snug into his body though. The good groove.

Today, in this dead-time of a Wednesday afternoon, she was slamming him around with that customary vigour but, with the charlie inside, he was answering in kind. Puff and coke was just the champion mix. True, the coke kinda shrivelled your dick, but it gave you a zest that was complemented by the strong durability-enhancing powers of the weed, so that you achieved this mad, new, squidgy kind of hard-on which could be maintained for hours. He felt like he had a bionic dick, like those Tantric Buddhists he had heard about.

After she had come he played around her pussy to loosen it up, then started bumping it hard. She took his seed, she took it neat. (Did that mean love?) His heart was thumping pitter-patter, pitter-pitter. He felt like he was on a rocket to the moon. A Bionic rocket, like some spectacular science-fiction.

When he finally burst his barrel it felt that every last pocket of juice and jissom was being yielded, all the reserve troops tapped and pressed upon, every bit of bodily control surrendered, and that if it did not stop now he just might have a coronary.

He fell asleep quickly enough. He was whacked. There was one magical moment, when he half-woke to find her seated on the side of the bed beside him, stroking his face and smiling. Her plucked eyebrows accentuating that slight air of distance that she carried, so that her smile became almost a knowing wink. Ah, but there was so much love in it! He looked at her disorientatedly. The moment had the weight-lessness and soft-focus of a dream.

It was evening but still light outside when she prodded him awake. 'Get dressed. You've gotta come out to play.'

Dele yawned. 'Where to?'

'I don't know. Somewhere. Let's get out of town.'

Dele puffed out his cheeks. Since their lightning raid on France about two weeks ago, Andria had got the taste for exotic trips. That had begun as a journey to pick up some goods for her mother from a food caterer's in Kent and ended up with them driving to the coast and taking the ferry across. The avowed intention was two-fold: to allow the air over there to course through Andria and enhance her gastronomic future, and to bring jungle to the continentals. They seemed dying to be freed from the mediocrity of MTV Rock and the techno-pop banalities of Euro-house. But time was short and by the time they had reached Paris, early the next morning, they had enjoyed a morning's sightseeing and then turned back.

There had just been time for the two to have a quarrel over navigation, and for Andria to storm out of the car in the middle of Pigalle. Dele had got worried. He had been listen-ing to the airwaves and had been surprised to see that discussion of immigration in France hadn't got beyond the prehistoric levels of north Africans smelling and cooking funny, and he didn't want *les flics* taking her for some kind of fair Arab.

But that apart, and the usual tussles with passport con-trol, the most memorable incident of the trip had occurred on the Metro. This tall, distinguished, elderly man had stood by Dele and looked at him intently. He was an old Army Man, with a beret on his head and a string of medals on his jacket. The carriage was pretty rammed and Andria was a little dis-tance behind Dele.

'Vous êtes Africain?' asked the old man quietly.

He had studied French at school and he was still pretty up to speed with it, but this query was hardly taxing. Dele nodded.

'Mais, j'adore les Africains! Les Africains, ils sont *chauds*. Ils sont *chauds*!' the old man smiled an emphatic rotting-toothed grin and shook his hand.

He was being chirpsed by some veteran of the SIS death squads. Sacré Bleu!

'Vous venez d'où?'

'Je suis touriste.'

'Ah, bon!' the man looked content. 'Mais, vous êtes jeune, si *jeune*! On pourrait se voir? Ça vous intéresse?'

Dele glanced around. The locals were clocking them closely, wondering what this unlikely couple could possibly have in common. He spied his girl, turned to his new friend and said, 'Monsieur, je suis avec elle et là, nous descendons. À bientôt!'

Later, he had replayed the scene to Andria, to much merriment, and the incident had added to their stock of impressions and nonsense word games. They were currently hooked on French words that ended in -isme.

'Andria, you know we can't do that,' he said, reaching for his trousers. 'One, I thought you were working tonight at that "Summer Madness" thing – '

'So, obviously I buzz Janet and Dina. Them two can cover for me.'

'Two, financially, it's not happening for either – '

'We can go to Italy. You get monopoly money out there. Millions of lire. We can stay with my relatives.'

'Look, baby, you know I've got to hold the fort down here. I've been going out all over already, as it is. God knows how it looks.'

'Okay. Fair enough. Forget it.'

Dele went downstairs to wash the plates and field a call from his mother, bearing the latest no-news bulletin from the hospital. He still wasn't used to his Mum not being here at this time, organising the house, putting the food on the table. It was ironic that it had taken this crisis to get some flexi-hours into her life. As he chatted to his Mum, his father pottered around, fixing up something cold. His old man still wasn't speaking to him so he tried not to cross his path too often. He guessed his Dad was probably marvelling at his son's frivolity, messing around with this girl, playing the fiddle while Rome burnt. He wondered if his Dad knew that Andria had been staying over some nights. Probably. But he had communicated no displeasure through his mother.

And Dele was kinda surprised too at their situation. Oh, he understood why he liked her so much. She was sussed, she was a looker, she powdered him, he slept much better when she was around. He knew he'd been lucky to meet her. But he was angry and confused, and he could not tell whether Andria had something to do with it. All his points of reference had been scattered and everything was up for grabs. He did not know whether this was the worst part or just the beginning of how everything would be. He hated the police and the system and all those white things and didn't know where Andria fitted in all that. She wasn't rich, she wasn't even middle-class but then neither were the Old Bill . . . Were their differences more important than what they had in common? Fuck it. He, the Oxbridge man, was more establishment than she and yet what had befallen Dapo, and his parents in other ways, assured him that mere papers counted for little.

And it was still possible that the major lesson to be drawn from this all was about him. *His* chickens coming home to roost. And again he did not know where Andria made sense in all of that – whether she was part of his past (he had come to her, after all, with unclear intentions, none of them serious and most of them bad), or whether she could be part of something that could be assembled from the wreck. But when would that be? Not now when he was clueless, and frightened, and doing too many drugs. He felt angry that she had brought him this kindness when he could not use it.

The two of them had imagined their own little air pocket of sweet things, tossed amongst his own turbulent currents. It was heady but it could not save him. He did not know how long the deluge would last but it would take time. She should flee and leave them all behind.

They didn't go out. They played chess instead. He was teaching her and they had been playing plenty of speed games, to make Andria familiar with the actions of the pieces. As they played he probed her about her relationship with Wale, that ex of hers. Andria shrugged. She couldn't see the need to discuss it. Wale, she said, was a bit different from other people she knew. Most people just sat around, moaning and having kids, or just hung around at the same old places. They didn't want you to better yourself, they just wanted everyone to remain at the same level. But Wale! He had encouraged her to train as a chef and helped her fill out forms, and he had plans for himself too. In business, eventually.

'See you can come to me with no money, and a life of hard knocks or whatever! But if all you wanna do is diddly shit, yeah, and agonise about housing and social, yeah, and run your mouth off about what Tammy said or did with Andria's cousin, yeah – then I ain't interested!'

Wale's problem was that he had tried to control her. He didn't like her smoking, nor going out and seeing her friends too much. He could do those things but she couldn't. And, since he was asking, yes there were similarities between them. 'You're both real hung up on your Dads. Wale was forever going on about him, saying "Oh, I'm nothing like my Dad. You English women couldn't survive with me if I was. I'm the nice guy!" But he tried to put me under manners same way! And I'm sure he was a dog too – I never saw anything, mind! – but you boys, his Dad, your Dad, all of you, you don't change.'

'I'm no dog!'

'Oh, honey,' she snorted, 'are you sure? You was dogging them two girls you was with the night we met! I know you, Del. When you have the smoke in you, you wanna fuck every fish in the sea! But, if you dog me, well, I ain't gonna suffer to anyone at all. You'll be a fool if you do.' And she stared defiantly at him. She didn't really like guys and she had taken to him. It must be going deep. They would have to be very careful.

'I'm not gonna dog you,' he said.

At about eleven p.m. she took her leave, bound for stall duty at the dance on Highbury Fields.

'I've only got five words to say to you,' he said at the door, as he waved her off in her Wolsey, 'Le jungilisme . . .'

'Le jungilisme?'she enquired, smiling.

'Le jungilisme est une humanisme!'

Dele carried on spending his time shuttling from one world to another. He went on further spiritual trips to Plaistow with his mother, answered his bail, and stood in the cold night outside Brixton police station in a vigil with twenty others. The benefit date for Dapo was now only a fortnight away, and the event seemed to mushroom daily. Sol took him to upmarket restaurants in Fulham, with pin-spot lighting and neo-classical decors in pastel colours, where hostesses in G-strings greeted you in the toilets. Tasty nibbles of a *dolce vita*.

What with Gabriel not really checking for Sol, and Dele still uneasy with Celia, Gabriel and Dele saw a lot less of each other and kept in touch mainly on the phone.

He received a postcard from Helena, out of the blue. They had not exchanged many words since the night with Cheryl, but the card was entirely free of rancour. She was staying with a college friend of hers, living the high life in Bombay. Next week she was travelling south to Goa. She had received three marriage proposals, she said. He could barely bring himself to read it through.

Andria and he rumbled on in their fashion until two incidents gave him much pause. The first took place in Brockley. They had made early moves one Saturday to drop an amplifier round for a friend of hers down that way. Her car had had one of its frequent seizures so they were standing by a bus-stop when this guy approached them. Late twenties, tall, Caribbean, he must have been a postman – he definitely had on one of those blue jackets with the official insignia. As he drew level he lunged out, grabbed Andria by her jacket and threw her against the wall of the building behind them. He stepped back and glared at Andria's shocked face for a second, and Dele used the moment to jump in between them. The guy faced him off evenly for a second, then pulled out a blade from his back pocket, and just held it in his hand. He didn't wave it about or point it especially, just held it in his right hand, and walked backwards, keeping his eyes locked on Dele, before slipping the blade back and stepping into The Crown and Kettle on the corner. Dele thought about pursuing him but he knew that that particular pub was a den of vice. It was like a shopping precinct – you could buy anything in there – and stabbings and shootings were not uncommon. He thought twice of it and went to attend to Andria who stood, arms folded, shaking her head. Her face was drained of colour.

She said she was alright, but on the top deck later she punched him and cried, 'Why didn't you do anything?' Her Majesty's postman hadn't known anything about them, he hadn't robbed them, so it could only be racial. Just his luck, he was thinking, to come across some Carib with a dose of black rage. South-east London was always fucking him up! He speculated on what could have happened to him to make him do that, but it could have been so many things really.

He paid a little more attention to where they went after that. Luckily the jungle scene proved a safe harbour. What was so sweet about the dances was that it felt they were all renegades. The heads could come from Dalston or Tottenham, but it wasn't as if any interested outsider could go to Kingsland Road, take its temperature and know anything more about these particular people. Here, they were all on some other shit.

Even so, he found himself steering them more towards the second of the two distinct camps which were developing – where the sounds were more hardcore and the crowds more mixed than the dances where the tunes were more from the ragga side.

The second altercation took place down Willesden way. They were seated in the waiting-room on the platform station with ten or so others, all white apart from one Moroccan, when a man with old eyes on a young body sidled in. He had picky hair and was quite strangely dressed – a long coat with a handkerchief stuffed in his breast pocket, jogging bottoms-cum-trousers, and white shoes. Dele took him in quickly and looked down again. Francophone African, he guessed. Côte d'Ivoirean maybe.

'Niggers! Niggers!' the guy shouted. He sounded drunk and deranged. 'We're fucked-up. We're lost.'

There was total silence. With that sinking feeling, Dele looked up. Everyone else was shuffling nervously. This type of thing didn't happen in their worlds. How far was this man gonna go?

'Don't look at me!' he yelled, advancing towards the couple across the cubicle. 'Look at your white pussy! Yes, that's right. Enjoy it! You think you've achieved something? You think you're so great?'

Half of Dele was taking this in, the other half was thinking 'Oh Lord! What a disaster. I'm sweatin' bad. What a public shame! Am I gonna have to take action? Am I gonna have to take action? Ah fuck, I'm gonna have to take action.'

Dele got up and flung his arms around the man's midriff, pinioning his hands at his sides in a kind of lock, and half-dragged, half-carried him out of the cubicle and on to the platform.

'Get off me. Get off me,' the crazy was screaming. 'I will dagger you!'

Dele put him down and glared at him. For an instant he thought about smacking this guy in the ribs. What was really irking Dele was that this derelict guy was darting eyes up at him, with a superior contempt. What gave him the right when he didn't know anything about his life?

'Tell me what you think you know, old man!' Dele sneered. He turned and walked back up the platform where Andria was waiting.

As the train pulled in, the greys in the carriage who had witnessed the scene dropped him meaningful looks of sympathy and pity, but this enraged him further. It was like they thought because he was with a white girl, and had acted how he did, he was one of them. Well, fuck that! Don't come to me with your slimy looks! But Andria's instincts, as usual, were good, and she motioned to him to follow her down the train, far from the madding crowd.

They had laughed about it at the time, and concluded that *le Nubianisme* most definitely wasn't *une humanisme*. But all these episodes were undermining the fragile edifice within which he and Andria made sense. He couldn't stand the vulnerability their affair made him feel; the sense that the power of judgement hung over him, ready to be wielded by any man, jack, black or white, on the street. And when white people let on to him when he was with her, making overtures, happy to see him basking in the mainstream, it made it worse. He found it harder to disentangle Andria from the people out there. These people that had produced one big humiliation for his family, and who knew how many small humiliations had escaped his knowledge, beginning with his father in his schooldays. And all that just set him thinking about Oxford again – just thinking about it made him feel faint. He just wanted to draw a fat red line under that whole period. Hadn't he said that Helena would be his last, even before all this? He wanted no intimate connection with those people anymore. It should just be strictly business from now on.

And always ticking away quietly was his other runnings that Andria didn't even see, couldn't really see – Sol and the whole package he came in. There was a home and everything was in place for him there. Sol had never said anything directly, but Dele was no fool, and he could tell there was sometimes a tone of quiet rebuke, a bemusement that Dele did not seem interested in having it all. He felt under increasing pressure from most of his worlds to find a woman who befitted him.

He couldn't square the circle. He had always been some kind of black. But now was a new stage, and he was finding out what demands this latest leg would place on him, and which needs he had to satisfy. At the very least, he had to put the two of them on hold. He pottered around his room, very depressed, and drafted Andria a letter:

Darling Andria,

I have for some time now been worried about the strange trips I get off on when I'm with certain people. I was even thinking bad thoughts about you until I basically realised what a wonder you are. I have stopped giving white people the benefit of the doubt and this is horrible for me, because I'm turning into something I never thought I would become. These problems and the other bigger grief are for me to sort out and confront now, straight in the face. Until I do, I cannot make you happy. I just feel very cold. I am so sorry.

Much love,
Mista D

He read it and tore it up. In the end, he just sent her a short note:

Andria dear,

I cannot see you now for a while. I really like you but there are other factors. You know all this shit I'm under! Please leave me alone for a while. I'll give you a ring soon, I promise. I'm really sorry.

Much love,
Mista D

He posted the letter then took the tube down to the hospital. Melanie, the physio, was ensconced with Dapo when he went in. She attended his sister daily; turning her over in case of bed sores. On to her back, her side and then the other side.

Dele perched at the foot of the bed, behind Melanie. He looked at the rows of numbers on the drug charts, but was listening to Melanie's little patter as she tweaked his sister all over.

'How are you feeling today, Dapo? I'm going to move your arms now. Can you feel that? Yes? No? Okay, I'm going to your hands now, Dapo. I'm going to have a look at your fingers . . .'

After a time he turned round, tapped Melanie on the shoulder and joined her.

community service

YOU COULDN'T quite call it an argument but they were certainly the first serious cross words the two had exchanged. They came at the end of a lengthy meeting of the Friends of Dapo group. There were five of them present: Sol, Michael, Sam the YCA accountant, Dele and Ketsia, a friend of Dapo's that Dele had brought on board. Together they bashed out the final arrangements for the benefit evening, two nights away. All that remained was the straightforward matter of rubber-stamping Backstreets as the support band who would be introducing Easy Roller, the American hip-hop star. Easy, along with Lieutenant Lipman, a London sounds veteran and a killer DJ credited with the fastest tongue in the West, were the two main musical attractions. It had been a coup to get them, albeit at some cost.

Dele was just starting to add his nod to those of the others when he checked himself. If that was gonna be *all* the acts . . . 'Hang on! How about Bushy? When is she coming on?'

Bushy was this young folk singer with a big, deep voice. Her family had come to Tottenham from South Africa when she was a kid, and here one of her brothers had hanged himself and another was sectioned in hospital. She riffed off all these histories with this stage act that was snatches of chant and melody and trancy interludes. On the times when the crowd was vibing and working with her, you could just be spirited away.

Michael was looking shifty, so Dele knew something was up. Sol returned his gaze evenly.

'Dele, I thought we had discussed this. How often have we said that there was only gonna be time for three bands max?'

'I can remember telling you from the off that Bushy and Dapo were tight and we had to fit her in.'

Sol looked pained and shook his head. 'Well, I can remember you saying something about this girl then, but nothing since we've sat down and dealt with this business properly.'

'I know I mentioned Bushy to everyone here and I just assumed it was sorted.'

This was serious. Because Bushy's stuff was so left-field she was dependent on the kindnesses of the north London polytechnic circuit and was desperate to play to a crowd nearer to home. Dele had promised her. She would be gutted.

'Look Dele, you know how I've been going back and forth with Flatbush on all of this. Backstreets are opening for Easy Roller when he does the tour dates here proper, so they wanna raise the profile – '

'So you're saying we can't have Roller if we don't have Backstreets? Is that what you're telling me?'

'That's it, man.'

'Okay. Then we're gonna have to drop one of the DJs or that comedy act.'

Michael spluttered as he said that they couldn't do that. They had already sent out flyers saying men like The Architects would be playing a selection, and Phoenix was doing an auction for them, donating all these T-shirts, so dropping him was out of the question.

And besides, everyone knew NW10 was the DJ capital of the land, so they weren't gonna put some crazy freak-show out there –

'It's not crazy. It's standard African and Brazilian song, just given her own blend.'

'Whatever it is, Del,' Sol smiled the smile of the victor, 'it sure ain't popular.'

'And so? The future may be unpopular! I thought we were doing something for Dapo, not the pissin' choice charts . . .'

Sol puffed his chest wearily. 'We're all tired, I think. Do you want to put this to a vote?'

Dele nodded, trying to catch Ketsia's eye. She was staring blankly ahead, seemingly unresponsive to the delicacy of the situation. You're not here to play dumb, he thought, you're here to represent Dapo. That's all. Dele was reminded sharply of how his sister used to complain that, Parmesta apart, getting some spiritedness from the rest of the SSS clique was like getting blood from a stone.

'Who thinks we should keep Backstreets and Easy Roller, and/or thinks we should go for Bushy and her people instead?'

Well, Dele was sure it was a bluff, but put like that the choice was ridiculous. Sam sniggered. Too late, Dele realised that this was a silly vote to have, and chided himself for ever having accepted the position whereby votes were used to settle disputes. And when had that happened? At some earlier point somehow in this flippin' meeting . . .

It was two to one against Dele. Sam had no vote and Ketsia abstained. She said she couldn't make up her mind.

'Jesus!' cried Dele, and threw up his hands. He was beginning to get the impression, this past week, that Sol was dissing him. First of all there had been the discussion over the location. Dele had made enquiries to various good-sized venues around Tottenham and knew they could hire out a place at a cheap rate. He was prepared to go for an alternative that was more centrally located, say Camden or the West End. Well, Sol and Michael had wanted to do the benefit here at Carlton Vale, on the grounds that the YCA had their office here, they knew the directors well, so best to hold the event on friendly, convenient turf. Which sounded reasonable enough, but Kilburn was no more central than Tottenham, and not especially accessible to the punters, many of whom would probably be coming from the north-east side. Plus Dele was worried about the bad local press concerning the Centre's 'financial irregularities'. The stories had mushroomed from a murmur and some shit was clearly about to blow up. He didn't want Dapo's thing getting affected by any of that. Sol had said it was white man's press, and Dele was being over-sensitive, and he had conceded maybe. Then Ketsia had asked what was the damage and Booksman Sam had said eight hundred pounds and Dele had exlaimed 'What!' and that he could get the Rosebank and Gary's for three hundred and fifty and Michael had said ah, but this included security, and Dele had said what do we need security for? How were they going to raise the necessaries for the scholarship for a medical student and the legal action if they were splashing out on security? And anyway, he thought that the YCA were directors or something here? Couldn't they get freeness, or at the least get a fat discount? And Sol had angrily denied they were the bosses and where had he heard that? They just paid their rent like everyone else. But they had gone away and done some consulting and, the next day, Booksman said they had managed to get a squeeze and now it was four hundred pounds all in. But still Dele wasn't altogether happy, until finally Sol had flashed listen, he hadn't wanted to bring this up before, because he didn't like to chat about another man's business, but the fact was that Lieutenant Lipman had enemies up at The Farm, and *no way* would he head up anywhere near those parts. And obviously you couldn't really argue with that, although it seemed that Sol had just pulled this so-called fact out of a hat, like the white rabbit.

Dele felt cowed and green, outflanked at every turn. He could barely look Sol in the face as the meeting broke up, and Sol kneaded him on the shoulder. 'D'you wanna come and meet this youth I was telling you about? And then we'll buck up with Roller at his hotel.'

Dele nodded. The YCA had been running this outreach project, called Proud Minds of Tomorrow, for which they received funding from Brent Council. It consisted of two youth-club leader types taking a weekly two-hour group with teenagers. One of them was a boy who had recently come over from Nigeria and was having trouble settling down. Sol said the boy seemed the sensitive type, and could Dele please have a word just to see what was up with him?

They walked down the stairs and down the hall that ran along the large exhibition space to the Conference Room. About fifteen people sat around in a circle listening to a coffee-coloured woman called Ella. She was bulky and dressed in a voluminous, flowing dress, with her hair up in a wrap. She was apologising for the fact that this week's was a lunchtime session, only Fabian, whom Dele presumed was her co-leader, couldn't make the evening because of family business. A suit, with Council Observer written all over him, was seated behind the circle and nodded to Sol as they came in. They perched themselves further down the row from him.

Proceedings began with these name games, which Dele assumed was an exercise in self-assertiveness. Each PMOT member had to stand up and say their name, complete with an adjective or a sentence that they felt described them or their aspiration. So you had, 'I'm Shanice and I'm gonna open a hair salon', or a youth rephrasing a popular song, 'My name is Trevor and ladies, you need a man with/ Sen-si-tiv/ I-ty, a man like me/, to sniggers all round.

After that, the psyching-up continued with five minutes' silence for meditation before Fabian announced that the subject for today's meeting was mixed-relationships and anyone who thought Race *should* get in the way of love should sit on that side and those who didn't should sit on this side. Boy! Wherever I go in this town I just can't beat this rap, Dele was thinking.

The chairs were divided up so that they were facing each other and nearly everyone, the group leaders included, trooped off to the far end of the room, on the side for the motion. Only the youngest members of PMOT, three thirteen-year-old mixed-race girls, and a black girl who was clearly a mate, stayed put.

Then the Nigerian boy strode in, apologising for being late. At first sight, he didn't look the shy, confused type. He was a chunky seventeen or eighteen, wearing a Fruits of the Loom sweatshirt and a baseball cap under which hung two long, elegant plaits, beaded at their ends. He sat in the middle, a couple of rows in front of Sol and Dele, and the man from Brent.

A woman in dungarees, who looked too Caucasian to be called black anywhere except America, kicked off, announcing that she didn't check for the type of romance that had brought her into the world at all at all. Her main point was that, in a relationship, when things turned bad, partners were bound to bring race into the beef. Others chipped in to say that no way would they bring a mixed-race child into the world, because they were invariably fucked-up. Dele looked at the four young girls on the other side. Two of them had their heads in their hands.

Asians really gave the PMOTs the hump. They were stepping out with all our men at college, strutting like they had something special the guys wanted, and hadn't a whole bunch of them gone down to the Jodeci concert. You wouldn't believe how many you saw down there.

When the other side came to speak, they were just steamrollered over. It didn't help that they were so young, or that they got up to see Fabian and Ella staring stony-faced at them. The black girl, in what sounded like an apology, said 'Well, I go out with Phil. Some of you know Phil, innit? And er, well, he's never called me "black anything!" . . .' and she was followed by a friend who pleaded along can't-we-all-just-get-along lines. Weak. Very weak.

Dele sat there thinking how bizarre this all was. What struck him was that there was no serious talk of culture, just of colour. There was plenty about how white women couldn't bring up a black kid because 'she just don't know, ummmm culturally an' that . . .' and 'As an African brother, I want my African sister,' and Dele thought aah, so it's African culture that you feel will be the stumbling block for other folk. He listened to them all and waited for them to say one thing that would indicate to him that they were on the same cultural planet as, say, his father or even that they had ever related to flesh and blood Africans around them. Dele knew what your average African mini-cabbie would say, faced by this gathering here: that they were all mad lucky to live in a country where the education system was free, so why didn't they stay in it instead of pissing off at fifteen, and don't come into my house until you've got a degree.

The parade seemed to rest on the premise that communities were automatic gifts, not something that had to be imagined and then made flesh. Did these people think that because they were all black they were guaranteed anything in advance? Dele looked up expectantly when his countryman finally raised his hand to speak. Can you save us today? Dele wondered.

Victor introduced himself and spoke quietly, with his head bent slightly down and his braids bobbing about. He said that he was sat in the neutrals section because he had too recently arrived in the country to have an informed opinion, although, judging by the number of 'You get mes?', he must have been around for a little while.

He said that when he saw a mixed couple on the street he just thought, well, probably the black person hadn't found their ideal partner as yet. But, really, he couldn't see what all the fuss was about and, personally, he would jump at the chance to date anyone nice. For this, he was vociferously condemned by those supporting the motion.

The session broke up shortly after Victor's intervention. There was no need for a vote. No one had switched sides. Sol went off to find the Man from Brent, who looked happy enough, whilst Dele spoke to Victor. Victor asked him what he had thought and Dele looked around for Sol, lowered his voice, and said 'Bogus bullshit. It's like we're the children of the world!'

Mainly though, they chatted about soccer. Victor said he was a Bendelite and Dele teased him about how Nigeria stood no chance in next year's World Cup because the team was packed with Bendelites and where were the Yorubas?

Victor said his school didn't have a sixth form so he was about to head on to an FE college, and was that a good idea? Dele said just make sure he got quality A-Levels, don't be fobbed off with Mass Communication Studies and HNDs, and don't listen to all the rubbish people were saying to him. He gave him his number and said they should keep in touch. He felt like the catcher in the rye.

'How is he?' Sol had wandered over.

'What? Victor? Oh, he's fine. I don't think he's got any big problems.'

'Good. Listen, I think Fabian may be leaving us soon, and I'd like to see you getting involved in the scheme. I want you to think about maybe taking over from him. I think you and Ella could really get on, you know. Would you be interested?'

Would I? Would I fuck! Dele was thinking. You really don't know me at all Sol, do you?

'Errr, possibly. I'd have to have a think.'

'You do that.'

Meeting Easy Roller wasn't quite the trip Dele had hoped for. Draped in a white Polo shirt and a striped pair of linen jeans, he was propped on the bed in a split-level suite in Paddington's Intercontinental Hotel. He was bleary-eyed and munching from great vats of Kentucky Fried Chicken. He muttered that if his boys didn't get their acts together and rustle themselves up he might just have to deal with the whole feast himself. They had flown in from Rome last night, after miming to their hit single at an MTV bash, and headed straight out, raving until the morning. It was their first time over here, but it didn't sound as if they were planning on passing by St. Paul's Cathedral somehow.

His girlfriend, dowdier than had seemed likely, was fretting around all these Oxford Street shopping bags and complaining in her Brooklyn drawl about how expensive clothes were in London. This thickened the furrow on Easy's brow deeper. He was staring, in puzzled fashion, at a spread of notes in different currencies on his pillow.

'You mean you have to change these notes when you go

to Paris or Rome or London?' he enquired of the two.

Sol confirmed that this was indeed the case.

'For real? Damn! Falana – you hear that? Europe is some deep shit!' A ray of pleasure peeked through the bloodshot eyes, before Easy buried his head in his beans.

Dele wondered at the rap world's rising star, this shy twenty-year-old ghetto boy from New Jersey, only now dis-abused of the notion that Europe was all one big country. Was the immediate future of the hip-hop nation really safe in his hands? Not that Easy had come as a philosopher. He had blown up by erecting a curious, East Coast citadel of Californian wave-your-hands-in-the-air, it's all good-ness, but still, you had hoped for more.

Easy looked less than pleased as Sol went over the details for the benefit evening. Dele wouldn't have bet on him turning up at all but Sol snorted and said he surely would. 'His manager Orlando and me go back, you get me.'

'Is it?'

'Yeah-yeah. Plus don't forget him and Backstreets are gonna be touring together. They know it'll be the best kind of exposure if they give us a little assist.'

Sol offered to give him a lift home, but Dele said to drop him at King's Cross. He had had enough of BMW culture for today. He would tube it the rest of the way.

When Dele finally reached, towards six in the evening, it was to the sound of his parents' raised voices in the dining-room. There had been far more shouting and cross words of late. He even thought he had heard the first slap and lick-down of his mother in quite a while early the other morning – confirma-tion that his family's descent, which had stabilised after the initial aftermath, had now gone exponential. It could not have gone any other way, really, but it felt that he had been unpre-pared even for this.

The well of visits from his wider family and friends had all but dried up in the month since the incident. Auntie Bola still dropped round, but most others kept in touch by phone, if anything. Today was the first day his mother had ever taken off unpaid from her workplace. They had been good but they could not make allowance for her indefinitely. Even his public sector Dad could not get away with his irregular attendance much longer. Given how he would have budgeted for both his children pouring holiday pay-packets into the family coffers, Dele guessed the financial situation must be bleak.

His floor hummed to the customary mélange of Yoruba and English. What were they creating about? He could hear the reciting of a familiar litany of schoolfriends . . . now it was Haringey Council, and . . . yes, now it was money. They were hurling figures at each other.

Dele unfurled the cigarette's worth of powder, wrapped in tissue paper, on the table. It was all that remained of a wade he'd bought two days ago. This last smoke and that would be it. He was returning to purity, hadn't he promised her? No more women, and no more of *that* stuff until *this* stuff was over. He was restless. Since he and Andria had done he had so much more time on his hands. It was quite frightening this way but clearly for the best. He could concentrate, now that the smoke-screen had lifted, on attending to these unlanced sores.

Andria had kept on ringing since she got the note. The first few occasions he had parried her frantic questions with mumbled evasions, until the conversations descended into vicious two-way harangues. Then he had taken to putting the phone down when she belled, but that hadn't stopped her, so now the family was having to handle erratically-timed nuisance calls on top of everything else.

She had sent him a card in the post too: A4, stark black, except for a window at the top from which brooded a pair of eyes. Underneath the eyes she had printed inside: 'Big Sister Is Watching You, Big Sister Is Watching You . . .' about ten times.

He did not realise for some minutes that he had been moving his precious lump of tissue around different parts of his room. From his table to the top of his records, then the hide of his drum, and now buried beneath his pillow. It was good this was the last one. He had begun to get severe stomach cramps, like his insides were gnawing at themselves, when he woke up in the mornings. He gathered his bits and crept outside.

On the garden steps he got para with a crushing sequence of visions. He wondered, contrary to what Dapo and he had always gambled, whether things wouldn't in fact get better once they left home – that this was quite possibly the best already; that they, and all their investment, were at the beginning of a clattering descent down; that it would end with him being destroyed like Maudsley Makanje and how many other casualties out there impaled on their crosses.

The chat upstairs had died to a murmur, leaving the opaque, musty house air all around. But reading its signs was no mystery for him. He could smell that they were at the edge of the precipice. It was something over a month now and they had hinted there wasn't much coming back after six weeks, hadn't they? It still felt as if it was in their hands. So, until someone showed him the way, all he could do was work harder.

Back inside, he belled Gabriel. Gabriel said he wasn't really doing anything and, sure, Dele could drop round.

Dele waited until he knew the old man was *in situ* in the lounge – to avoid one of their embarrassing silent encounters – then sought out his mother in the dining-room. Her eyes were a dull yellow. She said they were thinking of selling the house.

'Selling?' He didn't even know the place was theirs to sell. 'And go where?'

She just looked at him.

'Somewhere else here? Or you mean go back back?'

She shrugged. She would have loved to go home. The passage of the children through to university had always been the light at the end of the tunnel. Dele had come through safely and Dapo . . . well, if that was not going to happen then there was nothing for them here. But she doubted her husband, despite their talk, would turn back now. He had envisioned the trumpets blaring on his return, after an honours-strewn stay abroad, to the cosy bosom of his school-mates and the top table of a civilian administration. Mere proceeds from a house sale, after the mortgage was paid off and funeral arrangements done (and where would they bury the body?), would not be enough in his mind to save him from the taunts of failure.

'Aiy – Dele! What have we done, enh! Who can do something for us now?'

She carried on clucking her tongue and staring into the middle distance when he gave her a hug and told her he was going out and she shouldn't wait up for him.

Gabriel lived in a little block of low-cost black housing association studio flats at the Vauxhall end of Wandsworth Road. He had only recently moved in after four years doing the tasks meted out at members' meetings and the place was still spanking new. It was minimally furnished, with black wood surfaces and varnished floors. Not that you could see much of them underneath Gabriel's clutter. Photos and contact sheets, and unmarked audio tapes, and hi-tec Aiwa equipment rigged up in Heath Robinson contraptions that you had to tread round to reach the kitchen.

Gabriel was fingering with exaggerated disdain one of the two little bottles of Cisco that Dele had brought. 'You won't mind if I don't join you?' said Gabriel, pulling a Guinness from the fridge.

Dele had been to the flat once before but that had been a while back and he now rocked on the end of a beanbag feeling awkward. He had come for advice from a wiser, sympathetic head, specifically on whether he should take up this part-time work with the YCA and PMOT, but maybe it was a little cheeky. Between Andria and Sol, he hadn't really been keeping up to speed with Gabriel and he wondered whether he was still entitled to privileges such as flopping out on his beanbag, and conducting the conversation with one eye closed, as he currently felt like doing. His eyes flitted around, past the mini pool table in the centre of the main room, and ended on the dinky stepladders leading up to a bunkbed at the back.

'You got ants in your pants or something? You can't

keep still,' said Gabriel, which was a little rich seeing he was already interfering with one of his cherished bits of technology, holding this three-mile-radius scanner out of the window and tuning it to the sounds of the police.

'Sorry, man. I'm just checking Celia doesn't creep up on me from a crack in the wall,' Dele joked. 'You still getting trim there?'

Gabriel snorted.

'I'm about finished there, you know! The way she's always carrying that attitude around with her like a pitbull. I was just embarrassed for people to be thinking she was my woman.'

'Tell me about it!'

'So I'm just gonna shut it down swiftly. Can't have that situation hanging around my head with carnival coming up . . . And you? Is it "Andria"?'

Dele shook his head. 'Sacked.'

'Ah, that's a shame. I liked her. What I saw of her.'

'Did you?' said Dele. He hadn't known. It would have been useful to know. Ask me one more question about Andria, Dele was thinking, and I'll give you the juice: Andria, Sol, all the worries and the pain, the whole nine yards. Ask me one more question in the next ten seconds. Otherwise we'll leave it.

One, two, three . . .

Gabriel reached above his head to the ledge, pulled down a weathered, patterned box, and fished out a bag of bush.

Four, five, six . . .

'Hrmh!' he grunted.

Seven, eight . . .

'So who sacked who? 'Cos it was looking like a little vibe there for a while!'

Dele smiled with relief. He leaned back on the beanbag and whipped off his shoes. Now they could have a chat!

Gabriel continued with his sideline bits of business – crouching down to record some of the noise picked up on the scanner, then racking up the balls on the pool table.

They played game after game as Gabriel listened to the breakdown of the Friends of Dapo meetings and winced.

'Sounds like you're geting shafted, man. Have you had a look at your accounts at all?'

'The accounts? That's a thought actually.' Dele pondered, then laughed. 'I'm saying I don't take to how Sol gets his way in meetings and you're telling me he's a full-on gangster!'

'I'm not telling you anything, Dele. You know I've had no brief for Sol from day one, but it's not that I've heard anything conclusive about him. I'm just saying we know the guy is knee-deep in a place where a lot of money has gone missing, we know the man has got a whole heap of runnings. You go to bed with a hustler you're gonna get shafted somewhere! So all I'm saying is check your accounts.'

'Okay, okay. No, you're right.'

'I mean, how much do you expect to clear if this thing goes well?'

'Well, at ten pounds a head, say we get five hundred paying people in . . . About five thou on the door and whatever else comes from the raffle and the auctions. Say between five and ten.'

'Well, that sound healthy enough. But do you know how much you're paying out to the acts, or any other bills you'll suddenly get landed with? There's plenty of scope for some Harlesden fly-by-night merchant to sink his fangs into – '

'I don't think he's from Harlesden, man.'

'Near enough!'

'The thing is, their Booksman and I actually went down to set up the account, and the way I think it works is that we both have to sign any cheques that are paid out – '

'So who did you actually recruit on to the team?'

'Ah, just this Ketsia fool.'

'Not Concrete?'

'Uh-uh.' Dele breathed out deeply. 'I don't know where his head's at these days. It's like he's pretending to be better than he is and worse than he is. On the one hand he's this Mr Johnny-Come-Lately-Nubian, and on the other he's hanging out around those 33s – '

'The 33s?' Gabriel was puzzled. 'To judge by the sound of them, they need the scanner more than I do!' he said, after Dele had given him the lowdown. 'Wait a minute, though . . . Hang on.'

He got up and disappeared into a little cupboard-cum-darkroom at the back of the flat. Dele was just wondering what species of DIY gizmo Gabriel was digging up when he returned with two crisp, A5-size black and white prints.

'I took these on the day of the march. Less than a minute before that guy got stabbed. 'Cos I told you some youth tried to thief my camera bag, right? Recognise him?'

'Oh shit!' said Dele, staring at a teenager with razor cuts at the top of the picture, running away from camera. He was wearing a Georgetown University basketball jersey, number 33. 'That's one of the same people with Concrete that morning. And you say you saw him circulating at the time?'

'A-ha. Him and mate. I haven't put my mind to it since then. I didn't even look at everything I develop 'til last week. It was just you talking back there that got me thinking.'

'Fuck, man.' An ugly line had started its trace across Dele's head. 'Are you thinking the same way?'

'That these hooligans may have been involved? It's starting to look like it. I can't believe I was there that day and I couldn't see it!' Dele had cast his mind feverishly back to the snatch of conversation he had heard those two girls exchange at Carlton Vale. They had mentioned the 33s – was he sure? Yes, for sure. Something about cutting up a man on the 'line . . . He got up edgily, pacing around and catching the two pictures in the corner of his eye. 'I'm just wondering how far back the connection, if there is one, goes?'

'Well, you tell me Sol is paying Concrete and Concrete is running with these boys – '

'So you think Sol's a killer now?'

'*Me* you asking? He's *your* bloody business partner! Do me one favour. The next time you get in tight with someone, make sure he's not a psychopath.'

'Don't say that, man!' A cold flush hit Dele as he remembered the card he had sent Dalton's family. And the phone call the other day. His widow had rung. God forbid he should be somehow tied up in that! He scurried around for his cigarettes and the phone.

'Who are you calling?'

'Concrete. To find out what the fuck's been going on – '

'Is that wise? He's not gonna tell you even if there's anything to tell, is he?'

'I know Concrete, Man, believe me. I'll be able to tell.' He left a message on his bleeper service, leaving Gabriel's number and saying Concrete should call him soonest. The activity calmed him down somewhat, but their conjecture continued uncurtailed.

'Okay, let's say Sol did have a hand in it. He would do it for one of two reasons,' said Gabriel. 'Either he had a personal grudge against Dalton, which is unlikely and there would be far easier ways to sort out a problem like that, or there could have been a general wish to sabotage the march.'

'But Dalton was BFB and BFB are Sol's clients. So – '

'True. But ask yourself who has benefited most out of this whole mess? Answer: the BFB and, by extension, the YCA. Look at Fitzroy Lara. That retard has been everywhere – they've all rushed to accommodate him! And him going on about how when we go to college they chop us down at a bus-stop, we march to support a sister and they lick us down on Railton Road, you know, talking it all up. And remember, Sol gets ten of all their action for starters, isn't it?'

'But what a way to get it. I just can't see it, you know!' Or could he? He *could* just about form an image of Sol – the devotee of action films and books like *Cataclysm* – getting the germ of some Big Idea. Of course what this was, if true, was pure Malcolm X. That spectacular double-agent trauma. He knew Sol would have read the book, watched the film, and probably sold the T-shirts by the truck-load. But Sol was the kind of conspiracy zealot who'd think the CIA did it.

So he just couldn't tell. Gabriel was right. How could he have shared this key project with this man and not even know?

Just letting his mind run now unlocked the whole

Pandora's box. The funny thing, he hadn't even much taken to Sol that night he'd met him. So what was it . . . He came round the next day . . . Oh, the records and Genevieve. Slick Rick and a pretty girl. Just that.

'Un-fuc-kin-believable!' murmured Dele, shaking his head. 'I've just been doing all this by whimsy.' He was thinking even beyond this, to Cheryl and Helena and those times.

'Relax. You weren't to know, and it may all be alright anyway. If Concrete calls, he calls. Otherwise, we'll find out tomorrow.'

Gabriel played him a tape of live, local culture that he had amassed over the years. Plenty of cursing – cab drivers and their fares, lovers' tiffs, men being men – all recorded at different speeds. He reckoned that seeing jungle, where the drum was basically the melody, was tearing it up, it meant that now everything was permitted and maybe the world would soon be ready for 'Uncle Gabriel's Real Street Sounds!' Dele laughed and said if even Bushy, who was still in the old school where melody was the melody, couldn't get a decent gig, what chance had he? Gabriel replied ah but, at the end of the day, he wasn't a performer.

'I don't need an audience of thousands, just an audience of one. And from the time you realise that about yourself, and you've got a roof over your head already, then no one can fuck with you.'

His clothes were retro, but all his talk was of the future. Very keen on science-fiction was Gabriel. Before long he had whipped out his marker pens, and they were on the floor drawing storyboards for a black remake of *Alphaville*, while Sun-Ra played in cosmic fashion around them. As they sat there doing the spliff-riff – messing around with fantasy projects that would never see the light of day – Dele was struck by a sweet *déjà vu* of that first time they'd met.

Lord, if he had thought he was in a bad way then . . . At least he had not been afraid to be unusual. That was what had been missing. Since that time he'd just been all over the place, giving it up like the neighbourhood pussy. Wide as the Blackwall Tunnel. Just look who he'd been dealing with: all the politicos, Ella and her Proud Minds, Carl the rocksman and Eton lover, all those places, uptown, downtown . . . He'd just been surfing really. How many could he seriously take with him?

Gabriel was hooked into his scanner again, tuning it for the breaking dawn sounds.

Dele was just thinking he couldn't afford to stay another whole night away from the house of pain when there was a knock on the door and two of Gabriel's neighbours, Freddie and another guy whose name Dele didn't catch, strolled in. They had been out at an after-hours place and heard the voices and music and did they want to come down and get some breakfast at the McDonald's up Battersea Rise?

They nyammed up the food: hash browns, scrambled eggs, orange juice. Nice! He hadn't eaten with such an appetite since the days of Andria and Banoffi pie. He cleared his plate and beamed all round. After, Dele headed home and slept the dreamless sleep he had been longing for all this time.

He didn't wake much beyond eleven. He got up quickly, washed his face, had a good look at himself (he was worried about his eyes mainly – could he resurrect them or were they irretrievably mashed) and jumped into the bath. There were many things to do, but he knew which was first. He needed his mother to be around and he knew she would be stepping out soon for her half-day at work.

Her greeting took the familiar follow-up that he should speak to his father. 'Tch. But Dele! Why are you so stubborn? Ai!'

'Mommy, I'm already fighting this big battle over Dapo. I can't fight any more battles now.'

'I am the mother, enh, I know what he has done. But it is not for him to apologise – oh.'

As usual, he muttered 'Sure, sure,' to kill the issue off. This morning, though, he took a deep breath and stepped into the sitting-room. His Dad stood with his back towards him, gazing out of his favourite window, right leg slightly bent and supporting his weight. Dele looked away from him to the college photos and shields on the walls alongside the 'Bless This House' scroll, and wondered whether it was possible for them to find a new organising principle. He coughed again.

It had been a long night for his father too. His reverie yesterday evening had been disturbed by the sound of the phone and his wife calling to say that it was Tayo Adeniran, Enitan's son, for him. He had exclaimed 'Aa-aa!' and got up. He had read about Tayo's artistic exploits in the papers, made enquiries and had it confirmed that, yes, it was the son of the same Enitan who had been his junior at college. He had not followed Tayo's work closely, but doubted it could be earning him much money, and hoped that, if Tayo was so good with his hands, he had taken the precaution of training as a doctor as a decent living to fall back on. It had crossed his mind that he might expect to get a call at some point, even though he had not seen the family in twenty-five years. Certainly, it was not his place to call Tayo.

With all the respect and unction that Tayo knew was required before you could usher in weightier issues, he handed on his own father's greetings, and apologised profusely for not calling before, only he had been rushing in and out of the country ever since he had moved here. But what had reminded him was when he had met his son at a function the other day and could he say, sir, what a charming and bright son he had. He had been thrown off-balance by the remark, poignant as it was to him. To have answered it properly would have required a frankness that he did not consider fitting, so he had contented himself with saying that, yes, his children had worked hard and done well, but there was a certain Englishness infecting their psyches – an ill-disciplined something. But, as Baba Dele went into compare-and-contrast mode, and bounced his remembrances of upbringing down the line, Tayo tugged away, gently. If his children did have these taints, then surely it was the price he had to pay for their schooling here? It was all around them, wasn't it? That children like his were dual nationals, in the sense that they were bound to inherit the liberalism of their British peers in many ways. And it was less relevant that they survived at some future point in Nigeria, than that they flourished here, where such thinking was the norm. And he could not really say, but Dele seemed a boy who was trying to prepare himself seriously for the world outside, and maybe needed a little encouragement.

It can be the little things that set you off. For Tayo, it had been a means of killing two birds with one stone. He had got into contact with a family friend and put in a good word for Dele. He would have done it sooner but had kept on delaying for he could remember that Dele's father, like his own, loved to talk. You had to make sure you had a couple of hours spare. His benign brand of community service done, he went to sleep and thought nothing more of it.

But for Dele's father, who had been trying to incorporate their tragedy as part of the grand, over-arching themes with which he furnished his world – he had gone to his Genesis and re-read the Abraham-Isaac story how many times – it was the key to unlocking a hitherto secret side door. He brooded over the call for hours and forged – from the fierce love that had always been there – a new concession. He finally allowed that, where once he had only seen peevish adulterations, his children might actually have a point of view. Maybe all it had ever needed was for somebody with a link to his own late-great-days to nudge him in the right direction. Whatever, both were ready as Dele advanced a few feet and cleared his throat a third time.

His father's back was to him, still impervious, like a slab of stone. Dele took one final step forward and half-tugged his arm. The tension under his touch ebbed away as his father turned round. His eyes were heavy and his body rocked with great man-like tears. He threw his arms around Dele, the flats of his hands on his back. There was no dignity. It was wonderful. And they stood there for a little while, as Dele's right shoulder became sticky and sodden.

'I have gone cap in hand to Scotland, to Ireland,' his father finally said, his voice breaking, but still with its characteristic tone, so that it seemed he was neither talking to you nor himself, but explaining to a third party, 'to interviews for jobs which they would not consider me for and which I did not want! We have spent our last pennies on rooms with dirt and damp, your mother and I have borrowed, we have begged, to the bank, and to the council, at the workplace. Henh! But it was hard, so hard!'

He shook his head and broke down again. Dele gripped him more tightly. 'But they cannot ask me to bury my child. How can I bury my child? That's not the way. It's totally devastating. A child should do better than the parent. Are you with me? Eh? A child should eclipse the parents. That's all I wanted.'

Dele's mother came in and exclaimed at the sight in front of her. 'By God's Grace, you see it now. You see how we love you!' she said in her babytalk voice that she used when she anticipated resistance on a matter. She kissed Dele's head and patted it and sung the special song she would chant when he returned for the college vacations. And his father pulled off his specs and dried his eyes, and bade Dele fetch his Bible and the hymn book from the bedroom.

He was praying it wouldn't be Revelations when his father said to turn to John 14 and read aloud:

> Let not your heart be troubled.
> Trust in God, trust also in me.
> In my Father's house are many rooms:
> If it were not so, I would have told you.
> I am going there to prepare a place for you.

Then his father led them in prayers, and they ended by singing 'The Rocky Crown', a spiritual which Dele would have swopped half the music he owned to be able to do justice to, for it swirled and swooped like a bird. So he hummed quietly and tuned into his mother beside him for guidance.

When the service ended, his father sat down heavily and stared into the middle distance. He looked broken again as if the mighty effort of reconciliation had drained him. He muttered absently that he would no longer interfere in his children's lives. Dele went to fetch some juice from the kitchen. His mother said that today was special and she would cook Jollof Rice when she came home that evening. Dele pressed the glass into his father's hand and returned upstairs. Tomorrow was D-day, and there was now so much to confirm and confront. Time to get busy.

the
emperor
has no
clothes

D-DAY MORNING Dele woke up with the cramps. He had
felt his stomach churning up for a few hours before actually
opening his eyes, and a dozy commitment to doing something about the discomfort had buzzed around and invaded
his dreams, so that he'd scarcely got any quality sleep at all.
He sat bent over on the edge of his bed. The pins and the
tightness in his stomach were making him wince. It felt like
his belly was eating itself. He hobbled to the bathroom. All
the charlie had really laxed him up but he could only force
out dribbles that burst and stung his ass. He squatted on the
toilet and ran his hand across the sweat on his forehead.

The day before had seen him stalled at every turn.
Neither Concrete or Sol had returned any of his messages,
which made Dele all the more certain something was up. He
hadn't had time to chase them in person. He'd had enough on
his plate fielding a deluge of calls from every acquaintance
that Dapo or he had ever clapped eyes on on Green Lanes,
begging some freeness for the benefit night, and was it true
that Lipman and Roller would be playing? This was ironic,
given his earlier spat with Sol over the acts. To some he had

said, fair enough, I'll stick you on the guest list; about others he had thought, you really have no shame, and had to restrain himself from balling them out. The whole experience had been trying.

He had made some discreet enquiries with those contacts he had as to whether there were any rumours that the 33s, or any black person, had been involved in the killing of Dalton, but had drawn blanks. He had even belled Victor from PMOT, and described the two girls he had seen chatting at Carlton Vale about a stabbing, and asked if he knew them, but he didn't. The problem was he didn't really know people with their ear to the ground of south London's action. The only guy he knew who would know for sure was Concrete.

After he'd bathed he faced a mini clothes-crisis. He didn't know how to represent himself today. He felt to don something cultural. Either his white, patterned *agbada*, topped off with the burgundy crown of a cap, or else another kris Nigerian two-piece that glittered in yellow and gold. But he suspected there would be a lot of cult-nats in similar attire, and he wanted to disassociate himself from that tendency. But it was right to think smart, only there were various items he could not wear because he had been losing so much weight. In the end, he went for his tan shoes, red chinos, a white shirt and black waistcoat.

In the kitchen, he was sipping some tea and trying to decide if he could force some *gari* down his throat before heading out. He wasn't hungry but he thought he should try, for his tummy's sake. He was shuffling to the cupboard above the fridge when the doorbell rang sharply. It was a shock when he opened the door to Andria. The dark moods evidenced in her glare had sent a glow to her face. Her breasts stood up firm and perky in a grey halter top. She was looking mighty fine, but fiery and possibly unhinged.

'Where have you been?' she said.

'Where have I been? I've been here.' Where have I been! You say that and expect me to – what? To crumble? You're gonna have to do better than that, girl!

'Get out of my way, Dele.' She pushed past him and stormed up the stairs – to his room, he presumed. Dele blew his cheeks out and returned to the kitchen.

He should have guessed Andria might try a dawn raid. He returned to his *gari* and water, and was wondering whether his father had heard the bell, when he heard Andria run down the stairs and come in behind him. He carried on chomping at first, but then got one of those lucky presentiments and turned round to see Andria bearing down on him with homicide in her eyes and a saucepan in her hand. He was still seated, which prevented him from gaining sufficient springiness to grab her before the saucepan came whirring about his head. He managed to duck under most of the impact, and jumped forward to knock her off balance so they both fell tumbling to the floor, head to head, his knees clacking against hers. He was still doing his best to use what the self-defence pleaders called minimum required force, when she kneed him in the midriff, shaking him off.

'What's this, Dele? What's this?' She was holding something by her thumb and forefinger. He peered at it – a long, single strand of straight black hair. It certainly wasn't his.

'I found this in your bed! On your flippin' sheets! Who is she? Tell me – ' And she came at him with her fists again. He had to grab her and shove her against the wall.

'What the fuck is wrong with you! I don't know where it came from. Shit!' He could hear his father's quick, angry steps upstairs.

'Aa-aah! De-le! What is going on?' Baba Dele boomed from the top of the landing.

'Nothing, Daddy, nothing. I'm just here with a friend and I fell over.' There was a little silence before he heard his old man returning to the bedroom.

'It didn't just land there, did it?' said Andria. 'I want a proper answer.'

Dele told himself to stay calm, and answered sardonically, 'Andria, I don't know how that hair came on to my bed. I assume it got on to my clothes, maybe on the washing-line or sometime I was outside – I really couldn't tell you – and got deposited from there on to my bed at some stage.'

'Come with me,' she said, and grabbed his hand and led him upstairs. His clothes were scattered on his bed, and she had emptied out half the contents of his green folder marked 'Personal'.

'It's her, isn't it!' Andria pointed to the postcard Helena had sent him from India. 'You're back with her?'

Dele stared at her and laughed at the craziness of the charge. Boy, Mista D, you can really pick 'em.

She accused him of dealing with half the people they knew, including girls whose heads this hair couldn't possibly belong to. He didn't respond to most of it. He selected tapes for his Walkman and took a tie down, folded it and stuffed it in his waistcoat pocket.

'Andria. Not now, alright? You know what day it is, for God's sake. Now, if you have some love for me, would you get out of my life, please?'

'Not until you explain what you've been doing to me – '

'We've been through all this time and again but, if you want, I'll give you a call tomorrow and we'll go out and sit down and have a chat. Alright? I'm outta here.'

He went downstairs to the front door. Andria followed him.

'Where are you going?'

'Brixton.'

'I'm coming too. I'll drive you down. I'll floor it – '

'No, you won't.'

He was walking down the street by now. She called his name out then caught up with him and began tugging at his arm. 'You're not going anywhere. Listen to me – '

'Tomorrow, Andria, tomorrow,' he spat, under his breath, moving away, fearing that this counted as a scene already.

'Tomorrow's no good to me.' She was pulling at him again. 'I've been waiting a week. It's not fair! What about the chess an' Paris an' that?'

'Paris? You're talking to me about Paris! Fuck Paris, Andria! Paris was a joke.'

'How can you just put yourself above like this? Talk to me, Del.'

There was such hurt on her face he was shocked at how he could refuse it.

'And you can piss off!' she snarled to a group of three at the bus-stop, who were wide-eyed at the scene.

'Alright, tell me this. Is this it then?'

His head and back were damp. He was screwing. He couldn't believe this was happening to him on his own street. 'Dead right it is! You think I'll go back with you? You're fuckin' crazy! If you don't leave me now I'll thump you, I swear!' he hissed and walked on at a lick.

After a few seconds he realised she was running after him still. He turned down a side street. All he could think of was to get this shame off the High Street at least. He trotted for about fifty yards down Hilton Road, stopped and looked up. Oh no! Here she comes again. He waited until she was about halfway towards him, then took a left and clattered down Stamford Street. Already, he was beginning to pant. His lungs had never been the best. He shared a smile with a couple of workmen toiling on the pavement opposite, before he dived into another side street, just to be on the safe side, and followed it up to the main road.

He was just slipping on his Walkman, congratulating his long-time latent athleticism for giving her the slip and think-ing 'Say what you like about Andria, but she's got balls,' when he scanned the not-so-middle-distance and there she was, somehow manifested up ahead. She must have hit upon byways that he didn't even know! She grinned at his look of bafflement with a *schadenfreude* that did not inspire confi-dence in her mental well-being, and he turned round to flee as she sprinted towards him.

He hurtled past the workmen again, trying desperately to disconnect his headphones from the clanking stereo in his pocket and not break stride. The situation had plummeted into slapstick routine territory. He took a right, another right then busted a left. Still there! This woman was superhuman! He found himself bearing down on the main road again, a quarter mile further up, grimacing at the stitch in his belly. He was fast running out of options and out of steam. Across the road was a bus that he might just be able to reach. He didn't know where it was going, although he feared it might be the Chingford one. He cut in between the pedestrians and the slowing cars. It was a high-risk strategy. If she managed to make it too . . . Her and him in a confined, moving space with forty passengers and it would be all off! The bus was pulling away as he reached and he banged on the doors. The driver, a friendly guy with floppy twists, pressed them open. For one grisly moment it looked as if this too-benevolent man was going to leave the doors open long enough to accommodate the rather striking young thing pelting through the traffic in their direction. But, just in time, the doors clanked shut and the bus stepped off, to the rat-a-tat-tat of a lady knocking on its windows and throwing her hands up in extravagant Latin gestures of frustration.

Dele leant forward, eyes closed, gasping for breath. His shirt was rumpled and moist. And he had looked so fresh only half an hour before.

Dele hunted around for some tissue in his pocket. Lord have mercy! Mista D, you're going to have to keep your wits about you today. Take it one step at a time. First thing is to get out of Chingford.

Concrete wasn't up by his college, or by his Mum's. Dele had the idea of checking out a flat near to the Loughborough estates that he had seen Concrete frequent in recent times. Maybe it was a new place to hang out. He wasn't quite sure of the house number, so he pressed a few doorbells. After a bit he heard a window being pulled up.

'Alright? Is Concrete there? It's Del,' he shouted up.

Eventually a bulky guy with bumpy hair, who looked as if he'd only lately stirred, opened up. Upstairs, Concrete was sat cross-legged on the edge of a nasty mattress, fixing a coke cigarette. Behind him lay a fluffy dumbo elephant with floppy ears. Redundant bottles stacked with butt-ends dotted the bare brown floor. A man, who looked Indian-Caribbean, was programming chords and bass lines into a Yamaha organ and juggling with the levels on a ghettoblaster flashing with lights. He was locked into his work but looked up and let on. The big guy grunted, fell back on the mattress and carried on leafing through a photograph album that seemed to be full of pictures of maimed dogs.

'Easy, brer,' said Concrete.

'You didn't get my messages?'

Concrete nodded, his eyes still looking down. 'Yeah, yeah. I called. You was engaged.'

Like the house was engaged for a day and a half. Concrete was still clearly in his 'No Quarter' mood. He seemed to have stayed in character since the day of the trouble. Dele would have to hasten slowly. He looked up at the other two. He didn't want to discuss this in front of all and sundry but the others didn't seem to be listening. The big guy – who seemed to be a trainer for dog fights – was entertaining the muso with a story about how he had fallen foul of an RSPCA raid, and was due up in court next week.

Dele spun Concrete a yarn that he thought would appeal to his vanity. He said that Concrete knew how the police were chasing the wrong guys for the Dalton killing? And actually it was a black kid who did it? Well, some people were saying that it was just a simple argument that turned ugly. Others that it was a revenge thing, involving different gangs and a skank over a drugs deal. It was just that a friend of a friend of Dalton's family had heard the rumours that he was supposed to be a Mr Big Drugs Man, and had been really upset, and Dele knew Concrete would know what the real deal was. Just so's he could set her mind at rest.

Concrete offered Dele a puff but he declined. He scrutinised Dele carefully. 'So who's this girl that wants to know again?'

The question caught Dele a little on the hop, but he managed to invent a history.

'Seen,' said Concrete. 'No. It's just that my bredren got picked up on another ting, and the radics were firing him all these questions about that Dalton business. So someone's been going around with their mouth wide open.'

'A-ha. Are they gonna charge your man, do you reckon?'

Concrete snorted. 'Him a Supe. Him nah go down. Hear him now: "If you've got something on me, then charge me! If not, I don't want to hear about Dalton no more." And two-twos, he's out the door. He had nothing to do with it, anyway. I know the people, man, them guys that was involved. It was just a scrap, Del, a street ting. There was no background or drugs or any of that. I think maybe they tried to hassle the Dalton geezer, rob him or something. And, you know how it goes – '

Concrete shrugged. As if what he had just said didn't trouble him none. What has happened to you, Dele was thinking. The same thing that had been happening to him. Concrete said he was going to try to make it down to Dapo's do tonight. Only he was gonna be plenty busy later on. 'Touch?' said Concrete, holding out his knuckle to be rapped as Dele got up.

Dele looked at him. He wasn't going to respond in kind. He knew that, for the foreseeable future at least, this was it for them. 'Alright, man. Talk to you,' he said.

Outside he called Gabriel, who had said he'd be available throughout the day if Dele needed any help. The way it was looking he could definitely do with some back-up. They met at Vauxhall and tubed it to Kilburn.

At Carlton Vale Lenny, the security guard at reception, said no, Sol hadn't been in yet. Lenny was friendly, got on with Dele and had seen him come and go, so Dele thought he might fall to a piece of subterfuge. 'Do me a favour, Lenny, man. You know I left my wallet and all this stuff in Sol's office yesterday? I couldn't just grab the keys to open the place up a minute?'

Lenny grunted and fished around for the spare set. 'Seeing as it's your big day now. On your own head be it.'

Dele locked the door behind them and turned down the slatted blinds to cover the side of the office visible from the exhibition floor below. 'We've got to hurry. I don't know when any of them may be turning up – '

'So have you any idea where the books might be?'

'Well, that Sam guy sits over there,' said Dele, pointing to a little table wedged in against a wall at the foot of the room, 'but I've got a feeling they're more likely to be by Sol's desk which is the big one.'

Gabriel went through the Booksman's drawers but got no joy. Attention settled on a locked filing cabinet behind the master table. They tugged and peered at the two locks: one at the top and one at the side. Gabriel went to fetch a paper clip and they managed to pick the top lock pretty quickly. The side lock caused more trouble until Dele pulled out an old bank card, inserted it into the gap, and slid it up and down by the lock, hoping to slip it over the catch. It sometimes worked and yes, he heard a snap.

There were files containing invoices and financial statements on all Sol's clients. 'Friends of Dapo' was there, just before Backstreets. Heart thumping, Dele pulled it out and laid it on the table. It took a little while just for the two of them to figure out what they were looking at. You wouldn't have thought an initiative three weeks old could generate so much bumf! There were figures relating to the benefit account and to Witness – the name of the covering charity they had had to set up and register. Dele had prevailed on his Mum, an old secondary schoolteacher of Dapo's, Mr Lewis, and Molu, a library friend, to act as co-trustees along with him. Someone had mentioned to him that it was a little unwise being trustee and co-signatory on the 'Friends' account but he had thought he could handle it.

'Now what's this? Ring any bells?' Gabriel was pointing to what looked like a contract, on Witness headed notepaper, which stated that the undersigned guaranteed a loan of twenty thousand pounds made by New Age to Carlton Vale Centre. At the bottom were the names of all four trustees.

'I've never seen this in my life before.' said Dele.

'Do you know anything about this New Age?'

Dele shook his head. They scoured the stack for more.

They found a whole pile of bank receipts for cheques paid into the Dapo Benefit Fund by Yardcore Promotions and New Age, to the tune of about six thousand pounds, plus a nine-thousand-pound cheque paid out by the fund to Carlton Vale, with bogus signatures of his and the Booksman. Or of his, at any rate. The Booksman was probably in on it.

Dele ran his hand across his head. 'Is this as bad as it looks?'

'Well, you owe this place twenty thousand pounds if New Age don't pay up for a start. And given that you've never heard of them, when you're supposed to have been transacting all this business, I doubt they're the soundest company out there.'

They searched in vain for the New Age file.

'What do you think? Shall we photocopy some of this?' Dele was doing his best to think straight. He had one eye on the door.

'I don't know. Is there time?'

'I think we should. I may not get to see this again.'

Dele grabbed a sheaf of papers and scuttled to the copying machine at the end of the hall. His heart was pounding. When he returned Gabriel had tidied up most of the desk. They replaced the Friends of Dapo file, but Dele couldn't shut the cabinet properly. The catch must have snapped right off.

'Shit! We're gonna have to leave it, you know.'

'Okay.' He left the cabinet ajar. You couldn't tell it had been opened unless you walked right up to it.

They returned the keys and stepped outside into a mild afternoon to review the situation. Dele wanted to cancel the benefit but Gabriel said there was no point. It wouldn't solve anything and it was four o'clock already, don't forget. They tried to piece together what was going on. It was clear that Sol was using the Friends of Dapo either to paper over the cracks that had appeared in his Carlton Vale edifice, or to feather his own nest, or both. Presumably, the proceeds from tonight were also to be channelled in those directions. Apart from making sure that Dele got his own people on the door, there was no obvious action they could take in the short term.

'Green. Green like I just stepped off the boat yesterday!' he murmured.

'You weren't to know. How could you know he was up to this game?'

'I could kill the motherfucker!'

Dele said he had to go home to pick up one or two things. They arranged to meet by the main doors at seven-thirty. He took a cab back. He knew he had no money but what was an extra ten notes when you were facing a bill of twenty thousand. So these were the rules. All this while these were the rules and he hadn't been told. You see what happens, Miss D? You leave me on my jacks and I fall to pieces.

His Mum had left a note on the dining-room table, saying she and his father had gone down to the hospital. His father – that was a rarity. This must be the final push.

Dele pulled out his bedside drawer, ruffled through photographs and memorable invites to events that he had kept, and pulled out his knife. It had a ribbed brown base and a blade three to four inches long. It was the blade he took to clubs with dodgy clientele, especially in parts of east and south-east London. He had never had to use it.

His body was tingling. Part of him was frightened at the thought of the confrontation that surely lay ahead, and part of him relished the fact that he would shortly be drawing a red line under his dealings with these people, one way or another.

There was a moment of pure mystery. He flicked his lamp switch on, to no avail. The bulb must have gone. He tried it a few times then went downstairs to fetch a new bulb. On his return, the light was on! Merrily shining away. It was the strangest thing. He returned to the lamp, checking for a loose connection, trying to get it to go on and off, but it wouldn't. The key thing about electricity, as he recalled, was its inflexibility. It was not moody, it did not come and go. So he could only conclude that he had been visited by the supernatural. The episode uplifted him and a smile played on his face as he fingered his blade and nodded off for a short while.

The thud of the speakers carried the bass down the road, swelling the sprinkling of local people who habitually hung out on the patch of grass opposite Carlton Vale. At the main doors Dele told the four friends of his still holding out for comps that they would have to work a little for their reward. They agreed to go rotation on the door, taking the notes off the punters. They were only to hand the money over to him or this man here, he emphasised, pointing to Gabriel. There was some protest from two security people in YCA baseball caps, who said that this arrangement was not what they had heard. Dele said this had been sorted with Sol and he would get him to come down and confirm it soon enough.

The sounds were fading out as Dele and Gabriel went inside. An old man, with a shock of white hair, kente cloth robes, and clutching a stick, had begun conducting a libation on the left hand side of the hall. By his side Sol and Michael, also in robes, beads and kufi caps, looked on with due respect. Around them stood the early arrivals, fascinated with the goings-on. The white-haired man, in his role as Obuse Epanje, the senior elder, was pouring a clear liquid from a glass on to the ground, muttering some words in what the two presumed was Twi with every little shake. Beside him stood a litre bottle of Tesco Gin.

'Couldn't they find a brand with a bit more cred?' said Gabriel.

A guy, probably a YCA lackey, turned around and shushed them angrily. Dele and Gabriel shared a glance, amazed at the humbug of the scene. Carlton Vale's spiritual adviser ended the libation with a few sentences in English. He blessed the evening and the cause in which it was held. His English wasn't too tough. Dele hoped his Twi had been better. There was a burst of clapping and then the crowd drifted away. He was glad to see Sol disappear down the front of the hall to do some pressing of flesh. He was not quite ready for him yet.

'Come on, let's get a drink,' he said. 'That libation has got me thirsty!'

They leant by the bar. To their left were seven or eight tables where the VIPs, if any showed, could be seated. To the right was the stage from which the musical entertainment and the raffle of prized gold discs and sundries would be conducted. Right now, a couple of DJs from The Architects were standing by their booth behind the twin decks at the side of the podium, starting up their selection. Followers and associates of the crew laughed and loitered around them. Dele had heard the sound at house parties and they were safe; chatty and witty over the mike.

The plan was for The Architects to get people going, peak with the Lipman and Easy Roller sets, before the evening sobered up with the raffle and a speech by Ketsia about Dapo. (Dele had said he could not face making a speech but had briefed Ketsia thoroughly on what he thought she should include.) Finally The Architects would return to wrap the bash up at some point in the small hours.

'We playing tune for the gyaals and the boys. Tunes the pacemaker posse best avoid!' crooned the Architect in bud-burned tones, as the creeping bass intro kicked in on a tune. His selector, Infinity, added casual fillers over the rhythm, whilst he concentrated on the serious business of attending to the wheels of steel.

'Now this is a man called The Ar-chi-Tec' – '

'You nuh seh!'

'When me ah chat then hear your mother get vexed, To all you gyaals dem ah pretty – Listen we! Sound ah play, sound ah rock. Tune you nevah know, we give you tune you never stop.'

'When we seh – '

'Infinity, *In-fi-ni-ty*. Play your pretty music for you and for me.'

'You nuh seh – '

'Gyaals dem nice like ah sugar an' ah spice.'

'And ah – '

'Infinity, we have to play it twice!'

They restarted the tune, to the first shouts of 'Rewind! Rewind!' from some of the hundred or so already assembled.

'Rhythm come and ah rhythm come nice/ We gonna give you in ah de party style/ Special request going out to the one called De-le/ You know he know the area!'

Dele blinked up. He didn't know they were going to give him a shout-out. Probably got prompted. A few people were looking and smiling at him, and he turned to Gabriel, embarrassed but chuffed.

'Special request going out to the one called Don-na/ Me love mi Donna, me love mi Donna!' roared The Architect.

A ripple passed through the group of three by Dele. Donna seemed to be the one in the middle, with the glasses and band in her hair.

'Me have to hol' it down! Me nuh get X-rated . . .'

Listening to the antics of The Architect, and scoping the folk filling the hall, Dele's mordant mood fought for breath against a buoyant surge that would not be subdued. It was difficult to explain exactly. It was a feeling he'd first encountered that evening of the meeting at The White Rose, in the bar afterwards, and had had in moments since, that these people, some of whom he knew, most of whom he didn't, had come here to share the fact that the world *out there* was very different. That even if they had not been licked down by the police, they knew a man who did. That out there was sometimes hostile, ignorant or indifferent, but you could come here and maybe grab a good dose of the oxygen that you needed to survive. And this connection was not exclusive. Other people could come enter and that could be fine. But its upshot was that his biggest highs and lows were to do with these people. Even Andria and all that was to do with these people. It struck him that you could inhale the air from these occasions in this city without having to take up its body and soul as well. There had to be a way to live the life but not lose your head. He could rely on events like these for the joy of them and nothing more. But the joy should be the start of it.

'Are you alright?' said Gabriel.

'I'm fine, man. Just fine.' Dele looked up to Sol's office and saw the light on. 'I'm gonna go upstairs in a moment. You know the office is just up there, yeah?'

'Ah-hah.'

'If I need you, I'll come to the window and shout or make a sign. Okay?'

Gabriel nodded.

Sol was fiddling with his cabinet when Dele walked in. He looked a little agitated.

'Del! How's it? I'll be down in a minute.'

'Looking for something?'

'Eh? Nah. Someone seems to have tampered with my drawer, or tried to break into – '

'What makes you think they only tried?'

For the first time Sol turned round fully.

'You thiefed my fuckin' money, didn't you?' A definite trapped look passed across Sol's face. Only there for a moment but blatant. You see, thought Dele, you're not such a champion hustler. You couldn't even play poker.

'Just cool it, man. You can't come into my office with that low-mentality talk – '

'Save the bullshit for someone else. I want my money. I saw the documents, okay. I know all the fuckrey you've been doing. And I'm not leaving this room until I get my money back.'

'What money of yours is this? Have you put any money into any account? I seem to remember you owe me!'

'Well, for starters, there's the twenty grand you've put me and my mother in hock to this place, and then money to settle the Carlton Vale overdraft you've run up on the benefit account.'

'I wish you'd had a professional to look at those accounts with you – '

'Just *leave* it, man! I'm not Concrete, alright? You shat on me good and proper. Let's just sort what's mine, out and done.'

Sol stared at him evenly. He seemed to have regained his composure. 'D'y wanna sit down?'

'It's alright. I'm not planning on staying long.'

Sol leant back on the edge of his desk. 'I know you're cursing my parts but just hear me out. It don't sound like it, I know, but none of what you may have seen was as serious as all that. Look . . . all them "administrators" trying to knock the stuffing out of us, yeah? One of the things they were doing was calling on all these loans they gave the Centre to start up, including this one for twenty thou. Now, originally, seeing as I'm a kinda director, I offered to deal with this through our YCA account, but the bank manager I have, see, because there was a bit of a cashflow problem at the time, he couldn't sort it on that account. This guy and me been tight from time, only he's got somebody on *his* back now at the bank! He can't be seen to be treating me any different to the others, you understand? Alright, so we just had to find another account to guarantee the YCA contribution. But don't worry, dollars come in now, and we'll pay off this loan first thing next week. I know we took a real liberty with that guarantor's statement, and, really and truly, I'm sorry about that, Del. I was sure you'd be easy about it if we asked but, you know, your poor Mum is obviously under all this pressure. None of the other trutees knew us as well as you. They might not have been up for it. Carlton Vale was sinking and we had to act fast. That guarantee – you can tear it up Monday.'

'So where does New Age come into it?'

Sol looked flustered again.

'The guarantee was for New Age not for Yardcore.'

'Oh, yeah, yeah, yeah. No, you're right. New Age is just a . . . you know, promotions. Just another one of the promotions businesses that we run.'

'So Sam and Michael know about it, do they?'

'That's right.'

'Good, 'cos they're just downstairs. I'll get Booksman up, then you and he can sign me over some YCA or New Age cheques for the twenty thousand and the rest, now you're liquid again. Just for me to be on the safe side. I don't know the most secure way to do this legally but I can call my lawyer. Maybe he can even come over. This way, we can tear them all up Monday!' Dele moved forward to the phone on Sol's desk, continuing, ''Cos I don't believe a word you said. But, whatever. I'm not leaving without my money. Let me get Sam.' He reached for the phone, but Sol put his hand over it.

'Alright, Del. Let's talk, let's talk.'

'You've said that once before.'

Dele sat down finally and lit a cigarette. Behind him he could hear a massive cheer, and a chug-chug ragga rhythm. It sounded like the entrance of Lieutenant Lipman.

'We've discussed quite a bit about politics from time to time, isn't it? I know The Nation isn't your bag but one thing you can say about them, is they know that money is the one ting dat talks in dis Babylon ere, yeah? Black businesses, corner shops in our neighbourhoods, boom, boom, boom . . . And The Nation have serious collats. Believe! 'Cos when I think about the other cycles of Black Consciousness we've had here, you know . . . Rasta! Ras-ta-Far-I in the seventies! Rudebwoys, ruffnecks, suddenly turn dread. But Rasta – beautiful Rasta – ran out of steam and half the dreads go turn again. And you know why? Because of jobs. Rasta provided the pride and the look but it didn't provide the jobs. This is the reality we deal with. Everything else – from your marches to your friend Bushy – is people emoting!

'You know how many jobs I provide, Del? Guess. PMOT, YCA, the security side, plus people I've brought into the Centre . . . twenty people. That's twenty black families. I tell you, these are dread times we live, and I'm just trying to get it all together – the ideas side, the business side. Linking up internationally 'n' stuff. But you know how this country has to keep a brother down.'

Sol looked for a reaction but Dele remained impassive. 'Okay, I've probably burnt a couple of people in my time. But I've been burnt too and that's just the way out there, you get me? If it takes this benefit money to help keep our heads, this whole project, above water, then – '

'So you *don't* have my money?'

'At the end of the day now, what more can we do for

her? She's a martyr, Del. A big martyr. She's played a part.'

'Tell me one thing. Was Derek Dalton a martyr too? Was that the thinking? 'Cos I went to see Concrete today – '

'Ain't nothing to do with me. The Dalton thing was a complete accident. There was supposed to be maybe one minor victim that day. And I think Concrete thought his people could handle it. But when you deal with them low-grade, low-mentality types . . .' Sol sucked his teeth and gazed at him intently.

'So what are you saying to me, Del? The job offer still stands, obviously. I'm sure I could even get you something else.'

'A job? With you! Sol, you're not well. You're one sorry fuck! I let you in like you were family and you took this, my kindness, for weakness. I just want what's mine, alright?'

Sol's eyes went cold. 'I don't have it. You're too late already. When I do I'll get back to you.'

Dele yawned and went over to the window that looked down over the hall. Things were in full swing anyway. He could spot old Cheryl down there, and Gabriel still by the bar. The Architects were hauling up a record box for their short second set. And was that who he thought it was? Storming around with two friends to the bar and scanning vigorously. He could tell that walk anywhere. Andria. Did she not understand the meaning of 'I'll call you tomorrow'?

He was worried about the whereabouts of Sol's security, but one seemed to be dozing by the doors and the other had joined the groupies around the sounds' booth. His insides had that funny warm stickiness, but it felt like he could channel it. He slipped his hand inside his waistcoat pocket, slid his hand around his blade and made sure it could be accessed swiftly. He turned round and pondered this man with his masterplans.

'I want some cheques off you, Sol.'

'And I told you that I can't do nuttin for you. Wha'cha gonna do? Run around telling tales like a little bitch? Do your worst. Blow your pipe 'til it bursts!' he sneered.

Dele had picked up a piece of A4 paper from the desk

and was now busy scribbling. 'As I say, I'm not a legal man. But let's try this, and I'll speak to my guy later.' He shoved Sol the paper. It was dated and stated in neat block capitals: 'In consideration of a loan paid by the Witness Charity to Carlton Vale Centre the YCA agrees to pay Witness the sum of twenty-five thousand pounds.' Underneath was space for signatures of four witnesses to the agreement.

'Me, you, Booksman and Gabriel. You start and I'll take it downstairs.'

Sol laughed. 'Is dis bwoy serious? And what are you gonna do when I don't sign? Go to the police! And even then what? There are two types of black men who go down, Rasta. The grasses an' that, and from they done their time, they keep well undercover, and leave the manor. And there are the ones the people check for still. Say "Respeck everytime to the brother!" They love me down here, if you don't know. Ah me mek the whole o' dem eat!'

Dele dipped his hand inside his waistcoat. He whipped the blade out so fast that Sol barely had time to flinch before the blade came whirring down on the table barely an inch in front of his fingers.

'Sign!'

Sol squinted at Dele, as if trying to figure how bad and brave he might be, then made a lunge. But Dele was ready, and he brought his knife up in an upwards slashing movement across his body. If Sol had not braced back as he saw the knife's motion, it would have ended up in his chest. As it was the knife sliced the right-hand side of Sol's heavy cotton top. The beads from his snapped necklace tumbled along the floor as he stood there in shock.

'I'm not joking, sir. Sit down and sign!'

Sol signed the paper in a shaky hand.

'Good.' Dele grabbed hold of Sol's left hand and pressed the blade to it. 'Now move your right arm as far as you can down the table.' He wanted to make sure Sol's weight was hunched forward and flat, to guard against a second lunge.

'Well, between this and the donzai on the door tonight I may be alright. Only there's one more thing on my mind and

I know, as a connoisseur of True Crime, you'll appreciate it.' He brought his left hand up to Sol's. All this was as easy as it looked.

'My aunt was telling me this story. Okay, she's driving through Lagos one night, nice Peugeot, mod cons, and she stops at this phoney traffic light and gets stepped on by robbers. You know how many bandits we got out there?' He slipped his fingers under Sol's chunky, silver sovereign. 'So anyway they took her bag and coat but still they weren't satisfied. They wanted the ring on her finger too. And she said, "Oh, but it's too tight-oh! I can't get it off." And they said, "That's no problem. We'll take the finger too!" It does have a happy ending, though – she got the ring off finally. The question is: will we be as lucky?'

Dele prised at the ring, using the blade and a finger. It seemed stuck to Sol's finger. He was trying to plan ahead for the next few moves. Snatch the ring, and run like hell. Jump into a cab, just floor it . . . Maybe grab his car keys, that's a good idea . . . The music was still playing. There would be people dancing. Might be a squeeze getting clear.

What's with the music anyway? It sounds distorted. Oh, it's the PA coming in and out. 'Message for Dele. Dele, please go to the bar phone. Is Dele in the house? . . .'

The two stared at each other. Sol suddenly tried to wrest his hand free but Dele grabbed it and jagged the knife down, splitting the webbing on Sol's finger. 'Don't fuckin' move.' He tugged at the ring again. It came clean off this time.

Dele held his blade out and backed to the door. The stickiness was now threatening to overwhelm him. He tried to sound like the victor but his voice was jumping all over the shop. 'This is a deposit and you'll get it back if the money comes through. Nice doing business with you.'

He turned and sped to the door. On the stairs he clattered into Gabriel hurtling up.

'It's a nurse from the hospital. You're to go there straightaway.

Dele looked at him.

'I don't know! She just said to come straightaway.'

Dele looked back up. Sol was approaching his door, flinging a jacket across his bare top.

'Okay. We've gotta shift it!' With one eye on their backs, they trod, jostled and weaved their way to the exit.

endpiece

DAPO WAS hidden from view when Dele came into the room. His Dad was there, talking animatedly with the consultant. His Mum was gesticulating and singing, walking up and down by the bed, and cradling Dapo's head in her arms. Maerag was looking on, beaming.

His parents rushed towards him as he half ran to the bed. They met up midway, embraced, and staggered together across the room.

Dele looked at his sister. She was fidgeting around, drowsily slipping in and out of consciousness. She didn't look any different, not a day older, like she had just been sleeping all this time.

'It just happened this evening,' said Maerag. 'I couldn't understand what was going on with the ECG – the levels were every which way. So I went to get Dr Hartson, and when we came back Dapo was already beginning to stir. Just her head and eyes slightly . . . so we can't possibly know yet what the diagnosis is for a full recovery . . .'

Dele carried on nodding vigorously, but he hadn't heard

a word the nurse was saying. He leant down and kissed Dapo. He buried his head in her chest, a babbling brook.

'Miss D, Miss D, my darling Miss D. I've got untold stories to entertain you! Oh, I can laugh about it now, but it was one troublesome summer!'

MY ONCE UPON A TIME
Diran Adebayo

Seven days to find a bride in the city for a mysterious
millionaire from the country. Fee: a cool one hundred
thousand. Sounds like a straightforward case for Private Eye,
Boy – that is, until he hits the streets and it begins to dawn
on him that this elusive woman is not the only one being
pursued . . .

'His prose is a joy . . . confident and swinging. The
contemporary English novel needs more Diran Adebayos'
Literary Review

'Gritty yet enchanting . . . a melting pot of voices talking in
Jamaican patois, south London streetspeak and educated
Englishman – are what makes this a work of art'
Sunday Express

'Boasting all the vibrant wit,
imagination and emotion of a true classic'
Straight No Chaser

'An urban novel of considerable style and impact'
The Times

Abacus
0 349 11442 0

FULL WHACK
Charles Higson

Dennis 'The Menace' Pike is going grey and going straight.
Then two old faces turn up from the past – the Bishop
brothers, Chas and Noel. Famously inept, they were bad
news then, and they haven't aged well. What's worse, they
need Pike's expertise on a scheme. Pike, still haunted by
what happened one reckless night all those years ago,
refuses to get involved. But when he finds his bank account
has been mysteriously tampered with, Pike is drawn back
into a world he spent ten years escaping.

A slick, razor-sharp novel, *Full Whack* is packed full of
searing wit, scurrilous characters and nefarious knock-about.

'Lively narration, a superabundance of action . . . gruesome
and hilarious'
Evening Standard

'Higson has the kind of ear for middle-England angst that
more established writers should be jealous of'
Nick Lezard, *GQ*

'The missing link between Dick Emery and Brett Easton
Ellis . . . a spectacularly fine combination of the crazed and
the macabre'
Vox

Abacus
0 349 10811 0

COMPLICITY
Iain Banks

COMPLICITY n. 1. the fact of being an accomplice,
esp. in a criminal act

A few spliffs, a spot of mild S&M, phone through the copy
for tomorrow's front page, catch up with the latest from
your mystery source – could be big, could be very big – in
fact, just a regular day at the office for free-wheeling,
substance-abusing Cameron Colley, a fully-paid-up Gonzo
hack on an Edinburgh newspaper.

The source is pretty thin, but Cameron senses a scoop and
checks out a series of bizarre deaths from a few years ago –
only to find that the police are checking out a series of
bizarre deaths that are happening right now. And Cameron
just might know more about it than he'd care to admit . . .

'Ingenious, daring and brilliant'
Guardian

'A remarkable novel . . . superbly crafted, funny and
intelligent'
Financial Times

'A stylishly executed and well produced study in fear,
loathing and victimisation which moves towards doom in
measured steps'
Observer

Abacus
0 349 10571 5

Now you can order superb titles directly from Abacus

☐ My Once Upon a Time	Diran Adebayo	£6.99
☐ Full Whack	Charles Higson	£6.99
☐ Complicity	Iain Banks	£7.99

———————————— (ABACUS) ————————————

Please allow for postage and packing: **Free UK delivery.**
Europe: add 25% of retail price; Rest of World: 45% of retail price.

To order any of the above or any other Abacus titles, please call our credit card orderline or fill in this coupon and send/fax it to:

Abacus, 250 Western Avenue, London, W3 6XZ, UK.
Fax 0181 324 5678 Telephone 0181 324 5517

☐ I enclose a UK bank cheque made payable to Abacus for £ . . . .
☐ Please charge £ . . . . . . to my Access, Visa, Delta, Switch Card No.

Expiry Date ☐☐☐☐ Switch Issue No. ☐☐

NAME (Block letters please) . . . .

ADDRESS . . . .

Postcode . . . . Telephone . . . .

Signature . . . .

Please allow 28 days for delivery within the UK. Offer subject to price and availability.

Please do not send any further mailings from companies carefully selected by Abacus ☐